Gwen closed her eyes tightly in an attempt to test whether this might be a dream, her imagination playing tricks on her.

After all, she was here again by this magnificent tree, with echoes of her past all around her. Could she have conjured up something she wanted to be true?

"Lady Gwenllian?"

Seemingly she had not. The voice that carried in the soft breeze did appear to be one that resembled Ralph's. Only it rumbled a lot lower, a lot deeper and belonged to a *man*.

Yes, it seemed very real.

Oh, God! Her knees felt like they might buckle beneath her.

He was filling in the silence as he continued to explain. "I did not mean to distress you. I know this must come as a huge surprise but...it became imperative that I had to tell you about this myself."

Gwen still could not find her voice, as her head swirled around trying to comprehend this new discovery.

"Is it really you?" she whispered.

"It is. Yes."

Author Note

Medieval tournaments were imported from France in the twelfth century and formed a significant part of strengthening a knight's command and prowess that he could later adopt in warfare.

They were also a great form of entertainment for both commoners and nobles alike, as they watched mounted and armored combats, or melees, fought in both one-on-one contests and in team events over several days.

Tournaments sponsored by rich nobles were also a way to make silver, provided the risk of injury was acknowledged, since many knights were wounded. This was the main objection to tournaments by clerics and some monarchs, including Henry III!— although not at the beginning of his reign, when this book is set.

The pageantry of tournaments also allowed the ideals of courtly love to be expressed, when ladies would gift a favor or token to their chosen champion. It is this, or rather the reverse, that occurs in this book when Ralph de Kinnerton returns a token gifted to him by his old love, Lady Gwenllian ferch Hywel, and inadvertently opens up the heartache from the past.

Can they find a way back to each other?

I hope you enjoy their story.

MELISSA OLIVER

The Return of
Her Lost Knight

HARLEQUIN
HISTORICAL

HARLEQUIN®
HISTORICAL™

PLEASE RECYCLE
THIS PRODUCT IS RECYCLABLE

Recycling programs
for this product may
not exist in your area.

ISBN-13: 978-1-335-40724-5

The Return of Her Lost Knight

Copyright © 2021 by Maryam Oliver

This edition published by arrangement with Harlequin Books S.A.

For questions and comments about the quality of this book, please contact us at CustomerService@Harlequin.com.

Harlequin Enterprises ULC
22 Adelaide St. West, 40th Floor
Toronto, Ontario M5H 4E3, Canada
www.Harlequin.com

Printed in U.S.A.

Melissa Oliver is from southwest London, UK, where she writes historical romance novels. She lives with her gorgeous husband and equally gorgeous daughters, who share her passion for decrepit old castles, grand palaces and all things historical. When she's not writing, she loves to travel for inspiration, paint, and visit museums and art galleries.

Books by Melissa Oliver

Harlequin Historical

Notorious Knights

The Rebel Heiress and the Knight
Her Banished Knight's Redemption
The Return of Her Lost Knight

Visit the Author Profile page
at Harlequin.com.

To my beautiful mother,
who is always in my heart.

Chapter One

1221—outside Castle Pulverbatch,
near Shrewsbury, England

He saw her then. The woman who had broken his heart all those years ago.

Ralph blinked beneath the iron helmet and felt his pulse quicken. He felt the blood drain from his face and not because of apprehension over the punishing exercise about to commence in the clearing. No, it was from the shock of seeing the familiar woman, with flaxen hair covered with a gossamer-thin veil, sitting in the spectators' area.

A lump formed in his throat, almost choking him.

Lady Gwenllian ferch Hywel of Clwyd.

He would have recognised her anywhere, but she was here at this tournament, outside Shrewsbury, after all this time. He hadn't seen her for six long years—the woman he had been betrothed to. The woman who had been his companion and to whom Ralph had thought he'd be bound for ever.

But it wasn't to be.

God, but he had hoped to have forgotten it all. And

for a time he had. After he had been attacked two years ago, near the small village of St Jean de Cole in Aquitaine, and left for dead, Ralph had temporarily lost his memory, but everything had come back to him, with a flourish. The loss of his father, the loss of his castle and surrounding demesne lands. And the loss of the woman he had loved. All gone within a heartbeat, leaving devastation and heartache in its wake.

'Is everything well?' His friend, Sir Thomas Lovent, acting as his squire, glanced at him from beneath a deep hood with barely disguised concern as he passed his shield and the blunt sword Ralph used for practice for a tournament such as this. Tom pulled his hood over his head to conceal his face further, but managed to give him a sly look, raising his brow as he waited for an answer.

'Yes, all is well.'

Ralph watched the assembled group of knights from the retinue of William Geraint, Lord de Clancey—of which he was a part—pitted against another lord's group of knights. They were all making last-minute preparations, flexing their arms before the tournament ceremony began with an exhibition in combat, where knights could test each other's mettle.

Suddenly, Ralph's head felt the weight of the encased heavy iron. He felt the tension around his jaw twist and tighten over the mangled scars on his face, making it ache. These he had acquired during an attack in Aquitaine two years ago that had left half of his face and his right hand and arm bloodied and cut in the frenzy.

'Can you loosen the leather ties around the neck of the hauberk, Tom?'

He felt Tom loosen it, making breathing a little easier.

'Better?'

'Yes.'

No. Nothing was better. Not now that he was back near the place he grew up in…so close to Kinnerton Castle. So close to home. And he certainly didn't feel better about seeing Gwenllian again after all this time. He'd hoped he would never lay eyes on her again after everything that had happened that last fateful night he had laid eyes on her outside Kinnerton Castle.

'Watch de Fevre's upward strike, Ralph. He bends low when he strikes, so remember to anticipate him in the way Will Geraint instructed us. And the man has chosen his favourite weapon, the mace, so be careful.'

'This is supposed to be a combat exhibition, Tom.'

'I know, but it doesn't mean that many of the knights here would view it that way. This would be the first time for you to be able to gauge the calibre of many of your opponents.'

Ralph scanned the clearing, before frowning behind his helmet. 'And what in heaven's name are they all doing now?'

'Ah.' Tom smirked. 'Naturally to gain a favour from a fair maiden, with the royal court here.'

They watched as a few of the knights, including a couple from their own retinue, sauntered towards the spectators' area and gallantly received a token of a piece of material or a length of ribbon from young maids in the crowd, to huge raucous cheers.

Before Ralph knew what he was doing, he stepped into the clearing.

'What's this? Are you following their example?' He heard Tom's laughter from behind as he marched towards the raised canopied area reserved for their royal patron— the young King Henry, who was in attendance and on tour in this part of England. The noise from the crowd merged with the roar in his head and the incessant drum beating within his chest.

A ribbon...

It was the first thing he had seen once he came to after the attack in Aquitaine two years ago. He had remembered it to be of great importance to him, as he tried in vain to recall what it was that made the blue and purple woven ribbon so significant.

And then gradually, he did. He remembered...everything.

But now, the faded purple ribbon he'd constantly worn around his wrist felt as though it was burning into his skin. And he wanted it gone and the memory of Gwenllian with it. He threw down his sword, the shield and took off his metal mittens, untying the ribbon, as his fingers shook.

Unlike the other knights Ralph didn't take off his metal helmet. It might be construed as lacking in courtly manners, even a slight, but Gwenllian ferch Hywel didn't need to know that it was him under the armour. She didn't need to know that he wasn't actually dead, even though he had so nearly perished two years ago. Nor did she did need to know that he was here pretending to be another knight—pretending to be his friend Sir Thomas Lovent, so that he could try to scramble together the exorbitant feudal relief tax that hung over Kinnerton, his ancestral castle, which had been seized by the Crown after his father's demise. That was *if* he could win enough silver in this tournament.

No, she didn't need to know any of it. Why would Gwen care after all this time, anyway? She had made her feelings perfectly clear to him the last time he saw her.

All that mattered to Ralph was his need for retribution and justice from men who had done him wrong—men like his cousin, Stephen le Gros—and to get back what was rightfully his. Besides, it had been six long years since he had seen her—Gwen was likely to be married now. Even if she wasn't, she was no longer of any importance to him.

Ralph took a deep breath and stepped forward in front of the dais where she sat and stretched out his arm, his fingers clinging on to the ribbon. He saw her properly the moment she lifted her head and his chest clenched tightly. Gwen looked the same, if a little older, and as achingly lovely as ever. But it was her blue eyes that almost made him gasp. They seemed lost, forlorn and strangely lifeless. As though she wasn't actually there.

He watched, transfixed, as a spot of colour rose in her cheeks, her brows furrowed in the middle as she recognised the ribbon he was holding out to her. A spark of heat shot up his arm as her fingers tentatively touched his when she reached out to take it from him, confusion etched across her forehead.

Even from where he stood, he could see the small faint scar above her eyebrow from that time, so long ago now, when they had gone for a swim. It reminded him of another time and another place, when there was the promise of those few treasured moments together.

The last time Ralph had seen Gwen was in the woods outside Kinnerton after his cousin had betrayed him and seized control of the castle. Ralph had had to make his escape quickly, fearing for his life, but Gwen had refused to go with him. She had maintained that it was impossible for them to be together since he would no longer be the next Lord of Kinnerton and told him that she had to put honour and duty first.

Ralph shifted uncomfortably. He couldn't linger there, drunk on the sight of Gwen. He needed to make a good impression here. This whole tournament could determine his very fate. Now that he had returned the precious token she had once gifted him, Ralph was resolved to forget Gwen. Forget everything about her and their shared past. He didn't want any reminders of the promise of a future that had been ripped apart.

It was his turn to put honour and duty first. He had bitterly learnt his lesson about where his priorities should lay. He bowed and turned away. He could no longer think about Gwenllian ferch Hywel. Those ties had been severed, a long time ago.

Gwen stared at the purple ribbon in her hand and let out a slow, shaky breath. She traced the surface with her fingers, remembering how she had carefully dyed the wool. Blending the colours to get the exact shade of the twilight hour at which she would meet Ralph de Kinnerton for their snatched moments together.

When had she gifted the token to him? Six, seven years ago, possibly longer. A lifetime ago...

Oh, Ralph...

She had refused to leave Kinnerton when Ralph had pleaded with her to go with him and had insisted that he left in haste. But only for his own protection. Not for him to perish far from home.

She knew only too well that had she gone with Ralph, then his devious, older cousin, Stephen le Gros, would have come after her, as he'd sworn he'd do, and kill Ralph. She could not have risked that and had stayed at Kinnerton Castle, biding her time before getting away a few days later, when no one was watching her movements too closely. Thank the saints!

Gwen remembered that day at court, some years later, when she had learnt of Ralph's death and pretended it had meant nothing to her. God, but she had felt his death on her conscience ever since. Yet, leaving England had been his only chance of survival. She'd had no choice other than to do whatever she could to get him to leave Kinnerton after everything that had unravelled around them so quickly.

Gwen remembered the first time she had met the sensitive, gangly boy who would become her best friend, and later the only person she trusted. The boy she was betrothed to marry, one day.

From the very first moment she had seen how caring Ralph was. The lives of ordinary people interested him far more than the complicated politics that he would one day inherit as a Marcher Lord, much to his father's chagrin.

It was this that the conniving Stephen had exploited for his own ends. His insidious words, constantly but casually undermining Ralph's character. Gradually, Stephen's ruthlessness created a wedge, not just between Ralph and his father, but the Kinnerton garrison and many powerful men in the neighbouring areas.

Worst of all was Stephen's unwanted obsessive attentions to *her* and his promise that Gwen would one day belong to him. And in hindsight, Gwen should have foreseen what was to come and warned Ralph. Had she done so events might have turned out very differently.

At least Gwen had managed to manipulate her way out of Stephen's clutches in the aftermath and get away from Kinnerton. He hadn't counted on that or the fact that, in the middle of the Barons' conflict with King John, the Crown would accuse Ralph's father, Lord de Kinnerton, of treason and seize both Kinnerton Castle and its land, as well as her wardship, to gain for necessary profit. Stephen had not expected that the accusation would be later quashed, even though Lord de Kinnerton had died on route to plead his case. With him dead, the Crown had settled a feudal relief—an impossible sum—that Ralph, as his son, would have found incredibly hard to pay off.

It was all so immaterial now, anyway. Ralph was also dead. The pain of his loss had been her only constancy.

And now she was back. So close to the place she had left six long years ago, with all its terrible memories. An area never normally granted licence for a tournament such as this, but then the powerful Earls of Chester and Hereford had petitioned the young King Henry, reminding him that his Uncle Richard, King before his father John, had meant the rules around tourneys as guidance only.

Not strictly true, but along with the fact that Henry was touring the region meant that he eventually acquiesced. And Gwen along with a few other ladies at court had been requested to accompany them.

But it was no mere coincidence that she had been dragged here. Her Welsh kinsmen had been putting pressure for Gwen's situation to be resolved. And with the huge burden of the feudal relief still hanging over Kinnerton, the possibility of being once again face to face with Stephen le Gros was highly likely, here, at this very tourney. After all, the tax still had to be paid and this tournament was an opportune way for him to try to raise the silver he needed, so that he could finally lay claim to Kinnerton Castle…*and her.*

The man had had to bide his time all these years, as the Crown profited from Kinnerton, and her wardship, without successfully reversing their decision. But now Stephen would be more ambitious than ever. Bile rose in her stomach at the thought.

Gwen was not a fool. Knowing the reasons why she

had been brought back here, she had to be very careful about what she did to get out of this mess. She had already put many of her meticulous plans into motion and had been saving the meagre silver that the Crown had given her as an allowance for years, knowing it might be needed one day.

Now, more than ever, there was a need for caution and patience.

Even before Gwen had arrived back in Shropshire, she had already secured her place at a convent where no one, including Stephen le Gros, would ever find her. And if the Crown were to finally grant the man her lands and wealth, then she'd happily bequeath them and renounce her claim to it all to avoid being tied to a man like Stephen le Gros.

She glanced at the ribbon again, her eyes brimming with tears. She brushed it against her lips and screwed her eyes shut, thinking once more of that awful time when she had last seen Ralph. She never properly explained the real reasons why she had not run away with him, and now she never could. He was lost to her for ever and all she had left of him was this…this ribbon.

Gwen snapped open her eyes and forced herself to focus on the exhibition tourney that had started in the clearing.

'Is everything well?' Brida O'Conaill, her companion and friend of three years, was smiling serenely beside her, acting as though it were an everyday occurrence for a strange knight to present a lady with a token. 'You seem a little out of sorts.'

'I'm perfectly well. I just had a little surprise.'

'Well, that is a blessing, but you may want to act a little differently to draw attention away. People are looking.' Her friend handed her a square linen cloth as she smoothed her grey woollen kirtle. 'Here, wipe your tears, Gwen.'

'Thank you.'

'Who is he anyway?' Brida muttered from beside her.

Gwen scanned the area until she spotted him. The man who had brought Ralph's token back to her—a knight from Lord de Clancey's retinue, judging by the standard he was fighting under. Who was he and what did he know about Ralph's demise? And why in heaven's name had he returned the ribbon to her? How would he know to do that?

Gwen would seek this knight and find out everything he knew about what had happened to Ralph. She hoped to God that he would somehow be able to ease her mind about how her betrothed had met his death.

'I don't know, but I mean to find out.'

Chapter Two

Ralph threw the blunt weaponry down on the ground of the sparse yet comfortable tent he shared with his friend and groaned in frustration.

'Don't say anything.'

The event might simply have been an exercise for knights to exhibit their skill and show their mettle, but it could not have gone any worse for Ralph. In front of the young King Henry and his court no less. Hell's teeth!

And all because his head was reeling from seeing Gwen again.

Tom loosened the ties on the back some more so that Ralph was able to get out of the hauberk before he helped him out of the constricting neck piece. 'I wasn't going to.'

Ralph took the helmet off his head, gingerly touching the scarred side of his face, and winced.

'Especially since you're in pain, my friend.' Tom passed him a linen flannel that he'd drenched in the bowl of scented water, perched on the small coffer.

He rubbed his jaw and patted the angry, gnarled skin that spread down one side of his face, from his forehead through his cheek, stopping short of his neck. Even after two years, it still looked as though a savage animal had clawed his skin, even though Ralph knew it was the work of a madman's dagger instead. He flexed his right hand and grimaced. More hideous scars were also visible on his right arm and the palm of his right hand, where Ralph had tried to defend himself against his assailant.

It had all been a timely lesson and a reminder of his woeful shortcomings as a knight—and the necessity to leave the pitiful man he once was firmly in the past if he were to succeed in his mission. He'd even gone to extreme lengths of learning to use his left hand, even to wield a sword, after his right hand had been left much weaker following the attack.

At times like this, when the skin was pulled and stretched taut on his face, it still felt raw to the bone. 'It's nothing that Lady Isabel's salve can't soothe.'

Lady Isabel de Clancey, or Adela Meunier as Ralph had known her in St Jean de Cole, had been his miracle two years ago. When he had been attacked and left for dead in nearby woods, she had tirelessly helped the old woman healer carefully stitch him back together, doing everything she could to help him with her ministrations, coaxing him to live. She had later left St Jean de Cole as Lady Isabel de Clancey, a wealthy heiress in her own right, making her way back to England to be reunited with her mother.

It was through Isabel that Ralph had found the courage to go on and forge his own destiny. And it was through her that he had secured a patron and mentor in her husband—William Geraint, Lord de Clancey.

'What happened, Ralph?' Tom asked tentatively.

'Didn't we agree not to mention it?'

'Yes, well, I know someone who'll want a word or two.'

'I know.'

Will Geraint…

'You may as well know that Hugh de Villiers, Lord Tallany, was watching as well.'

Damn. That was all he needed. The two men who had helped, instructed and sponsored him since his arrival in England were going to be heartily disappointed with that abysmal display out there today. Ralph dropped his head and expelled another groan.

'You know you're going to have to do better than that in the mêlée, Ralph, otherwise they'll insist that you're still not ready.' Tom frowned.

'I'll be ready, trust me.' Thankfully the tournament, proper with its two main mêlées had yet to commence.

Ralph knew his friend was right, but it wasn't through any lack of skills that he had performed badly today, rather the shock of Gwenllian ferch Hywel being present at this very tournament. And that shock had induced him to rid himself of the one thing that reminded Ralph of Gwen—her ribbon. It represented every hurt from his past and, try as he might, at present Ralph could not see beyond the events of six years ago and Gwen's part in them.

Mayhap it had been churlish of him to behave as he had in front of the court, especially as he had then subsequently embarrassed himself with his lacklustre performance. Nevertheless, it had been done and Ralph would think no more about the matter, or of Gwenllian ferch Hywel.

He moved behind a small partitioned screen so that he could strip the rest of his clothing off and have a wash.

Tom took his hooded cloak off and ran his hand through his hair. 'And just remember it's *my* reputation you're staking.'

'As if I could forget.'

They might look nothing alike, yet both men were of a similar tall height and frame. For Ralph, this made it easier to pass himself off as his friend, when he was dissembling beneath his armour.

It was imperative that no one knew that Ralph was alive. His enemies would be here at this tournament. Especially his cousin Stephen, who would, no doubt, want to find a way to convince the Crown, which had been reluctant to relinquish its control of Kinnerton Castle during the Barons' conflict, that he should be Lord of Kinnerton.

But Ralph would not give up his right to the castle and its land. And certainly not without a fight.

He had devised a plan with Tom and Will Geraint whereby Ralph would fight under the guise of his friend, hoping to win the champion's silver at the gruelling back-to-back double combat, or *mêlées à pied et cheval*, fought on consecutive days. Only then would he reveal his identity. Until Ralph had the silver needed to pay the tax hanging over Kinnerton and press his claim on the castle and his ancestral lands, hoping to thwart Stephen's ambitions, it would not do to arouse his cousin's suspicions. The man was a proven liar, adept at deception. Indeed, Stephen was capable of all manner of insidious, devious behaviour and it was far better to keep the truth from him for now.

They had all agreed that this plan would be an advantage over his cousin and the powerful men who backed him and could work in Ralph's favour. Let them all, especially Stephen, believe that Ralph was still dead.

Tom was watching him. 'It was the woman, wasn't it?'

Ralph snapped his head up. 'What?'

'That's why you couldn't fight as well you usually do.

The woman *you* gave something to.' Tom crossed his arms over his chest and raised his brows.

Damn, but the man was still talking. 'She'd have to be someone of great importance for you to risk everything you've worked so hard for.'

Ignoring Tom, he strode to the coffer and sloshed ale into a mug, throwing it back in one big gulp before slamming the mug down.

'Oh, no.' Tom's eyes widened knowingly before he shook his head. 'No, no, no! Do not tell me. She's *the woman*, isn't she? Lady Gwenllian ferch Hywel. Christ, Ralph, why didn't you say anything?'

'Forget it, Tom. It was a lapsed moment, that's all.'

'You know that it's a lot more than just a lapsed moment.'

'Think no more about it.'

'What if she finds out about all of this?' His friend swept his arms dramatically around in every direction. 'What if she finds out that you're still alive? That you… What was that?'

They both froze upon hearing female voices near the tent. Ralph had a very bad feeling about whom one of those voices might belong to.

One of the ladies spoke just outside the opening of the tent. 'Apologies, sires, but we were informed that Sir Thomas Lovent is here? If so, my Lady Gwenllian ferch Hywel of Clwyd would like a moment with you, Sir Thomas, if we may be so bold to solicit your company.'

Tom was shaking his head and mouthing something about this not being part of their bargain before Ralph practically pushed him out of the tent.

Thank goodness he had gathered his wits in time.

'Ah, Lady Gwenllian, how well you look,' he heard Tom's greeting.

Ralph stood inside the tent, trying to settle his erratic breathing, knowing how much was at stake. Knowing that Gwen stood just outside the tent, mere inches away…

'I am not Lady Gwenllian, sir. This is my mistress,' the unknown woman exclaimed from the other side of the tent.

'Of course, how remiss of me. But then when one is in the presence of two beauties, it is easy to do so.'

Of all the asinine things to say. The fact that the silence stretched for a painfully long time confirmed that the women had similar reflections.

A throat was cleared delicately. 'I'm pleased to make your acquaintance, Sir Thomas. I had to see you after you gave this back to me.'

God's breath. It had been a long time since he had heard Gwen's quiet, melodic voice that it sent his heart racing.

'Am I right in assuming that you knew Sir Ralph de Kinnerton?'

'Yes, my lady.'

'And he…he gave you the ribbon?'

Ralph's heart thumped wildly in his chest.

'Yes, that is…he did.'

'I see.' Her voice was almost a whisper.

'What is it that you would like to know, Lady Gwenllian?'

'Everything.'

'Everything?'

'Yes. Anything that you can remember about how…? About the circumstances in which…what happened when Ralph…?'

Tom's voice gentled. 'All I can say is that my friend is…*was* as noble and honourable as you last remembered him to be.'

Gwen hesitated before continuing. 'That is the issue, sir. We did not part on good terms.'

'Well, that is a surprise for he spoke warmly about you. I should say excessively warmly.'

Ralph's jaw clenched. Yes, he was definitely going to kill him.

'I am glad, Sir Thomas, as there were things said that should never have been said.'

There was something in Gwen's voice that caught. Could it be regret at how things had been left between them? Ralph was not certain, but there was a melancholy in Gwen, that he could not comprehend. Mayhap in the confusion in the aftermath of his father's death and the grab for Kinnerton, all might not have been as it seemed. But how this could be? After all, it was *she* who had insisted on staying behind six years ago, when he had been forced to flee Kinnerton.

'My lady, please do not distress yourself.'

'I am not, sir. I just need to know, whether…had Ralph…had he asked you to return the ribbon to me, before he…he…?'

'Yes, Lady Gwenllian, he had.'

'But why, Sir Thomas?'

That was a fair question and one that Ralph felt reluctant to examine. Even now, he could recall how her eyes had lit up when she had described the process in creating such a small, yet thoughtful token. How she had dyed the wool and woven the yarn before embroidering their entwined initials. Mayhap it was *that*—knowing the ribbon had been made and given with a love that no longer existed, that he wasn't sure ever existed—that prompted him to accept the blatant truth. That he no longer wanted it.

Seeing her again after all this time reminded him that

he should no longer hang on to her gift. It reminded him that he could no longer claim such sentiments...or claim her love. Not that her love had been what he'd believed it to be, since her friendship to him had been borne out of a deep sense of duty. Nothing more.

It mattered not, after all this time. But it could explain why he had acted so recklessly on this day.

'Tell me, Sir Thomas. Please.' Her voice sounded so small that he almost reached for her. Instead, he fought the innate need to comfort this woman as he once had. That would be a very bad idea. She meant nothing to him now.

He'd already compromised himself when he had given back the ribbon and look where that had got him. She had come here...asking questions about a past that should be long buried.

'What message had Ralph wanted to convey to me? Was he despondent, sad, reconciled to his circumstance or...or still angry?'

Yes... Ralph was still so angry and he'd die a thousand times before being reconciled to anything that happened six years ago. The pain was as palpable now as it had been back then, when he had been betrayed by everyone in Kinnerton, including the woman on the other side of the tent. And hers was the betrayal that had hurt the most.

'My lady, this area is reserved for soldiers, knights and their squires—men engaged in this tournament. It is not a place for a lady and certainly not for us to engage in such a conversation.'

'He must have said something to you?'

'Ralph said many things.'

'Be assured, sir, that whatever that may be, I am well versed in receiving unpleasant revelations.'

'Then allow me to say that I have no desire to deliver

any such unpleasantness, my lady. And nor do I have to, thankfully. But this is not, however, the place for these discussions. You should not be here.'

'That is what I keep saying to Gwenllian,' the other woman said.

'Then you give good counsel, mistress. We can continue with these discussions later when I hope to satisfy your curiosity, Lady Gwenllian.'

There was a moment of silence before Ralph heard Gwen's response.

'Very well then, I hope to see you in the hall later for the evening meal, after Vespers.'

'I cannot promise anything, my lady, but I shall try to meet you then.'

'Then that's the best I can hope for, sir.'

Ralph could not hear Tom answer, but heard Gwen's voice again. 'But before I go, how did you know it was me?'

'My lady?'

'How did you know to give the ribbon to me, Sir Thomas.'

'Ah, well…that would be from Ralph's vivid descriptions. And I was not mistaken, Lady Gwenllian. I…er… knew it was you.'

'I see. Until later, Sir Thomas.'

Ralph expelled a breath he had been holding before pulling a hood over his head and waited for a long moment, making sure the women had taken their leave before he ventured out of the tent to stand beside his friend. 'My thanks, I'm indebted to you.'

Tom shook his head as they both watched the retreating figures of the two women. 'Yes, but never fear, I'll be tallying everything you owe me.'

'Good to know.'

They both stood silently before Tom nodded in the direction of Gwen and her companion. 'You made a mistake there, Ralph.'

'So it would seem.'

'A mistake that might prove to have much wider implications. What if she realises that you're still alive?'

'I know. I should have thought before I acted.'

'You should have. She might be married. What if her husband hears of this?'

Ralph still wasn't certain what he had been thinking when he had approached Gwen. Not with everything at stake. He could not afford to dwell on Gwenllian ferch Hywel of Clwyd. Had he not welcomed the cold nothingness that had lodged itself in his heart since she had told him to leave without her six years ago? Yes, and it would do him no good to reopen up those old wounds.

He gave his head a shake. 'Come, I can see Will Geraint heading this way, no doubt to reprimand me for my other mistakes.'

He absently rubbed the rough distorted skin of his jaw, trying to relieve the tight tension. This day was going from bad to worse.

Later, as the day came to a close, Ralph stayed back in the open fields, relentlessly practising the techniques that had earlier deserted him during the opening exhibition in front of the young King and the Marcher Earls. He lifted his sword in different directions, tilting it in various angles and swiping it around his body as he circled a non-existent opponent. Over and over again.

Ralph could not lose sight of everything he had worked so hard for, all because he had set eyes on a woman who had once meant a great deal to him.

Not only had he made himself look bad in front of

the men who had helped and believed in his mission, but Ralph had left himself exposed to Gwen's curiosity after he'd given the ribbon back to her. Tom had been right— she was probably married after all this time and was not worth these reflections.

Ralph wasn't even sure why it had been so imperative to give that blasted ribbon back. Only it had.

Seeing Gwen again had brought everything to the fore—the loss of his father who had always been critical of him, the betrayal of his obsequious cousin, who'd turned on him so swiftly that it had made his head spin. And finally, Gwen herself, who had made it clear that she was staying behind.

She had always been so sensible, prudent and practical. Even that last time they had spoken in the woods. Gwen had explained her duty—to be the next Lady of Kinnerton, no matter who its lord might be. She had urged Ralph to run away and save himself. And like a coward he eventually gave in and left without her, hurt and confused that she would choose her obligation over him. That she had closed herself off to the love they'd shared. It had been like a dagger struck into his heart, a final blow following the madness in the aftermath of his father's death, leaving just a dark, hollow emptiness in his heart.

No more. He was now a different man to the one he had been back then and he could not lose sight of what was important here. He had to stop thinking about the past and look to the future. A future that could only be his if he was determined, resilient and focused enough.

Tom approached him, 'Come, let's retire to the castle and get some much-needed food. It will be quite the feast with King Henry in attendance.'

Ralph lifted his head and shook his head. 'No, I don't think that would be a good idea.'

'Ah, so you have reconsidered everything to do with Lady Gwenllian.'

'Yes, I do understand the need for caution.'

'If only you had thought of that before, my friend.'

'I do realise that.' Ralph sighed in exasperation. 'But I can rectify that now, by keeping away and avoiding her altogether.'

'And I suppose that would also include our absence from the hall tonight?'

Ralph nodded as he turned to his friend and placed his sword back in its scabbard. 'I've imposed much on you, Tom.'

'You have.' Tom smiled wryly. 'But I'm sure I'll live, without the good wine, delicious food and convivial company that I would surely enjoy. Who needs that anyway?'

'Who, indeed?' He nodded at him. 'My thanks, Tom. You're a good friend.'

His smile stretched to a grin. 'I know.'

The following day, despite their best endeavours to keep a low profile, Lady Gwenllian sought out Sir Thomas anyway. They were in an area, used by knights to practise with their various weaponry which they intended to use in the mêlées and tourneys. Here, the many Lords and their retinues were segregated by the tents dotted in between, but it was still a good a place to observe the competition and find possible weaknesses.

What it was not, however, was a place for a beautiful young woman like Gwenllian to be walking in with just her maid or companion, who was of a similar age. He could see the men's heads turn as the women strode in their direction.

Ralph pulled the rough edge of the hood of his cloak so that it draped over his head, keeping it bent low. 'Don't look now, but Gwenllian is here and heading this way.'

Tom groaned as he peeked over his shoulder at them. 'Oh, God, has the woman no sense at all?'

Ralph flicked a glance at her as she quickened her pace towards them, her head held high, the cream veil covering her head flowing softly behind her. 'Gwenllian has imminently more sense than you, my friend.'

'One would never know judging by this conduct.'

Ralph's heart pounded in his chest as she sidled next to Tom, with her female companion in tow.

'Greetings, my lady,' Tom said as Ralph kept his head down, staring at the ground.

'Sir Thomas.'

'And to what do I owe this pleasure?'

'Once again you find me seeking you in what you would, probably, consider an inappropriate place for me to be seen,' she said in a clipped tone.

'I'm afraid so, Lady Gwenllian.'

'You left me with little choice since you did not come to the hall yesterday evening, sir.'

'Ah… I can only apologise, my lady but I had much to attend to after a very poor spectacle in the exhibition event yesterday. In fact, I must beg to leave now, as I have to meet my Lord de Clancey.'

Tom began to move away with Ralph following him.

'Wait, sir, and hear me out,' she said in exasperation. 'I do understand the importance of a tournament such as this. Especially for a knight bent on making his fortune, Sir Thomas, but forgive me, sir, it was *you* who sought me yesterday. Or have you forgotten?'

'Yes, my lady. I suppose I did.'

'And I mean to find out why, sir.'

'My lady, I cannot say the reason to…'

'Please… Sir Thomas. I do not mean to intrude on your time, but if you would only give me your word that I would have the pleasure of your company in the hall this evening, with the promise that our discourse shall be brief… I shall not importune you any further.'

Tom didn't answer at first, but eventually Ralph heard him reply in resignation, 'Very well, my lady. Until this evening.'

Ralph then heard the soft footsteps of the women as they walked away. He lifted his head and pulled his hood down, rubbing his jaw. 'Well, then. So much for avoiding Gwenllian ferch Hywel.'

Gwen looked around the busy hall of Pulverbatch Castle—a castle that was familiar to her from when she lived at Kinnerton. Although, if memory served, it had always been usually uninhabited.

Yet, for the purposes of this tournament, the Earls of Chester and Hereford had jointly agreed to host the festivities here for the first time ever.

A makeshift solar with numerous chambers had been arranged for King Henry and his royal party, with bed-chambers arranged for the women, in the keep, with a constant guard at the entrance to the stone, spiral staircase to hold out any unwanted attentions from unscrupulous knights.

Gwen's eyes darted around the noisy, chatty room as people gorged and indulged themselves with the plentiful offerings of the evening feast. At the far end, the young King sat on the dais, looking bored, flanked by his guards and the two hosting Earls. The women sat demurely around the periphery in one corner, lending the banquet a semblance of formality, as Lords sat with their entourage of knights in small clusters around the hall.

'Thomas Lovent said he'd be here.' Gwen sipped ale from a mug as she continued to glance around the room.

'Be patient, Gwen, he did say he would come tonight.' Brida stabbed a piece of mutton with her knife and placed it on her pewter plate, spooning some of the accompanying sauce over the top.

Patience?

Patience was something she'd always be relied on to have in huge abundance. Not out of choice but of necessity. And on this particular night Gwen felt a certain inexplicable restlessness. She needed to know everything that had happened to Ralph, even though she feared it might be upsetting. She yearned to know that there was nothing she could have done to prevent it, though she knew that by letting him leave that night she'd done plenty to ensure his demise. Losing her appetite, she pushed her plate away.

She just needed his friend to explain more, which he strangely seemed reluctant to do. Why? Mayhap there was something that had happened to Ralph that was far too difficult and disturbing to disclose.

It seemed odd, however, that Sir Thomas Lovent would make such a public demonstration of giving back Ralph's ribbon at the start of an exhibition tourney and then avoid her request to talk about his deceased friend. There was no doubt in Gwen's mind that had she not pursued him again earlier he would have avoided her still. Yes, there was something about Sir Thomas Lovent that bothered her. It was the way he could barely meet her eyes as if he were concealing something.

'There—what did I tell you? He's here.' Brida took

a bite and motioned to the entrance of the hall. 'Admittedly, a little late.'

Gwen flicked her gaze to the tall, powerful, broadshouldered knight with golden hair and friendly green eyes. Sir Thomas spotted her and nodded in her direction before moving to sit with his lord's retinue. He was followed by another man, as tall and broad shouldered as Thomas Lovent, with a deep hood covering his face and his head bent low. He was the same man she had noticed earlier in the day when she had sought Sir Thomas in the practice area. Gwen frowned at them.

There was something odd about the hooded man. Something slightly unsettling. For one thing, he looked frankly a little too old to be a knight's squire. And another was that he seemed strangely familiar somehow. Gwen wondered whether she had encountered the squire somewhere before, but surely that was not possible.

She rose abruptly and looked down at Brida. 'Let us go now and get this meeting over with.'

'No, wait. Allow the man to settle before you bombard him with your questions.'

Heaven help her, but it was at that very moment that Gwen saw another man she certainly did recognise. Unable to move, she felt as though she had turned into stone.

Oh, Lord above...

Stephen le Gros sat across the hall underneath the arch with a group of Kinnerton hearth knights. And as usual, he was watching her in a way that made her skin crawl, assessing her in a manner that made her feel stripped bare. Exposed.

Gwen knew that the possibility of seeing the man was highly likely, but she didn't expect it to be this soon. His predatory gaze made her feel as though she were once again being hunted. God, how she hated him. Hated how he had changed her life irrevocably. She schooled her features and gave him a bold stare of her own as the man's lips curled up. He raised his mug and nodded at her, his smile turning into a sneer.

She wanted to turn her head, to look away, but, no… she was not going to give the man the satisfaction of seeing her affected by his vile attempts at intimidation.

Instead, Gwen rose and moved towards the area where Thomas Lovent sat. She might be reckless as well as a little foolish, but her patience had worn thin and, in any case, she had to get as far away as possible from Stephen le Gros's lingering gaze.

Gwen pushed the man out of her head and thought about what she hoped to achieve from this exchange with Thomas Lovent. She wanted peace—nay, she needed it after carrying the guilt of Ralph de Kinnerton's death around for too long. It might be irrational, but it never shifted. It never allowed her a moment to ease her conscience.

'Good evening, Sir Thomas.'

He stood and took the hand she offered, bending his head over it.

'My lady,' he muttered, without meeting her eyes. 'Come, we can talk here in this quiet corner.'

Yet the appointed corner held the tall shadowy figure of his squire or manservant, who had followed Sir Thomas into the hall and who stood rigidly in the dark, his head covered beneath a hood. Well now, it was hardly that quiet or private.

How strange.

'I had hoped this conversation would be in confidence, sir.' She indicated with a nod to the dark silhouette standing behind Sir Thomas.

'Naturally my lady, but please do not mind him. My

man is sadly a mute and an oaf, Lord help him, but he's loyal to a fault with the necessary brawn so extremely useful.'

'I see. Well, as long as you're sure.' She remained a little uncertain, but complied, nodding and conveying to Brida that she would be talking to the man privately.

'Now then, Lady Gwenllian, what is it that you'd like to know?'

'As I have said, Sir Thomas, I'd like to know everything. Everything that could fill in the gaps with what happened to Ralph after he left Kinnerton and then later met his…his demise.'

'Allow me first to offer you some ale,' he said as he poured into two mugs and handed one to her.

'My thanks. Now, please tell me about Ralph.' Gwen would not let him stall any longer.

'Very well,' he said softly. 'I met Ralph de Kinnerton a few years ago in Poitiers, where we served together in Lord Aligner's mesne. We became fast friends, being of a similar age and disposition.'

'I see.' But, no, Gwen didn't see. As courteous and gallant as Thomas Lovent seemed to be, he was evidently a powerful warrior and so unlike Ralph in every way, with his gentle nature.

'Ralph was increasingly uneasy, increasingly worried about threats that were directed at him alone, rather than our garrison…and yet there was nothing tangible that he could lay his finger on. He sensed there was danger around him, but never found out the truth.' Sir Thomas sighed, taking a sip of his ale. 'Then one day he went out with a small patrol of soldiers…'

'And never came back.' Gwen swallowed.

'Yes, exactly.' He nodded grimly.

'I presume you hadn't gone with him.'

He grimaced. 'No, I'm afraid I had not.'

They sat in silence for a moment before Sir Thomas met her gaze again. 'As for the ribbon, well, naturally Ralph left it in his possessions. When I saw you yesterday morn, I thought it may be best that I returned it to you. It was never meant to cause you any distress, otherwise I would never have given it back.'

There was something far too polished about his answer. As if it had been rehearsed, but that made no sense. Gwen's gaze shifted over Sir Thomas's shoulder to where his rather large squire stood rigidly, shrouded in darkness, and she swallowed uncomfortably. There was something disturbing about the man standing there listening to this discourse. She still wondered why it was quite so necessary that he be there at all. She couldn't shake the feeling that there was more to it…

She dragged her eyes back. 'Ralph told you about me?' she asked.

'Yes, Lady Gwenllian.'

'Well, then you know about how things stood between us.'

'Indeed.' He cleared his throat. 'But what I do not know and what Ralph never understood fully was why you refused to leave Kinnerton with him. He said something about doing your duty or some such?'

Was Gwen imagining that he had raised his voice a little louder?

And how was she to explain to this man? 'It was complicated.'

'I'm sure it was, Lady Gwenllian but I hope you can comprehend that, for my friend's sake…for the sake of his memory, I had to ask.'

'That was the reason in itself, sir,' she said slowly. 'It was for Ralph's sake that I couldn't run away with him.'

His brows drew in together. 'I am not sure I understand. Were you both not exposed to the same danger
that rose after Kinnerton Castle was seized and Ralph's
father accused of treason?'

'I can see that you know the whole of it.'

He gave his head a little shake. 'Yes, but I only know
everything from Ralph's perspective.'

Sir Thomas's squire shifted in an agitated way that
caught Gwen off guard. 'Is your squire well? Perhaps
he'd like to sit somewhere?'

'No, do not concern yourself with him, my lady. He
is fine where he is.'

'I suppose you know best.' Her brows met in the middle, uncertainty making it difficult for her to tear her
eyes back to the knight who sat in front of her. 'To answer your earlier question…no. The danger that I was
exposed to, as you put it, was very different to the real
one Ralph faced. For me, that same danger assured me
a measure of protection, strangely enough.'

'I do not understand.'

No one needed to know *that* part of Gwen's reasoning and she was in no mind to explain herself. No one
save Brida knew the truth of exactly what she had done
to ensure Ralph's safe passage. In any case, the risk she
had taken had somehow paid off, when she had managed
to leave Kinnerton Castle as well soon after.

'It's of no consequence, Sir Thomas—besides, I soon
became the Crown's ward, so the danger you allude to
never applied to me in the same way as it did to Ralph.'
She sighed. 'The truth was that I could not leave with
Ralph, as that would have been even more perilous…
for him.'

'You were—' he raised a brow '—protecting him?'

The man seemed incredulous that a woman would deem to protect a man.

'Yes. Much good it did me,' she said bitterly.

He watched her for moment before looking away. 'I am sorry for that, Lady Gwenllian.'

She suddenly sensed a presence behind her and snapped her head around to find Stephen le Gros standing over her. Yes, a very unwelcome presence.

She bristled with indignation that he was here, standing close to her, in such a presumptuous way. Yet she could hardly make a scene in such a public place, with King Henry and his court in attendance.

'And what exactly do *you* have to be sorry for, sir?' Stephen le Gros scoffed.

Gwen's stomach twisted in an angry knot as the knight who sat opposite her stood. And she prayed that was all the conversation that Stephen had heard.

Suddenly the air was charged with a palpable tension, emanating from not only Sir Thomas, but strangely from his man standing in the shadows. For some unfathomable reason, she sensed the menacing mood as a prelude to a brawl. And although she welcomed the intervention of Sir Thomas and his shadowy squire as they towered over Stephen le Gros, it would not do.

She shot up, addressing Sir Thomas. 'I thank you for giving me your time, sir.'

'It was a pleasure, my lady. May I be of service and escort you back to your husband?'

She smiled weakly. 'That won't be necessary—besides, I am unmarried, sir.'

Stephen le Gros stepped towards her and wrapped his clammy hand around her elbow. 'Come, my dear.'

She yanked it free as discreetly as she could manage

from the overbearing man and inclined her head slightly, ignoring Stephen. 'Good evening, Sir Thomas.'

It had taken all of Ralph's resolve not to go after Gwen and make sure that his repellent cousin was as far away from her as possible and that she was well. But he couldn't risk it. It had been close. Far too close. The fact Stephen le Gros was even touching Gwen in that familiar manner made his blood boil and almost made him act.

Almost...

The man had taken everything from him. Not that Ralph could prove that the insurgency and treachery against his father had been instigated by his cousin. But there was no doubt that Stephen le Gros had been behind it all, allying himself with his father's enemies. His cousin had his father's blood all over his hands as well as the attempt on Ralph's life in Aquitaine, two years ago. And the temptation to end it here and now had been shockingly inviting.

Ralph's hand had clenched tightly around a dagger, concealed by his hood, his knuckles white as he fought to control the urges to plunge it into the man's chest. Yet that would not help further his cause. Ralph had to somehow hold on to his temper, needing the patience he never had when he was younger. He would achieve nothing if he were to vent all of his anger, here, in front of the King, the Marcher Earls and his court.

God, but everything had changed the moment Stephen had come to live with them, years ago. From the first, his cousin had managed to manipulate himself into his father's high esteem. And be a constant reminder of what it meant to be a knight. The perfect shining example of the *heir apparent*, or so his father would say. And his cousin had exploited this to his advantage. He'd taunt, bully and put Ralph down at every opportunity.

Stephen had been everything that Ralph had not. Even Ralph's physical prowess had been questioned at the time. His cousin being older, so naturally bigger and much stronger than him. Although, judging by what Ralph had seen tonight, that no longer held true between the two of them.

Even so, Ralph had to tread carefully and not allow his animosity for Stephen le Gros get in the way of his attempt to restore his castle and lands.

Ralph might have been sorely tested this eventide after Stephen's unwanted attentions towards Gwen, but he could not lose sight of what he had to do.

Gwen...

Ralph's head was still spinning from everything she had disclosed. He was no closer to comprehending her reasons for refusing to run away with him six years ago than he was now. The certainty of what he had believed to be true was now being challenged even further.

It seemed that Gwen had not stayed behind for duty alone or because she had not cared for him and wanted to tie her ambitions to whoever would be the next Lord de Kinnerton. No, she had, by her own admission, done it as a way to protect him.

Protect him?

How exactly? He tried to recall what she had just said.

'I could not leave with Ralph, as that would have been even more perilous...for him.'

Had she really thought that he needed protecting? There was something both endearing and frankly disturbing about that. The idea that Gwen might have perceived Ralph too feeble to protect himself, let alone guard her from harm, was too depressing to contemplate. Had that been it?

There was also another disclosure that had taken him by surprise. She was unmarried, still.

Why?

Again, Ralph pondered on the circumstances of Gwen's life since they parted that fateful day six years ago. What had happened to her in the intervening years? Had she been looked after, protected from men such as Stephen le Gros, who it seemed was still in pursuit of her, damn it?

There was only one way to find out. Against his very own judgement that he needed to avoid her and banish her from his mind, Ralph realised something, then. He had to see her again.

Chapter Three

It was never part of Ralph's plan to seek Gwenllian ferch Hywel. As well as that, Will Geraint and Hugh de Villiers had warned him that he should not disclose his true identity to anyone and risk exposure. Not yet.

And God knew that Ralph could not afford to disappoint the two men, who could otherwise relegate him by dropping him off their elite group of knights in this tournament. They were right, too, and yet...

Yet Ralph knew he had to somehow see Gwen again only to satisfy *his* curiosity. Especially since he now understood, from her countenance and the sadness in her eyes, that Gwen had mourned him.

She still mourned him.

Ralph had been surprised by that. The pull on his conscience that she still believed him to be dead was beginning to sit heavily on his shoulders. He must inform her that he had not perished, if only to allow her some peace of mind.

More than that it was also becoming necessary to stop drawing attention to them. The fact that she had sought Tom not once but twice, in an open place and on the same

day, had certainly roused Stephen le Gros's notice and
was far too dangerous at this particular time.

Yes, Ralph would tell her the truth to satisfy her curiosity and he'd have to hope that she would keep his
secret before parting ways. But how to proceed without
rousing suspicion?

All throughout the following day, his mind was preoccupied with this difficulty and the best way forward.
But nothing had come his way. Gwen had not made any
further appearances. She had not come to the hall in the
castle for the evening feast and nor had not been seen
anywhere.

There was only one thing for it. He must take drastic
action. Which meant that, against his better judgement,
Ralph had agreed to an unwise scheme.

So, here he was with Tom in the middle of the night,
lurking outside the small arched window of the castle
keep, where they believed Gwen to be housed.

God help him!

'What exactly do you mean to do, if you see her?'
Tom muttered underneath his hooded cloak. They were
in the deserted part of the inner bailey of the stone castle, crouched low beneath the nearest shrubbery dotted
around the small herb garden that infused the moonlit
sky with its heady scent.

Ralph rubbed his chin and the ragged scar on his face,
soothing it. 'I'm not entirely sure, but I'll know when the
moment presents itself.'

'Let's hope that the happy event presents itself far
quicker than you anticipate because we cannot afford
to be careless and wake another group of maidens as
we just did.'

'And whose fault was that?' Ralph hissed under his breath. 'I know this castle as you do not.'

'By all means, go ahead, then, unless you feel inclined to climb that tree outside the window you believe may be hers and give the poor woman the shock of her life.'

'No, I think we should keep this simple, as we planned.'

But this wasn't simple at all.

Fate might have thrown them together again, but how was Ralph to let Gwen know that he was alive, without causing her more alarm and, yes…shock?

Ralph crept out from behind the shrub with difficulty and hurled the stone in his hand against the wooden shutters of the arched window of the upper storey before diving back. He could hear barking somewhere in the distance, but otherwise there was only the heavy stillness of a velvety night sky, as if in anticipation of the unknown.

Ralph took a deep breath, realising that he was nervous of disclosing his secret and how it might be received. He was a changed man from the one Gwen had known. Physically he was bigger, from his height to the honed muscles he had attained as a warrior, to the scars covering his body and, in particular, the mangled, distorted side of his face. Would she be repulsed by him and why in heavens should that matter? He swallowed in disgust. The purpose of all this was to unburden Gwen, reveal his existence and make sure that she kept away from him, afterwards. After all, they were as good as strangers now, even though they had once cared for each other. But that time no longer existed and neither did the boy he had once been. The boy she had turned away from.

'I don't think anyone has stirred.' Tom frowned. 'Do you want me to take aim?'

'No, I'll try once more.' Ralph crept out and threw a

handful of pebbles, one after the other, against the shutter, each one hitting with striking accuracy before he took cover beside Tom. Both men peered from behind the shrubs, but again there was no response. It seemed that no one within the chamber was inquisitive enough to find out the cause of who or what was persistently knocking against the window shutters at this late hour.

'Allow me.' Tom crawled out to stand and was about to take aim with the small stone clutched between his fingers above his head. Just then the wooden shutters jerked before folding out to open.

They saw Gwen's companion stick her head out of the arched window and look in every direction before she spotted Tom below, who had frozen in place, mid-throw.

'What is the meaning of this, Sir Thomas?' She scowled. 'My lady has retired for the evening and doesn't wish to be disturbed.'

'A thousand pardons, Mistress Brida, but we needed to…as in *I* have ventured to…to…'

'Yes? To do what exactly, sir?'

Tom took a step back towards the shrub. 'What shall I tell this prickly woman?' he whispered from the side of his mouth.

'Ask after Gwen, since we…as in you…have not seen her today,' Ralph replied in hushed tones.

'I wanted to enquire after Lady Gwenllian's health, since I must have missed her today,' Tom said to the woman. 'I thought the whole purpose of tonight was for you to reveal yourself,' he hissed to Ralph, still cowering behind the lush foliage.

'Yes, but *she* is not the one at the window.'

Tom pasted his most devastating smile and looked up. 'Could I trouble you, mistress to ask whether I may have a word or two with Lady Gwenllian.'

'You may, sir, but…er…sadly my mistress is indisposed. She does, however, thank you for your concern.'

The first rumblings of thunder could be heard overhead. 'What is it? Is Gwen unwell?' Ralph asked under his breath as he pushed down the branch to take a better look.

Tom flicked his hand behind, in a gesture that warned Ralph to stay back where he was hidden. 'I hope Lady Gwenllian is in good health?' he asked on his behalf, instead.

'Yes, sir, she is,' came the terse reply from the window. 'But my lady is not inclined to, ah…see anyone this evening.'

'Would there be a time she can see me, otherwise? Tomorrow, perchance, after the evening feast.'

'What are you doing?' Ralph hissed.

'Arranging a proper rendezvous for you with her,' he whispered from the corner of his mouth.

'Hell's teeth, Tom,' he spat, the needles of the shrub digging into his skin 'This is no jesting matter.'

'Did I say it was? But it seems unlikely that you are going to get past Lady Gwenllian's angry termagant tonight.'

'Mayhap I should come out.'

'Mayhap you should allow me to arrange this properly, rather than give the poor lady the fright of her life.'

Gwen paced inside the small chamber and snapped her head up. 'What is it that the man wants, Brida?'

The chamber was lit by only the last embers of the fire and the light of the pale moon outside, which was rapidly being veiled by dark clouds.

'Sir Thomas Lovent wants to meet you again.' Brida

turned her head around and raised her brows. 'But I cannot understand why.'

Neither could Gwen. Yet, there was much she still didn't understand about what had happened to Ralph de Kinnerton or the disconcerting manner in which his friend had given his ribbon back to her. And she could not shake the feeling that things were not all as they seemed. 'Could you ask Sir Thomas for his reason?'

'Certainly, but if I may, my advice is to be wary of the man.'

Gwen's fingers traced the edge of the coffer absently. 'Oh, and why is that?'

Her friend let out an irritated breath. 'All he's done since you met him is to drag up the past and upset you.'

'But I believe that sometimes it's a good thing to have the past dragged up, Brida. To be able to move forward, you have to be able to let go of the past.

'But to what end?' Her friend scowled.

'So that it can allow me to accept what happened to Ralph, somehow.' Gwen sat on the edge of the pallet bed. 'If that is in any way possible, then it can only be worthwhile. Do you not see?'

'Mistress? Would Lady Gwenllian meet me tomorrow?' Sir Thomas's muffled voice said from somewhere outside. 'Only it has started to rain...and it looks to become more persistent.'

'My lady wishes to know why you need to meet her again, sir.' Brida lowered her voice even more, so that only Gwen would hear. 'And for the sky to open and the rain to drench you to the bone.'

A corner of Gwen's lips curved. 'Does Sir Thomas bother you?'

'He smiles too much.' Her friend snapped her head

around in exasperation. 'And my mother always warned me of men who had a propensity to do that.'

Gwen burst out laughing for the first time for as long as she could remember. A welcome short reprieve, as it had been a particularly miserable day, which accounted for the reasons why she had wanted to be alone. And why she had been crying for much of it.

Meeting Ralph's friend had once again brought back everything that had happened between them. Brida had been right about that. Gwen had been upset ever since she had come back to this part of England and spoken to Sir Thomas, whose friendly eyes and easy smiles she was certain hid more than he was willing to say.

Yet, it somehow eased something inside her to be able to talk about Ralph with someone else who had also known him. Perhaps the more Sir Thomas explained about the life Ralph had led, after he had left Kinnerton under a cloud of danger and uncertainty, the more comfort she might possibly gain. Especially in the knowledge that he had not always been alone, that he has friends such as the man standing below in the rain.

Gwen inhaled deeply. 'Tell him that I shall meet him.'

If Sir Thomas needed to disclose more than he already had, then she would agree to hear him. One last time.

The following evening after the feast, Gwen scurried out of the hall. Tugging the wide hood of her long, grey, woollen cloak over her head, she strode out of the inner bailey, with Brida beside her, as a few bemused guards looked on. Other than looking them up and down, they didn't approach them, thankfully.

'I'm going to die of mortification, Gwen. They think we're women of the night.'

'Never mind that. Come along. It would be best not to give them a reason to stop us from leaving the castle.'

Huddling close to one another, the two women rushed through the gatehouse and along the path that circled around the castle, which eventually brought them to the edge of the nearby woodland. Here, as promised and sheltered beneath a tree, Gwen could just make out the silhouette of Sir Thomas, waiting patiently for them. They continued along the path until they approached him.

'Good evening, my lady.' He inclined his head. 'Mistress Brida.'

Her friend gave him a curt, dismissive nod as Gwen shuddered, realising that they were completely alone in the dead of night with this man. She hoped that she could trust him.

'Good evening to you, Sir Thomas. I hope you have not been waiting long?'

'Not at all, Lady Gwenllian.'

'Well then…here we are.' She swallowed. 'What was it that you wished to say to me?'

'Ah, as to that. I'm afraid I have drawn you here under false appearances.'

Her heart sank as she exchanged a quick look of concern with Brida. Had she been mistaken about this man? Other than being Ralph's friend he was, after all, a total stranger. 'Explain yourself, sir, and note we have not come unarmed.'

He held up his hands and looked solemn when she had expected his mirth. 'No, you misunderstand, my lady, it is not *I* who wish to meet you, but someone entirely different.'

'What do you mean?' She scowled, narrowing her eyes. 'You are talking in riddles, sir.'

He inclined his head towards the entrance of the

woods. 'The man who wishes to meet with you is there, within, waiting for you. If you take that path and follow it around, you will eventually reach…'

'The big oak tree…' she said slowly. 'Every path leads to that old tree. I used to come here a long time ago with…with…' She suddenly snapped her head up and gave Sir Thomas a withering look. Was this some kind of distasteful jest?

'What is the meaning of this?' She felt like punching the man. 'Is this a trick?'

'A trick?' Of course not.' He sighed. 'It's not a trick, or a riddle, or a miracle either.'

Gwen rubbed her forehead feeling suddenly weary. 'What are you trying to tell me, Sir Thomas?'

'Please, my lady. All shall be explained when you enter the woods…alone.'

Gwen could sense that Brida was about to object to his proposal, but something about this situation beguiled her more than she could say—more than it really should. It beckoned her forth as though it were pulling her by an invisible thread.

'Very well, I'll go.' Gwen lifted her head as Brida stepped forward to follow. 'On my own.'

'But, my Lady Gwenllian…?'

'Thank you for your concern, Brida. But I believe I shall be safe venturing here on my own. I am acquainted with this surrounding area after all.'

She took a deep breath and stepped tentatively into the unknown. She looked back behind her occasionally, knowing she could always run back, if she needed to. She walked along the damp sloping path, flanked by the dense copse and towering trees on either side. The air was heavy with a clammy stickiness and eerily silent apart from her thumping heartbeat and her rampant breathing.

The only light came from the incandescent moon, dancing on the leaves, illuminating her way to the tree.

Their tree…

She wondered whether she could still trace her fingers along the ridged, rough tree trunk and find their names—hers and Ralph's carved into the bark from another lifetime.

Gwen had never done anything impulsive and certainly not without good reason. Yet something had been bothering her since the moment Ralph's ribbon had been returned to her. Something that did not quite tally up.

Either way, she hoped to gain some understanding. Not that she could discern what that could be in these woods. Gwen did not even know who she was supposed to be meeting here. Possibly another friend or associate of Ralph's who might explain more to her, so that Gwen could finally close that painful part of her life.

Yet this was nothing new. Gwen had lived and lost before. First her mother, then her sweet, little sister who had lived no more than four short years. Her older brother perished a few years later and finally her beloved father followed suit.

All gone.

Before Gwen knew what had happened, she had been bundled away to live in Kinnerton, in England—a foreign land whose heir she was one day to marry. Gwen had only been a young girl, but that didn't matter, not when arrangements had been made by her desperately ill father and the ambitious Marcher Lord of Kinnerton. She was a pawn to be used for an important and strategic alliance.

But then something remarkably unexpectant happened. Something that managed to banish the hollow pain from the loss of her father…

Gwen found a friend in the young Ralph de Kinnerton.

A friend who would come to mean more to her than anyone had before. A shy, young reticent boy who was teased mercilessly for not being good enough, not being tall enough, man enough or even strong enough. But he was or rather he had been. He had been enough...*for her*.

Once again, however, the cruel hand of fate had dealt her a devastating blow as Ralph had also perished.

That elusive happiness was, somehow, always out of her reach and never to be hers. Now she no longer looked for it or even expected it. All she wanted was some semblance of peace in her solitude.

Gwen lifted her head and her breath caught in her throat.

There it was, the magnificent, sprawling, ancient tree. She blinked and adjusted her eyes more to the darkness, looking around to see who it was that she was supposed to meet, but there was no one.

So she waited...and waited. And waited some more.

But then she felt it. That strange feeling creeping up her arm, warning her that she was no longer alone. She swallowed, nervously.

'Who goes there?' She bit her bottom lip and let out a nervous breath. 'Show yourself. I know you are there.'

Again nothing, yet she felt that presence as if it were sliding down her body.

Then someone did speak.

'It's me, Gwen... It's Ralph.'

Chapter Four

Gwen felt as though every drop of blood had drained from her body. The world seemed to spin around her as she leant back against the trunk of the tree, her fingers digging in, seeking some sort of support. Her breathing became laboured. Her head was in a state of confusion. It could not be true, could it?

She closed her eyes tightly in an attempt to test whether this might be a dream, her imagination playing tricks on her. After all, she was here again by this magnificent tree, with echoes of her past all around her. Could she have conjured up something she wanted to be true?

'Lady Gwenllian?'

Seemingly she had not. The voice that carried in the soft breeze did appear to be one that resembled Ralph's. Only it rumbled a lot lower, a lot deeper and belonged to *a man*.

Yes, it seemed very real.

Oh, God! Her knees felt as though they might buckle beneath her.

He was filling in the silence as he continued to explain. 'I did not mean to distress you. I know this must come as a huge surprise but…it became imperative that I tell you about this, myself.'

Gwen still could not find her voice as her head swirled around, trying to comprehend this new discovery.

'Is it really you?' she whispered.

'It is. Yes.'

'I… I can't believe this. It seems so unreal.'

'Nevertheless, it's the truth, my lady.'

He sounded so formal. So distant, yet somewhere close by.

'Where…where are you?' she stammered as she opened her eyes and looked in every direction.

'That is of no consequence. All you need to know—all that is important—is that you need not concern your-self about me. Not any longer. I am hale. I am alive. And, thank God, in one piece.'

That was all she needed to know.

The man talking might have sounded like Ralph, but his words were so unlike anything the boy she once knew would ever utter.

'Where are you?' she repeated, but was soundly ig-nored as Ralph continued with his speech. He seemed to be in a hurry to finish whatever he needed to say.

'The truth is that, after I saw you for the first time in so many years, I felt compelled to give you back your ribbon. But I then realised you also had a right to know the truth about me.'

'You!' Her brows shot up. 'You gave me back the rib-bon?'

'I did.'

She frowned. 'But I thought… I thought that that was Sir Thomas Lovent.'

'You were meant to think that, Gwen.'

Oh, God, mayhap she was still dreaming. She edged

away from the tree and frantically stumbled from one direction to the next, trying to locate where the voice was coming from.

'Why would you need to pretend to be another knight?'

'It's best that you do not know that,' the voice murmured.

'Why would you not correct the assumption that you are dead?'

'You do not need to know that either.'

'I see that there's much I cannot be privy to,' Gwen bit out.

'Just so, my lady. It is for the best, believe me.'

Gwen frowned in confusion. *Believe him?*

She had a sudden impulse to laugh, scream or cry, whichever came first. Here was this man proclaiming to be Ralph de Kinnerton, presumed dead and actively courting danger by pretending to be someone he was not, with the added issue of his devious cousin also being present at this tournament. But far, far more than that was the way her heart was tumbling over itself from this incredible disclosure. Ralph de Kinnerton was alive and *hale* from all accounts. And somehow among the obvious joy that arose from this possibility was the sadness and hurt from everything that had happened between them in the past. In particular, how they had said so many harsh untruths before they parted ways that awful night in the woods outside Kinnerton. And with this, the bitter memory and subsequent guilt after learning of Ralph's demise. But that demise was not so, apparently.

Gwen moved slowly around the tree, chasing the shadow, hoping in vain to catch something more tangible…something that could confirm that he was real and much more than just a rumbling voice that rippled through her. Yet, each time she felt close to finding him, the shadow would shift and disappear.

'Why will you not show yourself to me?'

'It is better this way.'

'Is it?' She stopped momentarily as she dragged her palm across her clammy forehead, frustrated at having to play cat and mouse. 'I cannot see why. If you are truly whom you say you are.'

'You doubt me?'

'What am I supposed to believe when I cannot even see you?'

'It would be simpler if you did not.'

'How can I be assured that you are who you say you are then?'

There was no response. A hushed silence wrapped around her in the moonlight, making her shiver. And just when she was convinced that he was no longer there, he spoke again.

'Very well, as you wish.' The shadowy figure stepped out of the darkness and made Gwen take a step back and gasp. His braies and hose covered long, honed limbs and a short, dark cloak with a wide hood covered his head, his face invisible beneath it. Strapped to his back he carried two swords sheathed within its scabbard, criss-crossing his body.

'Well? Are you satisfied, my lady?'

She rubbed her eyes several times and felt her jaw drop, unable to believe that the man still shrouded in darkness was Ralph de Kinnerton. This man was huge in every sense—an embodiment of a powerful warrior and nothing like the long-limbed skinny boy she once knew. She took a step back, suddenly feeling more unsure about being in the middle of the woods with this…stranger.

'It *is* me, Gwenllian.' He sighed deeply, without making an attempt to come closer or revealing anything that she might recognise.

He remained in the near darkness, the outline of his tall frame the only part of him that was visible. There seemed to be a wide chasm between them as they stood some distance apart, facing each another.

'How can I be certain? You look nothing like the Ralph de Kinnerton I knew.'

She had expected him to move forward, to show his face, so that she would believe that his voice and this man—*Ralph*—were one and the same.

Instead, he stood pinned to the spot and took an exasperated breath before he spoke again. 'What would you like me to say, Gwen? Shall I recount that first time you came to Kinnerton, or remind you how you got that tiny little scar above your left eyebrow, in the brook not very far from here? Or what about the many times we would sneak here to Pulverbatch Castle, here to these very woods…to this very tree?'

'Oh, Lord, it…it is you.' Her hand shot to cover her mouth.

'Yes.' He expelled a deep breath. 'And after I saw you, I believed you also had a right to know the truth about me.'

Gwen suddenly found this—being in these woods with this version of Ralph—so unreal.

'I still cannot believe you're alive,' she whispered, pushing down a sudden wave of unfettered longing.

He shook his head. 'I very nearly wasn't. For quite some time it was debatable whether I would survive.'

'What happened to you?'

'You need not concern yourself about me any more, Gwen.'

She blinked, puzzled at the cool detachment in his

voice. It seemed that this was all the information she was to be offered. Yet, had she expected more because of courtesy? Familiarity? The friendship and love that they once shared? That no longer seemed to apply to their connection, after all this time. That, she was sure, she had quashed six years ago anyway.

Gwen gave her head a little shake as though clearing it. 'I see. Well, I'm glad that you have seen fit to allow me to know the truth, sir.'

'Just so.' His stance was so rigid as he stood with his legs apart, his back straight. 'Especially since your curiosity made you seek Thomas Lovent with more and more questions.'

Ah, so this was what this was all about. Her persistent inquisitiveness about what had happened to Ralph after the ribbon was given back to her risked the exposure of whatever scheme Ralph and his friend had devised.

Something else suddenly occurred to her. 'You are his squire, the man who followed Sir Thomas into the hall?'

'Indeed.'

She suddenly felt ridiculous that she had cared. That she had grieved over this man, who seemed more like a stranger now. God, but she barely recognised him.

'I should have realised there would be a reason such as this for you to tell me now.'

'I regret that my perceived demise caused you such anguish, but know this—once I saw you again, I knew that you had a right to know about me.'

'But not immediately, however.'

Gwen's jaw set, realising that he had seen her a few times and yet waited before informing her on this night. She could not help but feel a twinge of hurt, knowing that he had not done so until this moment in these woods, steeped in so many memories from their past. God, when she thought of the tears that she had shed, when she believed him to be dead. How she had mourned Ralph de Kinnerton and all this time—all these years—he had been alive, but had chosen not to tell her.

'You were obviously there, listening as I spoke to Sir Thomas, while I was still grief-stricken, believing you to be dead.'

He could have prevented the anguish, guilt and sorrow that had filled her heart when she had believed he had perished in a faraway land, but had chosen not to. Had she meant so little to him and been so inconsequential that Ralph could not have informed her earlier than this? Had their friendship, connection and love counted for nothing? Evidently not.

'I'm sorry for that, but it was a shock to see you again as well. I should possibly have said something earlier, but in truth I can trust so few people in my life that I wasn't sure that I should.'

Gwen could not help feel that somehow Ralph's reasons for withholding the truth all this time stemmed from the manner in which they had parted and his belief of her indifference towards him. This had been something she had painstakingly brought about, in order to get him to flee without her. God help her, but she had never fully considered the implications of the devastating wound she was inflicting on both of them.

'Even me?'

'Even you.'

'Well, then you honour me, sir.' She lifted her head. 'Yet not enough to tell me what it is that you are doing here?'

'No.'

'I see.' She felt a coldness trickle through her. 'Although I can only guess that this has something to do with the prospect of gaining coin through this tournament, so you can get Kinnerton back?'

'Can you blame me for trying?'

'Of course not. But in this highly furtive manner, when you're still presumed dead? While pretending to be another knight?'

'Never you mind about that.'

'Very well, but I imagine you believe that you're doing your duty.'

She could hear his quiet, hollow laugh. 'Oh, yes, and you know very well about *that*, Gwen.'

'What are you implying?' She suddenly felt sick in her stomach as it twisted tightly.

'Nothing, my lady. Only that the decision you made, when we last saw one another and parted ways, forced me to realise the importance of where *my* duty should actually lay.'

'Did you believe that the choices I took were easy?'

'You misunderstand me, Lady Gwenllian,' he said in a clipped tone. 'However, I cannot claim to know why you made the decisions you made.'

Gwen felt as though she had received a blow to the stomach. Where once they had known and trusted one another, her actions had made Ralph doubt and question everything about her.

'Yet, it was made with great difficulty, sir.'

'I can believe it was and I hope to relieve you now from whatever those difficulties may have been.'

Her smile felt brittle. 'As easy as that?'

'We can only do what we believe to be right, after all.'

'And did you?' She exhaled, unsure whether she wanted to know. 'Did you believe what I did was right? To stay behind here in England?'

'That is not for me to answer, my lady. Not now…after

all this time. Besides, it was a good lesson for me...a necessary lesson in the changes that I had to make if I were to be the man my father had wanted me to be.'

Gwen closed her eyes and let out a shaky breath. She felt bereft and saddened by this admission that Ralph had made. Had these changes that he had deemed necessary pushed out every last vestiges of the old Ralph? Indeed, did that side of him, the one she once loved and cherished, even exist any more?

'Tell me something, sir—why did you give me back the ribbon?'

He stepped back further into the darkness before answering. 'I could no longer lay claim to such a gift and the meaning behind it. I wanted you to have it back.'

'I see.'

But, no, she did not see.

It was the only part of his behaviour that seemed to conflict with the indifference Ralph now presented and the singular ambition that he pursued. Not that it really mattered now.

'Well, there's nothing further to say then.'

'No,' he muttered, allowing that single word to fill the silence for a moment. 'If I...if I may ask whether I can count on your secrecy regarding everything you have learnt tonight?'

'You may be assured of that. Your secret is safe with me.' She swallowed as she took a step back as well.

'Thank you.'

Gwen rubbed her forehead with the back of her hand. She suddenly had an overwhelming need to get away from here. From the secrets, the revelations, the lost hope. And a boy who had become a man. A man who was a stranger to her now.

She flicked her head to face him one more time. 'You have changed, sir.'

'I have,' he said, bitterly. 'In more ways than you'll ever know.'

Oh, yes, those old wounds seemed to be far deeper than she could have ever imagined.

Chapter Five

Ralph bent his head, ignoring the metal digging sharply into his neck from the back of his helmet. It penetrated through the many layers he was wearing underneath, making a visit to the blacksmith, who had taken temporary residence in the outer bailey, a necessity in order to fix the problem and smooth out the rough edges. Or it would once he had finished his training.

Ralph brushed his hands up and down his horse's glossy mane. 'We can do this…'

He squeezed his calves and heels against his faithful black destrier's lower flank, flicking the reins, making the animal sprint ahead.

Ralph held off until he got closer to the makeshift target of round, hollow, metal rings that had been suspended from a long-erected stand, until he lowered his lance. He shifted the angle of the lance as he clutched it firmly in his left hand, his eyes narrowing.

Closer. Closer. Closer, still…

And then it was there—the target swinging back and forth in the breeze. Ralph tilted the pointed sharp metal end of his lance towards it as he thrust through the hollow centre and caught it, making it slide down the pole.

He heard clapping to the side and knew it would be Tom, but as he glanced over, he spotted his mentor, William Geraint, standing with his arms crossed beside him as well.

'That was excellent, Ralph.' Will smiled, nodding at him as he rode towards them. 'Much better than your attempt yesterday.'

'My thanks—the technique of awaiting the target until I had it on sight was probably what made the difference.'

Will shrugged. 'That's really Hugh's gem of advice but it's a good one, nevertheless.'

Ralph passed the lance to Tom. 'Indeed, it is.'

'I would recommend, however, that you wait a fraction longer until you have the target directly in your sight.'

'Duly noted.'

Will rubbed his jaw and tipped his head at him. 'And bring the lance a little higher, in line with your ear. That way you can strike expediently in either direction.'

Ralph nodded. 'Anything else?'

'No, just keep up the practice, Ralph. I'm glad we're finally making progress here.' Will gave him a wry smile before turning on his heel. 'And lest I forget, Isabel would like the presence of your company tonight, so I hope to see the two of you at the banquet later.'

'My lord.'

Ralph was still perched on his mount with Tom beside the horse on foot, as they watched their patron's retreating footsteps.

Tom finally spoke. 'That went well.'

'I still need to go over it a few more times, if you would be so obliging to set it up again.'

'Certainly. Shall we try for an even smaller target this time? It might be interesting to see if you can rise to the challenge?'

'Very well.'

Tom looked up at him and pulled his hood over his head as Ralph turned his horse, Fortis, around. 'Don't look now, but Lady Gwenllian has just noticed you from afar.'

Ralph turned Fortis again in the direction that Tom had motioned towards and his breath caught at the sight of Gwen with her companion beside her, stopping and staring at them from beyond the training area.

It seemed as though their gaze caught and fused together even though there was considerable distance between them. Even though the back of Ralph's head and neck were encased within a padded coif and his whole face was covered by the metal helmet with only narrow slit openings for him to see through. It did not matter.

He saw her and his heart tripped over itself.

Ralph was meant to have felt much lighter, with his conscience eased after having disclosed to Gwen the fact that he was alive and back in England a few days ago.

He was supposed to feel relief from that revelation, so that he could move on with his life. Push her out of his mind, so that he could focus on what really mattered to him now—*this*.

Winning this tournament and somehow getting Kinnerton back.

He had to hone his skills so that he could pitch them against the best knights in England. And somehow prove that he was actually capable of becoming the Marcher Lord he was supposed to be. A Marcher Lord that many, including his father, had doubted he would be successful at.

Ralph had endured his father's criticisms throughout his life, but these were compounded more so when his cousin had come to live with them. Everything changed when Stephen had arrived in Kinnerton. He had taken an instant dislike to Ralph and revelled in exposing his inadequacies to his father. All in the hope of gaining favour and presenting himself as a far better candidate as heir. And although Ralph bitterly knew his shortcomings, coming from his own father it had been painful. More so, since there had been few who had not shared that perception of Ralph.

God, but even Gwenllian had probably doubted his capabilities all those years ago. It certainly explained why she had not fled Kinnerton with him. And if he had been honest with himself, Ralph knew that they had been right to doubt him. Back then, he had none of the necessary skills to command respect—neither in physical ability, his presence or through any leadership qualities.

Now he did, however. Now Ralph could show them just what he was capable of…he hoped. Indeed, he hoped that he was fortuitous enough to put everything he had learnt into practice.

He let out a slow breath as he pondered on the beautiful woman who plagued his dreams.

His reunion with Gwen had not eased anything and he had not achieved any peace of mind. Their whole encounter had been difficult. Ralph had wanted to let her know that he was alive so that it would cease any further interest in him. Her curiosity had to be satisfied and now, hopefully, it was.

But then that did not mean it had lessened *his* curiosity about her life and everything that had happened after they parted six years ago. The truth was that Ralph had so many questions of his own about what she had done since then.

And his disclosures in the woods had certainly not gone as smoothly as he'd hoped. In his haste to only tell her what he wanted her to know, avoiding her difficult questions, Ralph had inadvertently offended Gwen.

God's breath!

Although it might have not been his intention, it was probably for the best that she believed his indifference towards her. Ralph needed to cast aside those feelings which had resurfaced ever since he had set eyes on her. It would not do to rekindle any of them, however much he still desired Gwen, even after all this time. Even after the pain that she had caused him all those years ago.

Indeed, as long as they kept apart from one another, he would hope to eventually achieve some semblance of peace and equanimity regarding Gwen. Then everything would fall into place, as that last link from his past would also finally break and he could be the man he was always meant to be. The man she evidently hadn't believed he could be.

He blinked and made a small inclination of his head, which she returned before turning on her heel and walking away, her veil flapping in the breeze.

Yes, it was imperative that he did not allow himself to be drawn into any sort of acquaintance or familiarity with Gwenllian ferch Hywel.

'Come, let's get on with this.' Ralph scowled.

The day passed without further interruptions but Ralph was still distracted. And this was not made any easier now that he was under the same timber-framed roof as Gwen. He hadn't wanted to come to the banquet this evening, knowing it best that he kept his distance from Gwenllian. It was the only way to stop this incessant curiosity about the woman.

Yet Ralph could not deny Isabel de Clancey's company for the world, especially as she had only just arrived with her infant daughter to see her husband. Isabel was like a sister to him, whose warmth and interest in his well-being was as bewildering as it was humbling. He knew unequivocally that without Isabel's help and support he would not be where he was today. Hell, he doubted whether he would even be alive.

'I trust that everything is going as well as we had planned, Ralph?' Isabel's head was turned away from him as he moved forward to fetch the jug of ale while he performed his duties as a squire.

'Not quite. Have you not spoken with Lord de Clancey, Isabel?' he muttered as he poured some ale into her mug.

'Yes, but I'd like to hear it from you, Ralph,' she said quietly over the noisy clatter and din from the table.

'There is really not much to say except that I was suffering from a bout of nerves that first day. But now, thank the saints, I feel that I'm settling in it.'

'How are your scars?'

'Fine.'

'And your hand? Do you need more balm for it?'

'That too, Isabel.' He sighed. 'And I have enough. Thank you.'

'Good. And how is the training going?'

Ralph completed his duties before returning to hover behind his friends.

'As well as can be expected,' he muttered quietly.

'I'm glad to hear that, Ralph.' She sipped from her mug. 'And no one has guessed the nature of the scheme or your true identity?'

'No.'

Isabel titled her head away slightly as though she were talking to her husband. 'Then why is that beautiful, young woman with fair hair, sat at the far end of the hall, constantly casting her gaze in this direction...looking, I believe, at *you*?'

'I would not know,' he said, stepping back in the shadows.

'Oh, but, Ralph...' Isabel's voice sounded bemused '...you haven't asked which beautiful young woman.'

Ralph had kept Gwenllian from his friend, in an attempt to make that part of his past seem of little importance. Yet, he knew the way Isabel's inquisitive, intelligent mind worked. And he also knew how she would then insist on knowing more, if not from him then others, including Gwen herself.

'There's something you're not telling me here, Ralph,' she said over her shoulder. 'Such as the possible reason why the lady in question there is wearing *your* purple ribbon around her wrist?'

Hell's teeth!

Ralph should have thrown that damn ribbon away and destroyed it rather than returning to Gwen. It had brought nothing but aggravation since he'd made that blunder that first day of the tournament.

'Are you going to tell me?'

He closed his eyes, realising his mistake.

'Ralph?'

'Later,' he muttered under his breath. 'Not here, Isabel.'

'Very well.' This time she did turn around as he inclined his head deferentially. 'Be careful, Ralph. You cannot afford to risk everything you have worked hard for.'

No, that he could not do.

Gwen took a small bite from a soft bread roll that she'd dipped in meat juices before looking away. She knew she must be careful and that it would be prudent to stop looking in the direction of Lord de Clancey's retinue. Especially at the squire, who was far too large, far too broad and far too much of a man to be one.

Gwen should have realised something had been amiss with Sir Thomas Lovent's squire before. Deep down she had.

She stabbed the piece of meat on the trencher she was sharing with Brida with her knife.

'Is everything well, Gwen?' Her friend raised her eyebrow.

'Of course, why should it not be?'

'Because you have barely said a word since the evening in the woods.'

'It was just the shock of well…everything. Nothing more.'

However, it was far more than that. Gwen would never have ever imagined that the same squire would actually turn out to be Ralph. And neither would she have envisioned the changes in Ralph to be so huge as to render him so unfamiliar. Yet strangely those physical changes made her feel a little breathless. They made her stomach flip over itself every time she caught a glimpse of him in his full armour, dissembling as Sir Thomas, or dressed as a squire. And yet, she had not actually seen him at all, since his head was always covered. In truth, she would never have believed any of it had he not explained it to her himself. Such as it was…

Yes, Ralph may have wanted Gwen to know that he was alive…*and hale*, but no more than that. He had not thought it necessary to even show his face, seemingly preferring to be hidden within the darkness that night as he was now.

'Are you sure, Gwen?' Brida looked at her with concern. 'You do not quite seem to be yourself.'

'I'm just a little tired, that is all.' She felt the brittleness of her smile.

'You know that you can always confide in me. I am here for you, my lady.'

'I do know and I'm thankful for it, my friend. However, with everything that has happened I believe we need to bring forward our plans. We need to obtain the cattle we need for the journey ahead,' she whispered behind her hand.

Gwen had not intended to begin her journey to the convent for another few days and certainly not until the tournament was properly underway. And yet, ever since she had discovered that Ralph was alive and presently at this tournament, she had been uneasy with her confused, muddled feelings for a man who wanted nothing to do with her. Not that she blamed him. Indeed, it would serve them far better if she left as soon as possible and never saw Ralph again.

Brida gave her a reassuring smile. 'I'll see to it and make contact again with the groom and stable hand, who said that they would help.

'Good.' Gwen exhaled, feeling a little relieved.

'And what of Sir Thomas's "squire"? Do you think you shall see him again?'

'No. There is really no reason to.'

Ralph had welcomed no further connection or claimed any sort of acquaintance with her. He had been perfectly clear in the woods where he had effectively informed her that beyond his revelation, he owed her nothing. As she owed nothing to him in return…including her gift of a hand-woven ribbon.

'You need not concern yourself about me.'

If Gwen was honest with herself, that had stung. Ralph had not even asked about *her*…about her life since they had last seen each other. It was as though he no longer cared. And why would he? Not now, after all this time when he had far more important issues, such as succeeding at this tournament. That was what mattered to him, reclaiming Kinnerton, his lands and his title.

Well, she would honour Ralph's wishes and not seek him out any further. She looked down at her wrist that she'd foolishly tied the purple ribbon around and sighed, knowing she would have to get rid of it.

If Ralph didn't want it because it reminded him of a past that he'd rather forget, then neither did she. Gwen would do what Ralph should have done. She would throw it away in the hearth later. Then she would forget about him as he had asked her to.

After all, Gwen had important matters of her own to attend to, in carrying out her plans to escape to the convent sooner than originally planned, while heads were turned towards the spectacle of this tournament. She would use the distraction to put as much distance as she could between herself and Stephen Le Gros. Then and only then would she find peace and some measure of fulfilment, away from his avarice and ambition. An ambition that he made no secret of—to force Gwen into marriage, since he believed she belonged to him anyway. Her fingers absently touched the scar at the base of her neck.

Yes, she would keep Ralph's secret as he'd asked. Indeed, she wished him every success in his endeavours, but there was nothing more that would tie them together—not even a woven purple ribbon.

With a hollow feeling in her stomach, she got to her feet. 'I think I'll retire to our quarters now,' she muttered, but held her hand out, when her friend looked to follow her. 'No, no. You stay and finish your meal, Brida.'

'Allow me to accompany—'

'I insist. Please do not worry, I'll be perfectly safe. I just need a little time to myself.'

Gwen ambled outside before stepping into the keep and the cold, dank spiral staircase that would lead to their chamber. She absently noted that the guard who usually stood at the entrance was missing and reached for the torch from the metal sconce and frowned. The flame wavered, flickering in the night, giving her a prickly feeling that something or someone was nearby. She turned around, waving the torch in front of her several times in an attempt to see in the darkness.

'Who goes there?' she said, hoping her voice sounded more resolute than she actually felt.

Gwen could see no one, however. It was most probably a gust of wind since there wasn't anyone in the stairways or the passageway below. She dragged her hand across her forehead, feeling the tension ease a little as she began to climb the stairs.

But Gwen had not been mistaken. She heard the soft footfall behind her and knew instantly that she was not alone… It was too late, however. She spun around just in time as Stephen le Gros took her by surprise, grabbing her and pinning her against the stone wall, holding both of her wrists above her far too tightly in one hand.

'My Lady Gwenllian, how fortuitous for us to meet in such a quiet corner of this castle.'

'How can it be fortuitous when you followed me?' she said with quiet determination, not knowing how she'd managed to keep her voice even. Her heart was hammering in her chest, violently. 'Let go of me, Stephen.'

He stood a step or two lower, yet he still managed to tower over her.

'Not yet.' He tilted his head and studied her as he caught a stray tendril from beneath her veil, twisting it around his finger. 'Just look at the extremes I have to go to just to snatch a moment with you, Gwen.'

She felt bile rise as he pressed his groin against hers.

'Mmm, sweet as honey.' His lips brushed her skin as he nuzzled her neck, inhaling deeply as he held her tightly. 'You won't evade me any more, you know, once we are finally married, Gwen. God knows I've waited long enough for you.'

He could wait for all of eternity for all she cared...

'After all this time, you still believe that I would willingly tie myself to you?'

'Oh, but you will, my dear,' he sneered. 'After I triumph at this tournament, the Crown will be forced to accept me as Kinnerton's rightful lord, especially since I have the backing of the Earl of Hereford. Naturally, you shall also be given to me, my sweet. Whether you're willing or not is of no consequence.'

Oh, heavens, she felt faint!

'I asked you to let me go, Stephen,' she muttered slowly.

She could smell the wine on his breath as he smiled, his grey eyes crinkling in amusement. It was always like this with him, he revelled in the disgusting games he played.

Suddenly, the fine hairs on Gwen's body rose, with the sudden chill sweeping through. She could feel another's presence and knew instantly that someone else was also now in the passageway below. Gwen twisted her head around and saw a powerful-looking man, who looked remarkably familiar, even in the darkness.

Ralph?

He stood with his legs apart, his gloved hand clenched dangerously around something that looked remarkably like the hilt of some weapon. It flashed as he moved it beneath his cloak. He lifted his head, the wide hood of his cloak covering his head, edged in a pool of hollow darkness. She could make out the movement of his chest, rising and falling rapidly.

Oh, mother of Mary, she knew this could spiral into disaster, but when Ralph spoke, it belied his stance, that of a warrior ready for battle.

'Apologies, my good lord and lady,' he said in a deferential tone that might have belonged to a manservant. 'I mean no harm by venturing here to these parts, but only to do my duty by my mistress who sent me in this direction.'

Ralph lifted his head and she caught the whites in his eyes beneath the hooded cloak that he always wore. They held a murderous glint.

Please...please go, she begged silently in her head. *Turn around and leave. I can handle Stephen le Gros.*

She quickly faced the man still holding her, knowing she had to do something before this situation spiralled into disaster.

'I asked you to let me go, Stephen,' she muttered under breath. 'I'm not sure what the Chief Justiciar, Hubert de Burgh, or the Earl of Chester, who also have the ear of the young King, will make of this behaviour. I'd doubt it would help in your pursuit of Kinnerton, if it were known, even if you do have the backing of the Earl of Hereford.'

Gwen hoped that she hadn't pushed Stephen too far, beyond even his limited control. She watched the flash of anger glint in his eyes before giving way to amusement.

'Sir, would you allow the lady to pass?' Ralph's deferential voice, so unlike his own, boomed from below, but Stephen ignored him and watched her intently.

'You were always good with words, were you not? Always knew exactly what to say. I suppose that is how you evaded me, Gwen. By running away and using that talented mouth of yours to become the Crown's ward. Very clever, but no more.' He ran his thumb across Gwen's lips and then slowly let her go. 'Until later, my sweet.'

He inclined his head at Gwen and then turned on his heel, leaving through the entrance and barging past Ralph who had held his head low, covered beneath his hood.

Gwen turned her head toward the entrance and clung to the wall for a moment as Ralph stepped back in the darkness again. Yet she heard his rampant breathing, chiming with her own.

'Gwen?' he murmured. 'Did he…did he hurt you?'

'No,' she whispered.

No more than usual…

Gwen picked up the torch that had fallen by her side, her hands shaking, and sensed that Ralph was about to depart as stealthily as he had arrived.

'Thank you, by the way, for your assistance,' she murmured quietly. She wanted to say more, but the words were stuck in her throat. They stood staring at each other in the darkness, with only the sound of her heart beating wildly in her chest. Gwen inhaled slowly before she turned around and continued to climb the stairs as swiftly as her feet could carry her.

Chapter Six

The knights' procession the following day was a colourful spectacle filled with pomp and gallantry, demonstrating skill and commanding horsemanship. Apart from the exhibition and warm-up combat from the previous days, this would now usher the commencement of the *mêlée à pied*, the *mêlée à cheval* and the hand-to-hand combat.

The knights passed by in perfect formation, bowing in unison to King Henry, the silver metal of their armour and chain of their hauberks gleaming, as it caught in the sunshine. Deprived of their customary metal helmets, the exuberance and excitement were palpable on every young knight's face. The colours and heraldry of banners and surcoats paraded, marking out the various Lords' retinues that the knights belonged to.

Gwen was sat beneath the ornate canopied dais reserved for the King and the attending court, watching the knights mounted on their magnificent horses with a composed serenity. Yet inside she was in turmoil after what had happened the previous evening. She pasted a smile on her face and clapped her hands along with everyone else, as the knights marched past without really absorbing much around her.

Stephen le Gros had slithered into her mind, like a viperous snake, but then again, she had expected this from him. She never doubted that he could have changed over the years.

Indeed, she had been quite correct to have brought forward her meticulous plans to get away to the convent she had made prior arrangements with. And with the finer details settled, they would leave on the morrow. As soon as might be. It would allow her the opportunity to finally be free of the man for good.

Lifting her head, Gwen noticed a woman she recognised from the previous evening smile at her, a lady who had sat among Lord de Clancey's knights, talking to Sir Thomas's squire...to Ralph.

'Brida, is that Lord de Clancey's wife?'

'Yes, I believe that's Isabel de Clancey.'

The lady in question briefly looked at the group of knights passing with the de Clancey colours, including Thomas Lovent, smiling in his golden self-assured manner, as he rode passed. Gwen watched as Lady Isabel then flicked her eyes to Ralph standing as squire on the far side, his head and face covered, trying to look inconspicuous before returning back to her and inclining her head. Gwen flushed, but also bowed her head in return, her light blue veil billowing behind.

She realised then this lady must know about her...from Ralph. She swallowed down the mortification, feeling stifled, and turned her attention back to the parade. The sooner she could finally leave and be on her way from this place, the better.

Ralph watched Gwen from where he was standing and wondered once again at her cool manner after what he had witnessed the previous evening.

God, but when he had discovered Stephen le Gros holding and pressing her against the stone wall of the stairwell, he felt like raging against his cousin. And he would have had the man not let Gwen go. Ralph knew she had been shaken by the experience, but there was also something a little disturbing about the unfolding events.

The way in which Gwen had kept her nerve and not cowered, but had stood up against le Gros, had been both admirable and perplexing. In fact, she had been trying in vain to placate Stephen in a calm, measured way. Ralph had sensed Gwen's outrage and revulsion, but the lady had not been as surprised as he'd expected her to be in such a precarious situation. It was almost as though such a thing had happened before between Gwen and his contemptable cousin.

Ralph felt sick to the stomach just considering this to be a possibility. But then, Stephen had pursued Gwen, inappropriately when they had all been younger. Was there more that he had not been aware of? Had that been part of the reason that Gwen stayed at Kinnerton and had forced him to leave?

From a distance Ralph could see Gwen rise from her seat and steal away from the spectators' area. He darted his gaze in every direction, making sure that no one was watching him before slipping away in search of her. He found her of all places at the blacksmith's, talking quietly with her companion. At least the woman had accompanied her mistress this time, unlike the previous evening.

Ralph hesitantly approached them without getting too close and caught Gwenllian's eyes. He'd startled her, he noticed, as she flinched, then quickly recovered herself.

Gwen had not expected to see him and why would she? Had he not expressed that he no longer wanted to resume their friendship? Had he not pushed her away and warned her against any further interest in his life? Yes…and it had been necessary. Ralph could not fault his reasoning for his need to achieve what he had set out. He needed no distractions, just a resolute singlemindedness to right all the wrongs perpetrated against him. Yet Ralph was dissatisfied with how everything stood between them. With how there might be more to Gwen's apparent betrayal of him than he had initially believed.

In any case, he had not been able to push Gwen out of his mind since the moment he had seen her again, however hard he had tried.

'I did not expect to see you here.' She was talking to him softly, albeit discreetly. Both of them were faced away from one another, in different directions, and to any casual observer they would appear absorbed in anything other than this encounter.

'Nor I you.' Ralph ran his fingers across the smooth length of the blade as though he were examining the sword. 'I had not thought you would leave the knights' parade so soon.'

'Other matters needed my attention.' She narrowed her eyes. 'Do you not also have duties to serve your knight?'

'I do, but I wanted to…nay, I needed to see you after last night.'

She ignored him as her companion whispered something in her ear before walking away, presumably with an errand.

The big burly blacksmith wiped his hands on a dirty cloth and nodded at Ralph. 'Your helmet has been smoothed and would be ready on the morrow, as promised.'

'My thanks and I'll be delivering more of Sir Thomas's weapons for you in preparation for the mêlée, if you have the time to attend to it?'

'Aye.' He nodded as he turned to Gwen. 'And now, my lady…' the man inclined his large head awkwardly '…about what we discussed before… I can get everything that you need, ready and tight by sundown.'

'Thank you,' she murmured. 'You are too kind.'

Ralph watched with fascination as the big, gruff man softened his stance with a reticent smile on his face at being called 'kind' by a lady. He inclined his head again and resumed his work. Gwen returned his smile and bid the man farewell and began to walk towards the inner bailey of the castle. She took no notice of Ralph, intent, it seemed, on ignoring him even though he followed, keeping his distance, behind her.

'Tell me how you fare, Lady Gwenllian?' he said in a low voice, his head bent low.

'Thank you, but there is no need for you to concern yourself with me.'

He caught her elbow from behind and she stilled. 'Gwen?' he whispered softly.

'I'm well, but you had best go,' she muttered over her shoulder. 'It would be inadvisable if we were seen together, would it not?'

That he knew, but there was something she wasn't telling him. 'What are you up to, my lady?' She began to quicken her pace, ignoring him. 'What are these matters that need your attention?'

She stopped, but still faced away from him. 'They are of no importance. You and I are no longer…' She shook her head and exhaled deeply. 'Our lives run along different paths, now.'

'I know.'

'Well then, I beg you to leave it and continue to do everything you can to win Kinnerton back.'

'Gwen, I…'

'Go back, Ralph…forget me,' she whispered and resumed walking, almost sprinting in her hurry to get away.

Forget Gwenllian ferch Hywel?

He had tried to…all these years he had tried but, no, it appeared that Ralph could not forget her. No, he could never do that.

It was not too difficult to locate Gwenllian before dawn the following morn, getting ready to leave surreptitiously when most from King Henry's court and knights in attendance were still abed.

In fact, it had been shockingly easy to find out what she intended to do, especially with so many ordinary people whom she had sought help eager to talk readily in exchange for coin. Ralph had followed her trail in dismay. The impulsive foolishness of leaving, with just a young stable hand and her pretty companion, a woman as young as Gwen, no less, was nothing short of madness. Lord above, it was as though they were actively seeking trouble or at best naive enough to believe they were sufficiently protected.

They were not.

What he did not know was why Gwen was leaving now. But then again Ralph knew nothing of Gwen's life and what had happened to her after all this time. He wondered whether her reasons might have something to do with their meeting in the woods a few night ago. He hoped it had not.

Ralph stepped out of the darkness and into the gloomy, unlit stables that housed some of the finest horses in the land. Gwenllian and her small party were packing up their meagre belongings and attaching them to the saddlebags with quiet, efficient expediency. They were naturally in a hurry to get away.

He peered from under his wide hood and saw that she was surprised. Her eyes widened and she stopped and turned towards him.

'What are you doing here?' she hissed.

'I could ask you the very same question.'

Her lips twisted in annoyance, but she did not offer an answer.

'Well?'

Gwen turned away and continued to brush down her grey mare, uttering soothing comfort into the horse's ear.

Ralph looked her up and down and shook his head. She was wearing a dark woollen tunic, a padded leather gambeson, a wide hooded cloak, thick hose and matching braies. In fact, the apparel of a young squire, but Gwen looked entirely too feminine to pass for a young boy.

Her companion, Brida, strode through the entrance, wearing similar clothing. The young woman opened her mouth to say something to Gwen, but once she realised that he was there, she looked between them, worried her bottom lip and turned away.

'You still have yet to answer.'

'What I choose to do has absolutely nothing to do with you, Ralph de Kinnerton.'

'No, my lady.' He touched his hood, making sure that his face was still concealed. 'I did not say it did, but I would be grateful if you could oblige me, all the same.'

'Would you? And for what purpose?' She sighed in irritation. 'Why this interest in me and my movements now?'

He raised a brow. 'You believe that you are of no interest to me?'

'No, not from what you conveyed to me a few nights ago.' She shrugged. 'And, frankly, why should you, after all this time?'

Yes, he had clearly offended her that night in the woods.

Ralph tried a different tack. 'You seem to be in a hurry to get away, my lady?'

'We are, sir, so if you will excuse us, please. We would like to leave before daybreak.'

He caught her arm as she tried to walk past him and pulled her around to face him. Gwen's eyes fell to his hand touching her and Ralph quickly removed it, as though he'd been burned. Heat ignited through his body from such an innocuous contact. He swallowed, pushing the thought away, and stepped back.

'You wish to leave before anyone has a chance to find that you're missing? Is that it?'

She didn't answer him, but turned away to stand in the entrance and addressed her party.

'Simon, have you tied up the extra provisions?' She stood with her hands on her hips, addressing her companions.

'Yes, mistress, once I get this hack ready with the rest of the saddlebags.' A young male voice came out from behind the stables. Christ above, he was no more than a boy.

'Good, and what of you, Brida? Are you ready to depart?' Her companion made a single nod which Gwen returned before turning to attend her horse in the stable.

Ralph watched, turning from one to the other in disbelief. He had to try to make her see sense, somehow.

'What is this all about, Gwen?' He expelled his breath through his teeth. 'What are you running away from?'

'It really doesn't concern you, sir.' She frowned.

'Is it Stephen le Gros?'

She stiffened immediately. 'Even if it were, I do not need your help with him or anything else, Ralph.'

A muscle leapt into his jaw. 'You still do not believe that I can stand up to my cousin?'

'That is not what I meant. I am happy in the knowledge that you are doing everything you can to reclaim Kinnerton. And I wish you every success with this tournament, Ralph. I truly do.' She rubbed her forehead before continuing. 'But that does not mean that you are in some way obligated to me because of our shared past. You do not owe me anything.'

'Even so,' he said, standing in a dark corner, 'I can still be apprehensive about what happens to you. This, whatever it is that you are doing, is nothing but a fool's errand.'

'Not that I care for your opinion, sir.'

'You are putting the lives of your companion, the young lad as well as your own in danger.'

'And not for the first time,' she muttered under her breath, more to herself than to him.

'What does that mean?' He stepped towards her again. 'Gwen? Talk to me.'

She turned to face him, raising a brow. 'So, now you wish for discourse between us? I apologise, Ralph, but we simply do not have the time to tarry.'

'If I can discover that you're running away, with such ease I might add, then anyone can. I did it, effortlessly, in between the rigorous tourney practice, as well. Anyone intent on finding you would be able to, within a day or two.'

'I disagree. My departure is not expected and once it has been discovered that I am no longer here, it would be too late to pursue me.'

'Is that so? I'm not convinced, Gwen.' He grimaced. 'And if we leave that aside, what of other dangers that you're likely to meet on a long journey? For that is what I presume this to be?'

'Whatever danger we may face, it shall be a difficulty for *me* to bear.'

'"*Difficulty?*" I think it will be far more than that. What in heaven's name will you do if you are set on by bandits or outlaws, Gwen?'

'Please…please, just leave this be.' He could see the tension mounting in her shoulders as she screwed her eyes shut. 'I have been planning this for a long while, so you need not worry that this has somehow been decided on some whim. I promise you that it has not.'

'It does not matter how long you have planned and prepared for this scheme. It would still spell a disaster.' He shook his head and softened his voice. 'Are you this desperate to be away from here?'

'What if I am?' she whispered.

'Gwen…'

Ralph would never have envisaged Gwenllian ferch Hywel like this. Whenever, he had thought about her, over the years it had been with regret, heartache and, aye…bitterness. Anger towards her for not agreeing to run away with him and the reality that she had forsaken him out of obligation—for duty. Her practical, sensible and measured insistence, at the time, had left him without an argument to change her mind. He had left her behind, believing that her ambitions were tied to fulfilling a duty to be Lady of Kinnerton.

Yet now, after all these years, she was doing the very thing that she had refused to do back then. It made no sense and once again he was curious about what had happened to her these past six years. Guilt coursed through him, knowing that he still felt a sense of obligation towards her, no matter what had happened.

'Please let me…allow me to help you.'

'Why?' She flicked her gaze in his direction. 'Really, there's no need, Ralph.'

'That may be so, but I would like to give you any assistance that you may require.' He sighed. 'Despite everything you say, Gwen, I feel a sense of responsibility towards you.'

'Again, I must enquire the reason to that. Is it simply because I am unmarried still? Is that where your *sense of responsibility* stems from, because you can otherwise spare your breath.'

True, he had never thought Gwen to be unmarried, but there was a lot more to it than that. Without the protection of a husband, she was certainly at the mercy of every ambitious man with an eye to her wealth, including his cousin Stephen. Which again begged the question of how she had protected herself all this time and how she had managed to escape Stephen le Gros, when he had effectively taken Kinnerton to become its sergeant after his father's death. The man had mentioned something about her evading him and running away. Is that what she had done and if so, why had she not run away with *him*?

'There is much I don't know about you, Gwen, and I would like to rectify that, if you would allow it.'

'That is not what you said the other night.'

'I know…and for that I apologise. As much as you asked me to forget you, Gwen, it is impossible for me to do. I cannot just simply allow you to leave here without being assured of your safety.'

Her shoulders slumped and she expelled a breath. 'My thanks, Ralph but I just don't believe—'

'Listen to me, Gwen. This scheme of yours will lead nowhere other than disaster. Wherever it is that you're intending to go, I will pledge on my sword, on my oath as a knight, that I will escort you myself. But not directly and certainly not like this.'

She frowned, narrowing her eyes, not quite believing his words 'Because you fear for my safety?'

'Yes.' He inclined his head. 'It would be my honour to protect you, my lady.' And he meant it. Especially as Ralph could never have done so when they were younger—he could not have stood up to his cousin back then. Now, however, he would do right by Gwen as well. Yes, he would swear to protect her and escort her to wherever she wanted to go, but only after his future was determined one way or another.

Her brows furrowed in the middle, inducing a little crease in her forehead that he remembered from before. He pushed the memory away and tugged his hood forward, making sure that his face was still shrouded and hidden away.

'What happens if you do not succeed at the tournament, Ralph?'

His lips pressed down into a thin line. 'My success at regaining Kinnerton has no bearing on this. I would still escort you to wherever you need to go.'

Gwen didn't seem to believe in his abilities, even after all this time? Well, no matter, he would have to prove to her just what he was capable of.

'I know, Ralph. I did not mean to cause offence. I just…'

'And I shall protect you against Stephen. Upon my honour.'

She lifted her head. 'Your honour is not in doubt, but it isn't necessary for you to embroil yourself with Stephen. Especially if you do not want him to become suspicious of you and you don't, do you?' Her eyes narrowed. 'That's why you want him to continue to believe you are dead, I assume. So that you can gain leverage?'

'Something to that effect, but regarding this, Gwen, I cannot stand by while Stephen continues to intimidate you, as he did the other night.'

* * *

Gwen would like nothing better than to believe Ralph. But she was not certain that she would ever feel safe from Stephen le Gros. Not until she was far away from him would she feel secure from his advances. Yet…yet it was a relief to have this surprising offer of support and protection from Ralph de Kinnerton. Not since Gwen, as ward of the Crown, had lived with the family of the Lord Protector and Regent of England, William Marshal, had she felt safe. However, her situation once again became precarious after Marshal's death.

Gwen had managed to get away from Stephen all those years before, after the man had usurped Ralph and taken Kinnerton Castle unlawfully. He had foolishly believed that he would just be handed the castle, its lands and… *her.*

Yet, Gwen knew that his presumption and arrogance in believing that, with both Ralph and his father, the old Lord de Kinnerton, out of the way, everything would then belong to him would be his weakness. Stephen le Gros had underestimated her and she'd used that to her own end.

Gwen had persuaded Stephen that if he forced her into marriage, it would go against him and sit unfavourably with the Crown, who had by then seized Kinnerton as well as her wardship. Gwen had surmised correctly that the Crown would need the tax levies from both Kinnerton and her Welsh lands during the Barons' conflict and used this to get away from Stephen.

And her plan had worked.

Not only had the Crown continued its demand for a huge feudal relief that King John had set on Kinnerton before his death, but had not been willing to give it up so readily after the end of the conflict. Meaning that all this time, Stephen had no real way to raise the sum himself either, unless he did so by foul means.

It also meant that she had been free of Stephen le Gros until now...until this tournament with the possibility of huge sums of money to be won.

Gwen flicked her gaze to Ralph. All that had been before her knowledge of the man stood opposite being alive and at this very tournament. Could she trust that he'd help her? Indeed, she was at a loss as to understand why he would, after everything that had happened. And yet... This was still the same Ralph de Kinnerton, who had always been steadfast, resolute and loyal to a fault. She knew with absolute clarity that she could trust him with her life.

Before Gwen knew what she was about to do, she stepped forward and stuck out her hand.

'Very well, I accept.'

Ralph seemed to hesitate as if he couldn't quite believe that she had acquiesced, but then he regained himself and reached out to clasp her hand and lifted his head.

The sudden flash of heat flared from where their hands joined together, unexpectedly. She swallowed uncomfortably. Oh, Lord, mayhap this had not been a prudent decision after all. But it was then that Gwen felt the rough, jagged feel of his hand holding hers. She looked down at their joined hands and stared at the contorted, twisted muscles with gashed marks all over and gasped.

The hood of Ralph's cloak slipped back from his head a little as he let go of her hand and lifted his head, his face flustered and weary. He pulled the hood of his cloak to cover his head again, but not before Gwen had briefly glimpsed the scars on one side of his face.

'Ralph?' She reached out her arm, but he stepped back and inclined his head briskly.

'I will honour my oath to you. Now I must get back. Until later, my lady.'

And with that, he vanished just as quickly as he had appeared.

Chapter Seven

Ralph de Kinnerton had not just been hiding beneath his scallop-edged, hooded cloak in an attempt to conceal his identity, as Gwen had believed. No, he had been concealing far more than she could ever have imagined.

Lord above, but his hand, *his face*! What in heaven's name had happened to him? She had hoped that the reaction he had seen on her face had been one of empathy and not pity. However, there had been no conceivable way for Gwen to have concealed the surprise and shock she felt after feeling his hands grasping hers and the flash of the scars beneath his hood.

She could only imagine what Ralph had endured. What her desire to *protect* him had led to.

'I believe that you have made the right choice, Gwen.' Brida glanced in her direction as she continued to put all their possessions back in the chamber, as before. 'I am glad that I can say that freely now.'

'You were before. And I hope you're right, but only time will tell.' She sighed. 'And at least we shall now have Ralph de Kinnerton's escort when we eventually depart. Which will, God willing, relieve the worry of any possible danger en route.'

Brida stopped and turned her head. 'So, you still mean to go the convent of St Mary de Hogge?'

It had been through Isabel, Countess of Pembroke and wife of the late William Marshal, that Gwen had been given this lifeline. This small salvation to travel to a remote convent founded by the Countess's grandfather, in Leinster, Ireland, where no one would ever think to find her.

'After everything that has happened, there can be no other choice, as you know. And I am resigned to my fate. But what of you, Brida? Have you changed your mind about accompanying me? I had always believed that you'd wanted to get back home to Ireland?' Gwen continued to unpack her belongings, such as they were.

'No, my lady, I have not changed my mind. I thought that possibly you might have after meeting with…?'

'Of course not. I have no other option, Brida, and I am not naive enough to believe that my situation could change, now or ever. And the knowledge that Ralph is alive, when we believed the worst, makes the huge sacrifice that I took all those years ago even more worthwhile.'

'You're an admirable woman, Gwen,' she said gently. 'Not many would have had the courage to have done what you did.'

Oh, dear, she wasn't going to cry.

Gwen abruptly brushed away the tears that had fallen on to her cheeks at her friend's words and stared at her hands. The truth was that although the bargain she had made with Stephen le Gros six years ago had been one of the most difficult in her life, she would do it a thousand times again. It had not been for naught, as she had previously believed, since Ralph had managed to get away safely with the time she'd purchased. But it had left devastating consequences for her in its wake.

Gwen sat down on the edge of the soft pallet bed and smoothed away the crease in her brows, suddenly feeling a little weary. 'Nothing has changed beside the fact that we shall remain here longer than we had originally planned.'

After the nervous energy and the anticipation of leaving court, Castle Pulverbatch and this tournament, she was beginning to feel the strain of the day.

'We'll need to remain vigilant, Gwen. Far more than before.'

True, nothing had really changed, with Gwen's future just as precarious as before, but at least she now had Ralph's assistance and support.

Ralph...

She suddenly had a need to convey her thanks again to him and, more importantly, to find out more about the nature of his injuries.

'Come, allow me to help you out of those clothes, Gwen. You'll feel more like yourself after a wash and once you're back to wearing your own clothes.'

'Thank you but, no.' She stood up. 'There's something I need to do...that I must do before I can feel anything remotely like myself.'

'You're going out like that, dressed as a squire...in the middle of the day?'

'I am.' Gwen smiled at her friend. 'Apparently many do, in these parts.'

'I'll come with you.'

'No, stay, I shall return soon.'

Gwen stopped by the wooden arched door as Brida called out to her, 'Be careful, my lady.'

She nodded at her friend and pulled her hooded cloak over her head before leaving the chamber.

Gwen enjoyed the relative freedom and sense of anonymity she had acquired while posing, briefly, as a squire. It was quite liberating passing through the inner bailey and gatehouse without anyone's notice. She had even passed Stephen le Gros, who was coming back into the castle with one of his men, but, with her head bent low and hood covering her head, he had not even looked her way.

Letting out the breath that she had been holding, Gwen continued to stroll towards the furthest corner of the practice area, occupied by the de Clancey knights, trying her best to remain inconspicuous. Here on the edges of the clearing, red tents were dotted around, housing knights, with the largest red tent reserved for Lord and Lady de Clancey.

A sudden incongruous noise caught her off guard. Gwen snapped her attention in the direction of the two largest tents, curious to find the source of the sound of a young child giggling and a dog barking playfully. The noise intrigued her and was so out of place in an area held for the clatter and bluster of knights' combat practice. Her lips quirked upwards at the scene that greeted her when she made her way around the corner of the two largest tents.

A young boy, who looked to be no more than five years old, seemed to be teasing a little black and white dog by holding a wooden stick out of its reach. The dog wagged his tail as the boy made it sit before pretending to throw the stick some distance.

Gwen chuckled as the dog chased the stick that had not actually been thrown. The young lad turned in her direction at the sound of her laughter and stepped back with a look of uncertainty on his face.

'Please do not be alarmed, it's quite all right,' she muttered and pushed back her hood a little, so that he could see her face.

He blinked as he continued to look at her up and down, before sucking his thumb and nodding at her. 'You are a girl?'

'Yes, I… I am.' She realised how ridiculous she must look to a young boy dressed as she was. 'But these are not my usual clothes.'

'Don't worry, my mother likes to dress as a boy—a lot.' He suddenly looked up at her and frowned. 'You won't tell anyone though, will you? Papa says it is our secret.'

'I swear on the holy saints that I won't. You have my promise.'

He continued to watch her with his big green eyes and then smiled, as two big dimples popped out in his rosy cheeks. 'I'm William Tallany.'

She chuckled and made a deep curtsy. 'Happy to make your acquaintance, young sir. I'm Gwenllian ferch Hywel of Clwyd.'

'That is a *very* long name.'

'I suppose it is. I am originally from Wales, but I have lived here in England for a long time. Call me Gwen, William Tallany.'

'Very well.' He sucked his thumb and bowed his head. 'Do you want to play with me, Gwen? I only have Perdu, here, to play with,' he said, stroking his fur.

'Your dog is friendly.' Gwen knelt down and scratched the little dog's belly.

'Oh, he's not my dog, but Isabel's. Do you know her? She's very nice and gives me lots of honey cakes.'

Ah, he must mean Lady Isabel de Clancey. 'Honey cakes are my favourite, too. Tell me, William, why are you alone with just Perdy for company?'

'It's Perdu. Well, the truth is…' he shuffled his feet in the grass '…that I might have played a little, tiny trick on Brunhilde, she's my nursemaid—not that I need one now—and she has to lie down because I "sasperate" her. Isabel said I could watch the knights with her because one day I'll need to be as good as Uncle Will and my papa, but then I forgot about the secret, so now I'm here with Perdu for company.'

'Oh, dear,' she muttered, not completely following his tale.

'Do you like to dress like a boy, Gwen?'

'Not quite. I am pretending, you see, to be someone that I am not.'

He nodded, his dark curls bouncing around his plump cheeks. 'Yes.' He pulled a face, moved a little closer and whispered behind his hand, 'Everyone here is pretending, lots and lots. That's why I'm here and not there watching the knights.'

Gwen sunk her teeth into her bottom lip in the hope to stop from laughing. 'Did you do something terribly bad?'

He nodded again and pursed his lips. 'I shouted something I shouldn't have because it's a big *secret*,' he muttered in hushed tones. 'But it was only because I was excited that Ralph was winning. I forgot, you see.'

'I do see…and I can understand that it is not so easy when you have to remember so many secrets. But you know, William Tallany, it might be best to heed their advice since you would not want to betray a confidence.'

'I know and that is what Isabel and Uncle Will said. So now I have to play here because they think I might give away more secrets. Which I won't. I promised and everything.'

She felt a little sorry for the little boy. 'I am sure that it was an accident and that you have learnt your lesson now.'

'I really have, Gwen. I'm really, really actually good at keeping secrets,' he said, kicking a stone. 'I won't tell anyone that you like dressing up like a boy,' he assured her.

She was touched at how earnest the child was. 'Thank you, young sir. I am indebted to you.'

'And you'll keep my secret, too? You won't tell anyone about my friends, Ralph and Tom?'

'I promise.' She bent low and whispered in his ear, 'I'll let you into another one of my own. Ralph is also my friend.'

'Is he? No one told me that. Have you seen his scars? I'd want some just like his when I'm older. It would make me a lot more f'rocious.' He looked behind her and beamed. 'Isabel, this is my new friend, Gwen…' He looked up at her. 'Oh, I've forgotten the rest of your name.'

Gwen lifted her head and met the curious gaze of Lady Isabel de Clancey. 'My lady.' She curtsied, feeling awkward at being found having a conversation with the young William Tallany on her own and being dressed as she was. Isabel, however, smiled warmly and returned her formal acknowledgment.

'Lady Gwenllian ferch Hywel, I am very happy to make your acquaintance.' She held out her hand to the little boy. 'I came in search of you as your mother and I had wondered whether you might be hungry, William?'

'I am very, very hungry.' He skipped along with the dog jumping at his heels. 'Can Gwen come?'

'Oh, no, I would not want to inconvenience anyone.'

'Not at all, I would be delighted for a friend of… William's to join us for a light repast.' Lady Isabel smiled.

'In that case, it would be my pleasure, my lady.'

'Please,' she shook her head '…we do not stand on any formalities here. Call me Isabel.'

'Thank you and I am… Gwen.'

* * *

They had tucked into delicious rounds of cheese, sliced ham and chicken and dried fruits, washed down with a spiced wine, watered down so that young William could also partake in slurping it inside the tent that Isabel de Clancey shared with her husband. Gwen watched in fascination at the rapport and friendship between Eleanor Tallany and Isabel, whom were both quite different from the usual ladies at court. She couldn't help but warm to both women, as they insisted she accompanied them to watch the rest of the combat practice.

'Now, William, you will remember this time that you cannot shout Ralph's name, as you did before,' Eleanor Tallany admonished her young son as she passed her infant daughter to the nursemaid.

'I promise, Mama.' He raised his hand. 'I swear on the holy saints.'

The women laughed as Gwen flushed, knowing where he'd heard the phrase just moments ago.

'I'm sure you shall.' Isabel also relinquished her young babe to the older woman, muttering a few words to her before opening the entrance to the tent. 'Shall we?'

'Come on, Gwen.' William sidled up to her, pulling her by the hand. 'I have another secret. See Isabel's baby over there?' He pulled a disgusted face. 'My papa has told me that one day, when I am grown, I might become betrothed to her. Can you imagine anything so dreadful as being married?'

She smiled, surprised that a small lump had formed in her throat. 'I can only imagine, although she won't always be so little, you know.'

'Well, I won't do it.' He shook his head, his curls bouncing around his head. 'I'm going to be a famous knight instead. The best and the fiercest.'

'I am sure you shall, William Tallany. I am sure you shall.'

Gwen wondered, too late, whether it had been prudent for her to have sought Ralph, even though she was dressed inconspicuously. She felt self-conscious standing among his friends, who were naturally curious about her, especially Lady Isabel.

She chewed her lips, knowing that Ralph had also realised her presence despite being immersed in the middle of combat training. He'd looked in their direction a few times and the manner of his stance revealed that he was unsettled that Gwen was there and had made herself known to his friends.

Even so, regardless of her curiosity, she needed to speak with him and establish their bargain now that he had pledged to escort her to the convent in Ireland, once the tournament was over. It had certainly nothing to do with the pull of awareness she felt prickle through her.

Chapter Eight

$\infty\!\!\sim\!\!\infty$

Gwen watched as Ralph stormed off in disappointment at his performance which had seemed a little flat and disengaged. And she hoped it had not been because she had been watching alongside his friends. She waited a while before taking her leave from the ladies and young William, whom she had promised to visit another day.

Gwen pulled her hood over her head and walked over to the tent she now knew Ralph shared with Sir Thomas and waited outside for a moment to gather her nerves and calm her beating heart. Taking a deep breath before pulling the fabric opening to one side, she walked in.

She stopped abruptly and blinked several times at the sight before her. Her mouth went suddenly dry as she gazed at Ralph's sinuous back, broad shoulders, and large muscular arms still holding his weapon. Apart from the braies and hose covering his honed legs, he was very naked from the waist upwards.

'God above, I know it. I know exactly what you're going to say,' he said, shaking his head, evidently having heard her enter. 'But let's not get into it now, Tom.'

Mayhap she should come back another time. Gwen's

legs finally caught up with her head and she moved to leave, just when Ralph turned around.

'Gwen?' He stood to his full height, frowning at her. 'I thought you were Tom. What are you doing here?'

That was a very good question. At that moment, Gwen had neither an answer nor a voice to explain herself, so she sank her teeth into her bottom lip and swallowed in discomfort.

'Well?' He raised his brow, waiting as she looked him up and down. Ralph's back might have been impressive, but the rippled corded muscles of his chest, with the smattering of dark hair that ran down to his belly button, disappearing under his hose, made Gwen blush, furiously. She averted her gaze, but not before she had noticed his sun-kissed skin wet with moisture and glistening from being washed down or sweating or…

Oh, God, how mortifying.

She realised far too late that this was the first time she had properly seen Ralph since they were young. Of course, Gwen had been aware of the changes in him, from the moment she knew that he was alive, but she had only glanced at Ralph from afar or from snatched moments when he had lurked in shadows. Until this moment even his scarred face, arm and hand had been hidden beneath hoods and the many layers of clothing.

Well, not any more.

And nothing…nothing could have prepared her for this raw masculinity. Apart from the scars it had been his lean sharp features, the strong angular jawline with the days' worth of stubble and tousled dark brown hair. She looked up and met his dark eyes. He was still waiting for her to respond as he put his hands on his hips. Yet she did not know what to say.

So Ralph spoke instead. 'I suppose you can now see what I have also been trying to hide.'

Gwen tried not to dwell on the lasting image of his magnificently honed body which had greeted her only moments ago. Yet it was difficult to think about anything else.

'As well as concealing that you were still alive,' she managed to say.

'Yes...' he nodded '...that, too.'

Gwen could feel her face becoming hotter still and knew she should look away, but her eyes were drawn back to him every time she tried to glance elsewhere. Oh, for goodness sake, this was Ralph. And just because he wasn't fully dressed, she should hardly be reacting in this way.

'I had better put on a tunic,' he drawled eventually, with a ghost of a smile. 'I would not want my dishabille to distress you.'

'Indeed, I'm not accustomed to being in such a confined space with a half-dressed man.'

Why in heavens had she spoken so breathlessly? Honestly, could she behave more ridiculously than this?

'I am sorry to disturb your sensibilities, my lady, but this is my tent—mine and Tom's.' He pulled on a grey woollen tunic. 'And you did come here of your own volition.'

'You're quite right, I did. I'm sorry, I had better leave.'

'Wait, Gwen, I was just teasing you.' He caught her arm and then let it go just as quickly, as though his fingers were burned by the touch. He took a step back as they stared at one another.

Oh, God, what was wrong with her?

Gwen blinked, realising that actually there was no

measure to how ridiculous she could be. She turned to leave again.

'No, stay and have a mug of wine with me. I would be glad of the company.'

She wasn't sure whether that would be a good idea, but an unfathomable flare of emotion passed across Ralph's eyes, making her reconsider. 'Very well, if you wish.'

He walked to the coffer and poured the red liquid into two mugs, pressing one into her hands.

'So, tell me, Gwen. What brought you here?'

'I'm not so… Well, the truth is that I need to…'

His dark brown eyes glinted with mild bemusement. 'I hope that my scars do not bother you?'

'Of course not.' She gulped, hoping that she hadn't spoken too quickly.

'I wouldn't be surprised if they did.' He shrugged. 'They're not exactly a pleasant sight.'

'You are teasing me again, are you?'

'No.' He shook his head, the amusement fading from his eyes 'The scars are hideous and disgusted me the first time I caught a glimpse of them.'

Gwen could hardly say that she hadn't noticed them. They were there, glaring at her, and were not something she could have avoided. Yet it had been the changes in him and his body that had impressed upon her mind far more. Not something she could readily convey either.

'How did it happen?' she muttered instead.

'Sadly, the story of how I was left with these is rather lamentable.' He raked his fingers through his hair and sighed. 'Everything Tom told you about me, by the by, was true except for the part that I had died. I had been in Poitiers since I left England. One very ordinary day, two years ago, on a routine check in the area, my small patrol was set upon. The two men who accompanied me were butchered to death, Gwen, as would I have been had it not been for the local men of St Jean de Cole, who came to my rescue.'

'Oh, God, Ralph.'

'I woke up days later, not knowing who I was or what had happened, tended to by Lady Isabel de Clancey, who had her own story of why she had been residing in that small village in Aquitaine.'

'I met her earlier. She is lovely and extremely fond of you.'

'As I am of her.' He nodded. 'She is like a sister to me. I know for certain that without Isabel, I would not be alive and without her husband, Will Geraint, I would not be here. I owe them everything.'

Gwen was happy that Ralph had friends like Lord and Lady de Clancey and Thomas Lovent to look out for him and had not been alone as she had until she met Brida O'Conaill. 'It was fortuitous that you met them.'

'Indeed.'

'And do they still pain you, Ralph? The scars.'

He turned his head. 'I know they're repulsive to look at, but they remind me of what I nearly lost that day and still stand to lose. Every single one of these ugly, mangled scars is a reminder of the past and what I still owe my family name.'

Which wasn't quite answering her question, but telling, nevertheless. 'Do you blame yourself for what happened?'

'Naturally,' he said, bitterly. 'But these scars are also a good reminder of what I still have to do. What I must do to redeem the past and try to somehow gain everything that has been lost.'

'And that is why you are here.'

'Yes.' He nodded. 'That is why I'm here.'

'And the reason for your anonymity?'

'As you know I have not divulged the truth about myself yet. I may be under the protection of Lord de Clancey's household knights, but this is something that I need to use to my advantage. Why allow my cousin to have this knowledge, when he would manipulate it to his own end? I'd rather he tarried in a false sense of security, believing that there was no other who would challenge him for Kinnerton.'

'Although it sounds dangerous, it does make sense.'

'Indeed, and I can look out for myself, Gwen. But it needs to be carefully contained, until the time is right.'

She nodded. 'You can be assured that Brida and I will keep your secret.'

'I know and I thank you.'

'Oh, and by the by, they're not repulsive.' Gwen motioned towards his face. 'Your scars.'

His eyes locked on to hers, making her pulse quicken and the breath hitch in her throat. There was still so much left unsaid, so much Gwen did not understand about the events from the past, so much she could—she should—say, but all she could think about was how mesmerising those dark eyes were. But it really would not do. She gave her head a little shake and broke the silence.

'You say you woke up in Aquitaine without any knowledge of who you were?'

'No. My memory of both the attack and how I ended up in St Jean de Cole was very hazy. I could only recall… a few things at first and then very gradually every last thing that happened came back. Although I sometimes wish my ignorance about it all was permanent.'

'That would have been terrible, would it not?'

'Perhaps.' He shrugged and watched her for a moment. 'And what of you, Gwen? What happened to you all these years?'

'Nothing other than getting older.' Hardly the truth, but Gwen did not wish to dredge up everything that had happened to her.

'Some say that age and experience brings wisdom. Although you are still a young maiden.'

She took a sip of the wine and smirked. 'I may be that, but I'm not so certain about being much wiser.'

'That could also be said of me, but I hope to learn from my past mistakes.' He shrugged. 'Take today's disastrous practice. I'm certainly going to have to sharpen my skills if I want to have any chance at this tournament.'

'I am certain you shall.'

'We shall see. The very best warriors in the kingdom are present here, so it will not be an easy task. However, we were talking about you and not me.'

'If you mean to ask where I went after you left, then I would tell you that my aim was to get as far away from Kinnerton as I could.' As well as Stephen le Gros and all the bad memories, but Ralph didn't need to know that. 'I became the Crown's ward and eventually came to live in the Earl of Pembroke, William Marshal's household, where I acted as one of Isabel, the Countess of Pembroke's ladies-in-waiting. I also met Brida there.'

'And you were safe there?'

'Yes, indeed I was. They were happier times, but after the Earl's death, my situation changed once more.'

He tilted his head, watching her. 'And yet you never married?'

'No, and I hope I never shall.'

'I see.' He raised his brows. 'And that was the reason that you intended to run away?'

She made a single nod.

They descended into an uncomfortable silence. Gwen felt suddenly weary and a little exposed, as if she had been the one who was standing there, undressed as he had been just moments ago. Yet her own curiosity had been roused. There were six years that had passed. Six years of lost time reduced now to this awkward, frustrated feeling of not knowing what to say next.

But this was Ralph de Kinnerton. Surely there was enough of the boy she once knew there somewhere, underneath those scars and sinewy taut muscles of a powerful warrior? Yet that also meant that the girl she once was, the girl who had pushed Ralph away, remained, too.

'I should go.'

Ralph watched her for a moment as she stood uncomfortably shifting from one foot to the other. He didn't mean to make her feel guarded and so uneasy, yet he had.

'I did not mean to pry.'

He had wanted to understand Gwen a little more and the reasons why she had changed her stance on marriage as much she had. From everything he had known about Gwenllian, the promise of becoming a mother, having a family...and being a wife had always been of great importance to her and yet that no longer held true. Mayhap in the intervening years, her desire to take the veil could explain the reasons why she no longer welcomed what she considered the burden of marriage. In which case her need to get away made a little more sense, even though it made him feel bleak for some reason.

It seemed they were no longer the assured, sanguine young people they had both been. The hard lessons of life had changed them irrevocably. Yet he still wondered what lessons Gwen had learnt.

She cleared her throat. 'I would not wish to take up your time when I'm sure you have much to do.'

'You're not, my lady, and trust me, I don't. Well, not at this particular moment.' He took her mug from her. 'Nothing that cannot wait at any rate, especially after what happened in the practice field.'

'Surely you cannot be worried about the mêlée?'

He shrugged. 'And surely you saw my abysmal performance out there?'

'I am sure that is not an everyday occurrence, Ralph.'

He dragged his fingers through his hair in agitation. 'If only you knew.'

'Mêlées are notoriously unpredictable, are they not?'

'I'm afraid it has more to do with skill than that. There's a certain amount of luck that goes hand in hand with it, both of which have been lacking of late for me. Yet I have had a lot on my mind.' He briefly looked in her direction.

But Gwen was resolutely avoiding his gaze. 'I'm sure it has. What with returning back here and being so close to Kinnerton after so many years away.'

'Alas, it is not good enough of a reason. Not if I mean to succeed.'

'You are being a little too stern with yourself, are you not?'

'No, the time is nigh, Gwen. It is now or never.'

'Surely that cannot be?'

'With my cousin here as well, after the same thing? He gave her a grim look and sighed. 'I believe it must be. And this is not my first tournament, Gwen. I have been hiding for a lot longer than you know.'

Ralph poured some more wine into her mug and handed it back, his fingers grazing hers. He resisted the impulse to touch her again and stepped back, turning away. 'I was believed to be dead after the attack, two years ago, with my life still, very much, in the balance. Even then I believed it prudent to allow the fact that I was alive to remain concealed. Especially since danger was everywhere and I did not know who was friend or foe. But eventually, I managed to get a message through to Tom that I was convalescing in St Jean de Cole. He came into my confidence and agreed to help me. Soon we travelled around France, from tourney to tourney, taking it in turns to be Sir Thomas Lovent and his far-too-large oaf of a squire. Some tournaments we would win coin and many more we'd lose.'

'Then you returned to England?'

He nodded. 'Isabel offered us the chance to train as part of the de Clancey retinue of knights. It has been gruelling, challenging and incredibly difficult, but well worth the hardship. For one thing I had to retrain using my left hand since I could no longer use my right as effectively as before. I could barely grip a sword in that hand, let alone try to wield a sword.'

'That must have been extremely difficult.'

'I admit that it was challenging. Yet learning the art of combat from men like William Geraint and Hugh de Villiers has been, and still is, a great honour for me.'

'I am sure it has.'

'That's why I hate the idea that I could somehow let them down, Gwen. After everything that has happened that damn niggle, that I'm not good enough, has never seemed to have left me.' He expelled a deep breath.

That incessant disapproval from his father, from a young age, had left its mark no matter how much Ralph tried to eradicate it. His sire had constantly berated him for not being as good as other young men. Even now Ralph could recall that veneer of dissatisfaction in his head.

But why in God's name had he exposed himself, allowing his inner thoughts to be disclosed so carelessly to this woman whom he had once cared so much about? He screwed his eyes shut in embarrassment.

'That is probably because you are still carrying far too much on your shoulders. You always have, Ralph.'

And then he remembered why. Why he had always sought Gwen's opinions on different matters when they were younger. Why he had always wanted to gain her counsel. Why he always enjoyed moments where they could just unburden themselves to one another. Because she had so much faith and belief in him.

'You have many people here, Ralph de Kinnerton, who care for you and wish to see you to succeed. Lord and Lady de Clancey, your friend Sir Thomas Lovent… And even me. But you need to believe in yourself. Believe in your ability to be able to succeed.'

Ralph opened his eyes and stared at her in wonder… and then his eyes slowly travelled from her eyes to where her hand was inadvertently caressing his arm in comfort.

God, but she was lovely. This close he could see the silvery-grey flecks in her blue eyes looking at him with concern. This close her lush lips turned up slightly as a pink blush tinted her cheeks, spreading to her neck. This close her delicate floral scent enveloped him, reminding him of another time and place. He expelled another breath through his teeth, his good hand extending and covering hers. She stilled and blinked in surprise as his eyes dropped to her lips again.

Ralph had to remind himself that she had expressed a covenant wish to be a holy woman, a nun. He should respect her wishes, yet he found himself leaning towards her and bending his head. Closer and closer. Mayhap, just one kiss and if she pulled away then he would know that his attentions were unwelcome.

But Gwen didn't move. Her breathing came in quick, warm bursts as she tilted her head and met his eyes. There was pain, uncertainty but also longing. One that matched his own. He caressed her bottom lip with the pad of his thumb and felt her tremble before she closed her eyes in anticipation.

He moved in eagerly to cover her lips. Yes, just one kiss.

'Well, that went as badly as it possibly could.' Tom's voice carried through as he sauntered into the tent. 'What happened was quite—' He stopped speaking and looked from Gwen to Ralph as they pulled apart.

'I really should be going.' She tugged the hood of her cloak forward and made her way out so quickly and clumsily that she practically collided with Tom.

Ralph and Tom stared at the entrance to the tent, flapping for a long moment.

'Do not dare to say anything.'

'What about exactly, my friend?' A sheepish smile curled around Tom's lips. 'Your performance earlier in the training or what you were just about to do here with the fair lady?'

'Nothing was about to happen.'

'Ah, apologies. It must have been my imagination.'

'Yes.' Ralph stretched out his arms over his head. 'It must have.'

'So it would seem.' Tom grinned. 'And I am glad that you have reconciled whatever differences you may have had with Lady Gwenllian. I gather you have told her your sorry tale.'

'And what if I have?'

'Then it would go far to explain why I almost found

her about to express her sympathies in the most amorous of ways.'

'Damn it, Tom, that is not funny. And I will not have Gwen subject to your amusement.'

'Very well, but let us concede that it is a little funny.'

'Let's not.'

'Not even a little bit?'

'No.'

Tom grabbed an apple from the coffer and took a big bite. 'Well, in that case, I'll say no more on the matter.'

'Good. Now, I take it that Will Geraint has summoned me?'

'He has and he wants you in full armour, so expect another gruelling round.'

Ralph groaned, his body still throbbing in pain from the last round of practice.

'God, but this is going to be a long day.'

'Will wants to go through a few new techniques that he believes may suit your gait.' Tom helped him put on each layer of clothing, until he finally tied and secured his hauberk chain and handed the helmet.

'And do you know who I shall be challenging?'

'Yes.' Tom turned around and slammed his fist against his chest 'Me.'

'Oh, Lord, no. What is William Geraint thinking?'

'Come now it's not as bad as that. You do know that I shall allow you a fighting chance.' Tom grinned. 'And it's not as though I'm going to tell Will or Isabel what almost happened here.'

'I am warning you that if you say just one word about this…'

'Yes, I know, but try to harness that aggression to the field, my friend.' Tom slapped him on his back as they both moved to leave the tent. 'And I said I am not going to say anything.'

'As long as we're clear.' Ralph picked up his sword. 'Nothing happened here.'

'Whatever you say.'

Chapter Nine

Ralph persevered to sharpen his skills during the following day of strenuous training. Yet no matter how hard or diligently he worked, Gwen was never far from his thoughts. Her voice a constant echo in his ears.

'You are still carrying far too much on your shoulders.'

It was true, of course, but not something that he could readily shed. The weight of duty and expectation lay heavy on his shoulders. Besides, Ralph did not know how to break from those bonds, even if he'd wanted to.

What he had wanted, however, was a taste of her lips. Even the following day after their frank discussion alone in his tent, Ralph could not stop thinking about how much he craved Gwen…still…after all this time.

What kind of a man was he to have such base thoughts about a woman he had only just re-established an old friendship with? Especially a woman who had declared that she wanted to take the veil. God's breath, but none of it stopped Ralph from thinking about how he had almost kissed her and still longed to. Even though he was still baffled by the decisions she took six years ago and no closer to understanding how she believed she had protected him.

It was a blessing that Tom had walked into the tent when he had, since an entanglement with Gwen was not something Ralph needed to delve into. Nor could he imagine that it would be welcomed by the lady herself after a little reflection.

It had been wise of her to keep away—for his peace of mind and for hers. Ralph had not seen Gwen again properly, only snatched a glimpse in the hall during the evening feast. Yet he'd trailed her, when she was alone or with only her companion. He needed to make sure that she was safe and protected, especially from men like his cousin. He knew there was more to her association with Stephen and that whatever it was, was disagreeable and unpleasant.

'I think that would be it for this morning.' He nodded at Tom, who grabbed his sword from him. God, but the helmet felt heavy today.

'Good, as I need to break my fast…oh, and Will said he had a surprise for you this afternoon.'

'I can hardly wait,' Ralph said wryly.

'And neither can I, for it shall be something that would defy everything that… ah, hell's teeth!'

'What is it?'

Tom flicked his head around, his eyes filled with unease. 'Best keep that helmet on as your cousin is heading this way.'

'What? Where?' Ralph spun around, his heart beating furiously in his chest. 'Pull your hood forward, damn it. Stephen believes that he's about to parley with *you*, remember?

'As if I could forget,' Tom hissed, tugging it over and drooping his head low to hide his face.

'Well, well, Thomas Lovent, just the fellow I wanted to see,' Stephen le Gross sneered as he strolled over to them with one of his men in tow.

Ralph inclined his head, when what he would rather do was knock the bastard to the ground after everything he had done. Especially since he had almost accosted Gwen in the darkness of the stairwell only just a few nights ago. God, but it still made his blood roar that a man would use such intimidation against a woman like Gwen in the way Stephen had.

Ralph, however, kept his head with the metal helmet covering it, concealing his identity.

'I came to give you a fair warning, Sir Thomas,' his cousin spat. 'I have been noticing the way you stalk after Lady Gwenllian ferch Hywel and I'm here to tell you that I want you to disengage from your pursuit. The lady is my betrothed or, rather, she soon will be and I don't want you anywhere near her. I hope we understand each other?'

Ralph inclined his head again, but just as Stephen turned to go, he bent low and swung his shield under him, catching his cousin's ankle and making him hurtle to the ground. He should not have done it, as it only served to provoke the man. But the presumptuous way in which his reprehensible cousin had spoken about Gwen as if she were his property, as if she were truly his betrothed, well... Ralph just could not help himself.

Stephen got up, his face puce with anger as Ralph, with Tom beside him, stepped forward. God, but he would never cower to this man.

'God's breath...' his cousin barked, pointing the edge of his drawn dagger towards them. 'I'll let that go, but only this one time. Heed my warning, Lovent, and leave the lady alone.'

He got to his feet and strode away in obvious fury at

being made to look a fool. Even so, Stephen did not have to fall to the ground to accomplish that.

Tom pulled his hood off his face. 'There goes another to add to my ever-growing list of adversaries, chief among them Lady Gwenllian's companion.'

Ralph's brows shot up. It was on Ralph's mind to ask about the nature of the possible animosity that existed between Gwen's pretty young friend Brida and Tom, but thought better of it. After all, it was not his business to pry into another man's situation unless he was asked.

'I am exceedingly sorry to put you in this position, Tom,' he muttered.

'Think nothing of it.' He slapped him on his back. 'What I'd like to know is how the hell you are even related to someone so execrable?'

Ralph sighed, shaking his head. 'I have no idea, my friend.'

'He's dangerous. More so now that he has his eyes on *me*. I'll do my best to distract him, but you must take care, Ralph. He cannot know that you're alive. Not until it suits your interest or, rather, all of our interests.'

'I know, especially as it also puts Gwen in danger if he knew.'

'Exactly.'

'I thank you, Tom.' Ralph watched Stephen le Gros's retreating form before turning to his friend. 'But by God, the day of reckoning with that bastard cannot come soon enough.'

Gwen once again found that she was meandering to the practice area reserved for the de Clancey knights, as she walked beside Brida.

'Is there a particular reason we are walking in this direction?' her friend teased.

'Only because I promised young William Tallany that I would visit and I thought to further my acquaintance with Isabel de Clancey.'

'No other reason?'

Gwen ignored that. She had initially kept away, after the near disaster in Ralph's tent when he had almost kissed her. Although, if she were honest with herself, she had yearned for his touch. But that kind of honesty served no one and only led to further heartache. Indeed, the life she had once coveted was no longer possible for Gwen, despite any renewed feelings she might have for Ralph. What she had done six years ago to ensure his safety from his cousin in the aftermath of his father's death had sealed her future. For good. And nothing could ever change that.

Still, the moment in the tent did allow for the first proper discourse between them in a very long time. Gwen had been in earnest when she had told him that she believed in him.

Gwen wanted to know how Ralph was progressing, while pushing away other ridiculous notions about the man, which would serve no one.

They were greeted warmly by Eleanor Tallany, her young son and Isabel de Clancey. William rushed forward towards her and grabbed her hand.

'Good morrow, Gwen!'

'And to you, William Tallany. Come, allow me to introduce you, your mother and Lady Isabel to my friend, Brida.'

The small boy bowed. 'And you are wearing a dress.'

'Indeed.' Gwen chuckled as his mother shook her head at him.

'I'm happy to make your acquaintance, young sir, and you, my ladies.' Brida smiled at William, before inclining her head at Eleanor Tallany and Isabel de Clancey, who returned the courtesy.

'Welcome, Gwen, Brida. We are, as you can see, taking great interest in one particular combat.' Isabel smiled warmly.

'Yes, our friend, Ral—'

'William!' his mother admonished. 'Do not forget what we have spoken about.'

'Oh, yes, whose name we cannot speak,' he whispered behind his hand. 'He is doing really well.'

He pointed to the clearing, where many knights were engaged in hand-to-hand combat. And then she saw Ralph tower over a man while Lord de Clancey, Hugh, Lord Tallany and a hooded figure she assumed to be Sir Thomas, looked on, in obvious approval. She felt a fluttering in her stomach whenever Ralph happened to be in her periphery. She swallowed, trying to douse this unwanted awareness that confused and troubled her. She could not have those old feelings for Ralph resurfacing once more. That part of her life was over, with another awaiting her, if she could just bide her time. It was imperative for Gwen to not lose sight of that.

'You're right, William. I can see that he's doing very well.'

That did not, however, mean that Gwen could not be his friend. She hoped with all her heart that Ralph would find success in these endeavours to reclaim his birthright.

'He needs to tilt the sword a little higher if he wants the blade to have a bigger impact across the body.' Eleanor Tallany seemed more engrossed in the combat than any woman of Gwen's acquaintance.

'As you can see, Eleanor is far more at home here than in the bower chamber of any castle.'

'Absolutely, I have better things to do than stitch or

weave a cloth.' She chuckled before turning back to the clearing. 'That's it! Swipe the sword faster to his right, Ral—'

'Mother, don't forget the *secret*,' William Tallany said cheekily.

Gwen suppressed the urge to laugh as she watched Hugh de Villiers saunter back towards them. He picked up his son and swung him about before kissing his wife.

'Causing trouble again?' he asked quietly, making Gwen wonder whether he was addressing his wife or his mischievous son.

William shook his head. 'This is Gwen, Papa.'

'Ah, Lady Gwenllian.' Lord Tallany turned in her direction and smiled. 'I'm happy to make your acquaintance.'

'The pleasure is all mine, my lord.' She curtsied, along with Brida.

'You ladies must both join us for a short repast before we resume the training. Ralph will need every bit of strength for what we have planned for him.'

Just then the rest of the training came to a halt as, one by one, the men made their way back, but Ralph stayed back a moment longer. Gwen could swear that he stood watching her from beneath his helmet, but not before he tipped his head in her direction and made his way towards her.

'Good day to you both.' He seemed so large, looming over them in all his armour.

Brida glanced between them with a small smile before shuffling away to talk to the other ladies.

'That was most impressive, Ralph.'

'Thank you. What are you doing here, my lady?'

'Would you prefer us to leave?'

'Of course not, but I believe that your arrival has become a source of intrigue here.' He tilted his head, still encased in metal, towards where his friends stood. Gwen followed the direction and saw that their small party had stopped whatever they had been doing and observing them, as though they were some sort of epiphany.

'Come.' Ralph touched her elbow, guiding her away from prying eyes. 'Tell me, Gwen, is it Stephen again? Has anything happened? Is anything amiss?'

She smiled. 'Everything is well, I thank you. I'm grateful for your concern, as I am also for…the fact you seemed to be following me, sir.' She had sensed his presence on more than one occasion when she happened to be on her own or with only Brida for company.

'Ah, you were not supposed to know.' His lips twisted into a reticent smile.

'I didn't until you confirmed it presently.' Her eyes darted around for a moment before she addressed him again. 'I did not mean to intrude, Ralph, but only to see how you were faring.'

'Quite well as it happens. I've apparently got a surprise ready for me after the repast.'

She laughed, 'So I hear.'

'Will you stay and watch?'

Gwen had not intended to stay too long. It would not be too prudent to spend too much time with Ralph, when it would make her wish for things that she could no longer have.

She met his eyes and realised that, despite Ralph's insouciant manner, they also held a certain solicitation. He wanted her to watch.

'Yes.' She nodded, hesitantly. 'I would be happy to.'

'Good.' He bowed. 'Until later, my lady.'

This challenge was the greatest test that Ralph had had so far. It would also be his last until the *mêlée à pied* on the morrow. The unpredictability of the combat was one that made Ralph realise that he couldn't leave anything to chance...but then that did not mean he knew what William de Clancey had in mind to test his mettle.

Ralph quickly glanced at the clearing and noticed wryly the sight of the women standing on the periphery watching the spectacle. Even from where he stood, he could see Gwen chatting with the others. Her demeanour might have been a little reserved, but then Ralph had felt the same embarrassment she had in the interest they had induced from the others around them.

It had not been a good idea to give rise to any further speculation regarding the two of them, but Ralph had been glad that Gwen had come here, nevertheless. He was surprised to learn that he liked having her there. Her support meant a great deal more than it should. It gave him a sense of calm that he had not experienced in many years.

'Are we ready?' Ralph looked from beneath his helmet at Thomas, his opponent, and drew his sword out of its scabbard.

'I am, but are you?'

Ralph smirked as they began to clash their swords against each other, their movements agile and lithe. The two friends were evenly matched, being of a similar height and weight, but Ralph's tenacity was winning through.

'Not bad at all, Ralph. I can see you are tilting your sword in the manner Will showed us.'

'It apparently works remarkably well for knights who wield their weaponry in their left hand.'

'To good effect it would seem.'

'Indeed.' Ralph adjusted the angle of his sword as he lunged forward and struck against Tom's sword.

'Impressive, but enough of this.' Tom plunged his sword in the ground in front of him and tilted his head. 'I believe it's time to make things a little more interesting.'

'Is that so?'

'Yes, we need to make this more of a challenge.'

'Oh, and how do you intend to that?' Ralph said in between taking in big gulps of breath.

'Look around you, my friend.'

Ralph spun on his heel and saw Hugh behind him and to his left Will, who grinned and gave him a mock salute.

'All of you?'

'Indeed.'

'At the same time?'

'I'm afraid so.' Will smirked. 'But never fear, we shall go easy on you.'

How in heaven's name was Ralph supposed to fight his friend, an exceptional warrior in his own right, and two of the most notorious knights in Christendom, whose fighting skills were the stuff of legend?

'Now remember what we talked about, Ralph. You have every necessary skill.' Hugh thumped his chest. 'However, you must feel it here.'

'And you have to use your intuition.' Will nodded.

Ralph was circled by the three men and, one by one, they each lunged forward in attack, making contact with his sword as he used a deflective strike back. Round and round they prowled, as each attack came at him with greater vigour and speed. Ralph turned quickly, knowing he had to change the formation for his own advantage, so that he wasn't the one constantly being attacked. He pushed on his heel and stepped back expediently and found the three men now in a single line.

This was a little better than the feeling of being

hunted, but only slightly better than being surrounded by all of them.

'Not bad, Ralph.'

'Could still do with a little more refinement in your movement,' retorted Hugh.

'And the manner in which you swing your sword.'

'That's it. Much better.'

Hugh lunged forward with such force, taking Ralph by surprise, that he had to take a few steps back just to hold his position.

'Ah, I'd say that the contest begins in earnest, now.'

'Hardly fair,' Ralph stammered.

'Surely you can take on all of us?'

'Not by choice, I grant you. That would be madness.' He turned around to defend himself against Hugh's attack.

'Come now, you are much better than you think.'

'I would say that he is. Only he does not know it yet,' Tom bellowed over the sound of clashing of metal.

'Ah, that would be a shame.' Will shook his head. 'Since it would beg the question whether he is good enough to protect his fair maiden?'

'I am not certain.' Tom grimaced.

'No, indeed there are many here who would imagine that they are Lady Gwenllian's protectors.'

Ralph continued to defend each powerful strike coming quickly at him, as well as ignoring everything that was being said. It was not an easy task.

'She is after all a very beautiful lady. I have heard her described by many a knight here.' Tom smirked as he came at him on his weakest side.

He turned and struck out, his breathing becoming laboured.

'Would she even welcome such a thing from Ralph de Kinnerton?'

Ralph sensed the blood roar in his veins. But he couldn't allow his anger to overwhelm his senses. He had to block these words from penetrating into his head.

'Only the saints would know, but mayhap the fair lady would prefer another knight's protection.'

The surge of unfettered violence suddenly swept through him as he lunged at William over and over, pushing him back. His voice and the words he had uttered had crawled into Ralph's head, obliterating any rational thought.

'After all, Ralph de Kinnerton couldn't manage to protect her properly before. How well could he do so now?'

Ralph spun around and lashed out, not knowing who it was that he was fighting, only that he was battling everyone. The whole damn world and everyone who had done him wrong. The clamour in his head was so intense that he could hardly see. Beads of sweat tricked down his face and mingled with the rising mist of anger that seemed to make him hurtle out of control. No, he would not allow it.

He struck out again and again aimlessly, not caring whom the combat was against, only for the damn pounding in his head to stop. Only for these perpetual doubts to subside.

And then it happened. With his reflexes awry, he made a terrible blunder. Just when Ralph thought he might be able to repair his folly and stand his ground, his sword was met with such force that it flew out of his hand and he was pushed on to the ground, staring up at the tips of three blades pointing at him.

Hell and damnation!

Ralph lay in frustration and annoyance at his damn inadequacy.

Hell's teeth, but he had failed…miserably. And with Gwenllian ferch Hywel watching him. God, for the ground to open up and swallow him whole.

Ralph took the metal helmet off, his mouth full of spittle, and looked up as Will Geraint knelt beside him, holding out his hand.

'I apologise for resorting to that crass provocation, but it was a necessity, I'm afraid.'

'Was it?' He shut his eyes as he hissed an oath under his breath.

'Yes. Whether in a tournament or in battle, men will always seek to use anything they sense to be your weakness,' Hugh muttered, shaking his head. 'Don't allow them to, Ralph.'

It was true that this visceral need to protect Gwen from harm as well as his attraction to her allowed him to be far too distracted. Indeed, Ralph had to resist these feelings for Gwen that could threaten to overwhelm his mission here at this tournament.

'You must not allow anyone or anything to be used against you.' Will's lips pressed into a thin line. 'And you must use your emotions to harness and heighten your prowess, not the other way around.'

'There I was believing I was ready, but sadly I have been found lacking.'

'On the contrary, my friend, that was an excellent display of your ability. The fact that we had to employ those unsavoury means should act as confirmation of that.' Will smiled, pulling him to his feet. 'Just control that temper, Ralph.'

'How exactly?'

'Every man has his fears and weaknesses. The trick

is not to allow anyone to know what they are and, if they somehow find out, make them believe that you are impervious to them.'

Hugh clasped his shoulder. 'You must seek a way through this and conquer your demons.'

'I know, I know.'

'I have faith that you shall. Whatever you may believe, Ralph, you are a highly skilled knight. You just need to trust that.'

'And do not forget that sometimes it takes another's perspective and understanding to discover your own path, my friend.'

Was it his imagination or had Will just referred to Gwenllian? Could her insight and the truth she kept hidden be the key to unlocking the past for them both? Ralph gave his weary head a shake and bowed. 'My lord.'

Chapter Ten

The eventide came with a cluster of stars scattered across the clear, moonlit sky. It had been a long day that had stretched and yawned, draining every last drop of his resolve, with the onset of fatigue seeping in. Yet Ralph was about to climb the enormous tree outside the arched window of Gwen's chamber. He exhaled on a sigh before leaping up and grabbing hold of the branch, swinging his legs around so that he could gain purchase. Ralph looked up and realised that there was still quite a distance to climb, but gradually he moved from one sturdy branch to another until he had dextrously made his way up. He broke a thin, long branch and reached out and tapped it against the wooden shutter. Instantly it was pulled open as Gwen peered out, looking in every direction.

'Good evening, my lady.' Ralph could see, from where he stood languidly leaning back against the thick branch, that he had surprised Gwen.

'Oh.' She lifted her head. 'I did not expect you to have come all the way up.'

'You beckoned and I'm here. He grinned from beneath the canopy of leaves and branches. 'Besides, I thought it a safer and more discreet way for us to have this discussion.'

'I suppose so.' She chuckled.

'Now, how can I be of service to you?'

She peered out of the window. 'I wanted to find out whether you were well, after the practice.'

'Ah…' He rubbed his jaw, his fingers grazing the rough mangled side of his face. 'And you did not want to make your enquiry earlier, I take it?'

'I should have, but this was the only way to snatch a moment alone with you, Ralph.' His brow rose at that, but he didn't interrupt her as she continued to explain in a quiet, measured tone, 'There were just too many curious eyes turned in our direction and I wanted to speak to you with ease, alone.'

'And now you are.'

'Yes.' She sighed shakily. 'And now I am.'

They descended into silence for a moment as they felt the breeze rustle through the leaves.

'How do you fare after the practice, Ralph? You did well, you know, taking all of them on.'

'Did I? I'm not so sure, but either way it was a lesson well learnt.'

'Yes, but hardly fair.'

He shrugged. 'And neither is the reality of a mêlée or even a battlefield, Gwen.'

'So, you would consider what you had to go through a necessity?'

'I'm afraid so.' Ralph pushed away from the bark and moved tentatively closer to the window. 'It would be remiss of me not to explore every possibility.'

'I cannot comprehend your meaning.'

'To anticipate the cause and the effect of any given

situation could determine the difference between success and failure.'

'The cause and effect. Yes well, you and I have both
had to live with the consequences of that.'

No, he could not discount the truth in that. They had
both had their share of misfortune and grief in all its different guises. And seemingly survived their given situation in their own inimitable way.

'You will be careful tomorrow, won't you?' she muttered quickly. 'I would hate it if anything were to happen to you.'

'Anything can happen, that is rather the point, with
the uncertainty of the *mêlée à pied.*' Ralph realised his
mistake, noting that, even in this light, Gwen looked a
little ashen. 'But of course I'll do my best to stay safe. I
give you my word.'

It soothed his weary bones to think that Gwen still
seemed to care for his welfare, his progress…*for him.*
She might now harbour a different future for herself, but
that did not mean that she didn't want him to succeed or
that she didn't care for him.

'Let's talk of something else. Tell me more about yourself, Gwen.'

'What do you mean to know?'

'Anything, everything.' He crawled a little closer and
sat on the branch, his long legs dangling over the edge.
'Your hopes, your dreams…your greatest wish.'

Ralph wasn't really sure what had propelled him to
utter such absurdities. Yet, here, now…under the moonlight and those damned stars, the words seemed to spill
out of him.

'My hopes, my dreams,' she murmured as she leant
out of the window and sighed. 'Oh, they are of no consequence.'

'Of course they are.' He reached out and touched her elbow. 'Gwen?'

'I must go, Ralph. She reached out and caught his fingers and gave them a squeeze. 'Goodnight. I shall pray for your safety.'

'Wait, don't go.' Ralph grasped her hand, pulling her back. 'Tell me something else instead, anything that you like. Tell me something I do not know about you.'

'Surely you know all there is about me.'

'Six years have passed and we are now very different people from who we once were.'

'Do you think so?' Her brows met together in contemplation. 'In some ways, yes, I have changed, I suppose. It would be strange if I had not. But in essentials, I believe I am much as I was back then.'

'When you put it across like that, most people do not really change in essentials.'

'Even you?'

'With possibly my exception.' He turned her hand over and placed his palm against hers, his fingers bending over the top of hers. 'I have worked so hard to remove every last vestiges of the man I used to be, that I do not know any more, in all honesty.'

'You were barely a man back then,' she said softly.

'In every way that it mattered I was, however,' he said bitterly. 'Even though I appeared to be much younger than my years. Why do you suppose we never married at the time?'

'I knew even at the time why that had not occurred. Not that anything was ever explained to me. But know this—your father made many wrong assumptions about you.'

Ralph's lips pressed into a thin line. Yes, his sire had made many mistakes about whom he trusted and with the way he had administrated Kinnerton, but where Ralph disagreed with Gwen was in what his father had believed about *him*. Ralph knew now what he did not back then— how incredibly lacking he had been in what was required to be a Marcher Lord. And this more than anything had been what had driven him to change as much as he had. He'd needed to, in order to be the man he had to become.

'But we were not talking about me.' He raised his brow. 'Well, now. Are you going to tell me something about you, about the woman you are and have since become?'

Ralph wasn't sure whether Gwen would agree to his request as she seemed reluctant to divulge anything more about herself. That was one very notable difference about Gwen now—the fact that she was so much more guarded than before.

He watched her as the light danced across her face and then she blinked, a slow smile spreading on her lips. 'Very well. Come inside the chamber, then, and I'll show you.'

Gwen helped him climb through the small arched window. He stood up and scanned the small, serviceable chamber. The room had a large pallet with a cream coverlet with Gwen's signature floral embroidered over it, a wooden coffer against the wall and was lit by both the fire in the hearth and the light on the metal wall sconce.

'Where is Mistress Brida, this evening?'

'There's something she needed to attend to, but she'll return shortly.' Gwen beckoned. 'Come, I want to show you something.'

Gwen led Ralph to her makeshift workspace, lit by one of her only extravagances, a small beeswax candle. The others were seemingly scattered on top of the plain wooden coffer.

'So, Ralph de Kinnerton, pray tell me what do you make of all of this?'

She noticed as his eyes widened in surprise as he tilted his head towards her.

'What do we have here?'

There, on the coffer, were reams of parchment with sweeping letters, decoratively formed and illustrated, that Gwen had created using inks and powdered and crushed pigment dyes.

'These are what I had practised, before I transferred my work on to the parchment or even vellum.'

'You?' Ralph smiled. 'You created this…this exquisite work.'

'I did.' She shrugged. 'But this isn't really as impressive as you'd imagine. The true masters, training in monasteries up and down the country, produce the most breathtaking, stupendous artwork that you have ever seen.'

'And how have you come to be so skilled in such stupendous artwork?'

'Well, I do not know about that.' She chuckled, softly. 'But it was by sheer luck that I had the opportunity to learn.'

She watched his long fingers brush along the surface of the parchment, making Gwen swallow uncomfortably. The memory of how they touched her fingers in the moonlight still lingered. The warmth, so very palpable. She absently rubbed her fingers together before clenching her fist.

'I was lucky to have been part of the Marshal household, as I mentioned, after I managed to escape Kinnerton. One summer I accompanied my lady, the Countess of Pembroke, who travelled with her husband on pilgrimage. En route we stayed in St Albans Abbey.' She turned and gave him a small shy smile. 'The scriptorium at the abbey—oh, Ralph, it was the most splendid place that I have ever beheld.'

He grinned. 'I can see that it must have been, just by the way your eyes have lit up.'

'It was and it was here that we met Matthew Paris, a young talented Benedictine monk, who was very attentive.'

Ralph folded his arms across his chest and raised his brows. 'Was he now?'

She nodded. 'He showed us each different process to create the manuscript codices. From how the feather quills were prepared, creating oak gall ink and all the various coloured pigment to scribe and paint, and how the parchment and vellum were cleaned, stretched and prepared.' She inhaled before continuing. 'But my favourite part was gilding and binding each page to create the manuscripts.'

'It must have been fascinating.'

'Oh, yes,' she said on a sigh. 'It really was.' Gwen ran her fingers across the decorative jewel-coloured letter at the side of the parchment with bold gilded edges. 'The process for applying the colour and the thin gold leaf has over six intricate stages. Outlining the design using minium—here, can you see these faint orangey lines?'

He nodded, his attention on the artwork.

'Then adding the gesso, which raises the surface on the skin and is used wherever there is gold on the design. After which colour is added, using pigments made from lapis lazuli, woad and even dragon's blood.'

'Dragon's blood, eh?'

'Indeed—and used for the base, tints and shades, to highlight, and finally the black-edged outline is applied in stages.'

'Fascinating. And you learnt all of this from one visit to the scriptorium at the Abbey?'

'No.' She shook her head. 'The Earl invited a few monks to Caversham Manor to employ them in recording his family's history. I became an apt student and soon was allowed to finish some of the pages.'

'Quite the apprentice, my lady.' His fingers touched along the long thin stem of the quill. 'I'm impressed.'

'Here, let me show you how you can make a mark on this parchment.'

Ralph held up his left hand. 'I can only use this one though, remember.'

'Yes, of course.' She wrapped her fingers over his much larger left hand over the quill and gently guided it in the inkwell, dipping it in the brownish liquid before making long sweeping brushstrokes on the parchment.

'It must have been difficult having to do everything with your left hand.'

He was standing so close that his masculine warmth enveloped her, sending a frisson of awareness down her spine.

'In a manner of speaking.' Ralph shifted and shrugged at her question before exhaling irritably. 'I cannot even clench my right hand properly any longer, however hard I try.'

He tried to close his other hand, but his movement was limited and jerky.

Gwen reached out and brushed her hand over the rough mangled skin. 'Rest easy, Ralph. I can see how difficult it is.'

'It's more frustrating than anything although I do try to use it wherever I can. But, yes, I had to learn everything anew with my left hand. From wielding a sword to now holding this quill.'

'And doing remarkably well. Don't ever forget that, Ralph,' she added softly.

Their joined hands continued to make long, fluid shapes.

'I can see why you enjoy this. There's something quite soothing about making these marks.'

There was also something quite wonderful being this close to Ralph and being the one to guide his huge, strong hand. She watched the thick taut hand in fascination as his fingers flexed and stretched around the quill, yet creating light, fluid strokes.

'I suppose, but for me it is a little more than that.' She lessened the grip, allowing the shapes being created by the ink to flow through the nib evenly and allowing Ralph to take the lead.

'Oh? How so?'

'I have always enjoyed this… creating and making things that give me pleasure.' She shrugged. 'Or try to evoke that same pleasure in others.'

His hand stilled mid-air.

'You do not need to try, my lady,' he whispered.

'Sometimes.' Gwen darted her gaze at their laced fingers and her work strewn around the coffer. 'It feels as though that I am leaving little pieces of myself in what I create.'

She heard him take a slow breath and drop the quill. His hand turned palm against palm, his fingers curling around hers. She watched, mesmerised, as the pad of his thumb stroked her skin in a circular motion. Over and over again.

Dear God.

Without looking up, Gwen knew that his breathing had quickened, but then so had hers. She untangled her hand from his and took a step back, smoothing down her kirtle skirt.

'I seem to have got a little ink on my skirt. That teaches me to forget to wear an overskirt.'

'Gwen.' Her name reverberated in the chamber. She lifted her head and met his eyes, filled with confusion and barely concealed longing. They stood staring at each other for a moment. But it would not do. These feelings and emotions were ones that she could no longer afford to have.

'It grows late,' Ralph murmured, breaking the silence and seemingly this growing tension between them. 'I should go.'

'Before you go, I want to give you something.'

'You do not need to.'

'I know, but it's something I would like you to have, especially as I will not be able to give you my token openly tomorrow.' She strode to the coffer and opened a small wooden box, pulling out a length of green-coloured linen. 'I would like to be able to give you it now, as a symbol of our renewed friendship. Please...' she held out her hand '... I embroidered it myself.'

For a brief moment Gwen thought he would not take it, but his damaged hand reached out and caught it. She placed her other hand over the top and gave it a gentle squeeze, hoping he understood.

Friendship was all she could offer now. Nothing more.

Ralph bowed over their entwined hands, clutching her gift, and then turned, leaving the same way he came in, by climbing out of the arched window, without a second glance.

Gwen stared and stood in the empty, silent space, as a rush of tears filled her eyes.

Tears?

No, she would not allow these feelings that she had long forsaken to rise once again.

A knock at the door made her jump, breaching her miserable reflections. These futile worthless emotions that caused nothing but regret and misery. She wiped her eyes with the back of her hand quickly and pasted a ready smile on her face.

'Is that you, Brida?' Thank God her voice sounded measured and light. 'Come in.'

Her friend walked into the chamber, closing the wooden door behind her. 'I did not wish to intrude but I thought that mayhap now… Oh, Gwen, what has happened?'

She sat on the edge of her bed and sniffed. 'Nothing. I'm perfectly well.'

'You do not look well, my lady. Did you and Sir Ralph quarrel?'

'No, it's nothing like that. We talked and, well…that was all.'

Yet it was more than that. Gwen had shown him some of her most valued earthly possessions and spoke in detail of how she created them and the small pleasures they evoked.

'You told him?' Brida asked slowly. 'You told him everything?'

'No, no…of course not. Our conversation, thankfully, never dwelled there—in that terrible, awful darkness.'

'Then what is it?' She looked a little confused. 'What happened?'

'Truly, it's nothing, Brida. I am just a little fatigued.' And disheartened, desolate as well as so many other things she would rather not contemplate.

Hopes and dreams…

Well, hers had all but faded, replaced with revulsion coiled and knotted in her stomach for ever.

Brida sat beside her. 'It must be very difficult seeing him, knowing all that you have lost.'

'Yes, more than you can imagine.' Gwen leant her head on her friend's shoulder.

'Then why do you not tell Sir Ralph everything? Trust that he might understand,' she said softly, as they both stared at the fire spit and crackle in the hearth.

'No,' Gwen choked out, screwing her eyes shut. 'I cannot do that.'

'But he may just surprise you.'

'I do not want his pity.' Never that... 'Besides, this is not about any possible concern I may have relating to Ralph's feelings once he finds out the truth and what happened after he left Kinnerton. Only how it all affects *me*...still, after all this time.'

Gwen stood up and walked to the stone wall, leaning the back of her head against it. 'I can never countenance the terrible event from that time, only to acknowledge that it did happen and somehow I lived with it.' She rubbed her forehead and exhaled through her teeth.

'I can only imagine how hard it must have been. But never forget that you helped a good man escape certain death.'

'Oh, Brida, don't you see that, despite knowing that what I did back then helped Ralph get away, I still allowed Stephen le Gros to touch me, defile me, *mark me*. I would always carry that stain with me because I let him, Brida. I allowed that man to do it.'

Her fingers touched the base of her neck where Stephen had left the now faint scar that never failed to torment her. A permanent reminder of that harrowing time.

'It was a sacrifice that you were forced to make, Gwen.

You would do it again, too, if it meant you had to save Ralph de Kinnerton. Would you not?'

Yes, God help her, she would. In a heartbeat. Even though it meant that she would then live with the shame in perpetuity. As she was now.

'I would,' she whispered.

It had almost destroyed her before when she thought that it had all been for nought. When she had believed Ralph to be dead. Terrible as her actions had been, it had given Ralph a chance to get away…to live. To survive. And she had tried so much in vain to forget what had happened.

'And you are still a maid, my lady. Stephen le Gros did not take *that* from you.'

'Not for want of trying.' Gwen's lips twisted in disgust. 'And thank God, otherwise the man's claim on me would have been far greater and harder to refute. It was only by the grace of God that that did not happen and I managed to escape Kinnerton with the help of a few locals, otherwise the situation would have been far more dire.'

Yet Stephen had taken much from her. So much more than Gwen would ever care to examine. 'Either way, Brida, I do not want Ralph to know the sordid reasons why I must take the veil, however understanding he might or might not be. I cannot have him know the shameful side to what happened all those years ago. I could not bear it.'

'Yes, my lady.'

With all things considered, it might have been better if Gwen had not agreed to Ralph's escort to the safe confines of the convent walls in Ireland. It had been her pragmatic side that had conceded the need for more caution as well as the necessity for a strong warrior to accompany them. Had she known, however, that these unwanted emotions would once again resurface, she would not have agreed to Ralph's offer. Either way, Gwen must push them away, for his sake and her own.

Chapter Eleven

The following morn, after a restless night's sleep, Gwen found herself nervously watching the knights' procession before the start of the *mêlée à pied* in the royal spectators' dais. She wrung the material of her kirtle tightly in her hands in anticipation, knowing that it would commence soon. The dull thud in her chest quickened as she caught a glimpse of Ralph in full armour acting as Sir Thomas, in among the de Clancey knights. From afar, he seemed to have spotted Gwen as he inclined his head in her direction, raising his sword arm for her to see the narrow length of the token she had given him, tied firmly around the hilt of his sword. Why that gesture made her heart soar she did not wish to consider. She only knew that it did—very much.

Gwen had been so caught up in her musing that she had not realised Stephen le Gros's approach.

'My Lady Gwenllian, I hope I find you well on this bright morning?'

Yet she should have detected his reprehensible stench anywhere. 'Sir Stephen,' she managed to say, hoping for something akin to a composed courtesy when in truth she wanted to rage at him as she always did when he was close to her.

'I came in the hope that I could gain a favour, a token from such a fair lady before the start of this mêlée.' He knelt on one knee below her, to her utter dismay.

Gwen knew that this performance was as much for her benefit as it was for the royal court in attendance, but the very idea that she would willingly give anything that belonged to her to this man was repugnant.

'I beg pardon, sir, but I sadly have no favours to give,' she said, the smile brittle on her lips. 'However, I hope you find success in…your endeavours.' She lowered her head, hoping that Stephen would now go and ready himself for the mêlée, but instead he crept a little closer.

'Do you? Well, I must say that is good to know.'

Her jaw clenched so tightly that she almost ground her teeth together. She snapped her head away, ignoring him, hoping he'd leave, but it was wishful thinking. His very nearness made her want to retch violently. He always had this effect on her, making her feel the need to cleanse every part of her that came into contact with him.

He pinched her chin, turning her head around to face him again. 'Careful, Gwen. You wouldn't want anyone to think that you are opposed to your intended.'

'You are not my intended, sir.'

'Ah, but you very soon would be.'

She jerked her head away, not wanting his hand anywhere near her. She must not allow herself to rise to his jibes, knowing that was what the man craved.

'Come now, my dear. Anything would do.' Stephen grabbed her hand, clasping it tightly in his.

'I have nothing to offer you, sir, as I have explained.'

'Oh, but you must have something. No need to be coy.' His laughter seemed to turn into a snarl.

'I do not think so, sir. My conscience would never allow it,' she said through gritted teeth, trying to pull her hand free.

'Oh, would it not?' His fingernails dug into her wrist. 'You really are a tease, my lovely Gwen. Any other man might wither and run with their tail dangling from the legs, but not I. I find that your animosity and this reluctance to see sense, although beneath you, strangely heightens my desire for you.' He pulled her towards him, making it seem that they were having a quiet private moment. 'And you know I cannot wait until I bed you properly. Such a shame we were disturbed before.'

Gwen bit down on her lips hard, in the attempt to stop herself from screaming at Stephen. 'Unhand me. People are watching.'

'Let them.' He shrugged. 'It matters not since you shall soon belong to me anyway. But I'd wager that they believed we were having a more amorous discussion with our heads bent together so, anyway.'

'Stop this, Stephen. You are making a fool of yourself.'

'Alas, I always seem to, fair Gwenllian. Especially when it comes to you.' His grip on her tightened once more. 'But be warned, my dear. It has not escaped my attention that you seem a little enamoured of Thomas Lovent. Your eyes follow his progress whenever he is near. And while I may be a patient man, far more than most, I am not one to be averse to jealousy…but of course that may be your intention.'

The beat in her chest hammered faster. God, but she could not allow Stephen's notice of Sir Thomas otherwise he might soon realise the truth. That he wasn't whom Stephen le Gros thought him to be. It would be a disaster if he found out about Ralph before he should and Gwen would not endanger Ralph's plans for the world…

'Don't be so ridiculous. Your imagination has run away with you.'

'I do hope so, Gwen, for you would not want me to wreak my foolish jealousy on that young knight.'

'I hope that you are not threatening Thomas Lovent?' She narrowed her eyes.

'No.' He kissed the back of her hand before standing to his full height. 'Just a warning…for now, but heed my words, my sweet.'

Ralph could sense from a distance that all was not well with Gwenllian. She had sat with her back rigid, her jaw set and her face devoid of any colour. But it was only when Ralph spotted his deplorable cousin that he knew instantly the reason of her distress.

By God, but Ralph had had enough of the bastard's menacing, possessive behaviour towards Gwen. He would take any necessary means to stop Stephen if he did not cease with his intimidation.

Ralph pushed forward towards the dais in long strides when he saw that the man had moved away, to his relief, otherwise he would have had to see to Gwen's comfort and damn the consequences. The uneasiness that Ralph felt was still raw, still palpable.

There was something not quite as it should be with Gwen and his cousin. Oh, her revulsion and dislike of him was both visceral and intense, matching his own, but there was something else—a strange familiarity that revealed something far darker and more potent. Whatever it was, Ralph was determined to find out the truth in the hope he could somehow help alleviate Gwen's anguish. Stephen le Gros would not assert and impose himself on her even if he did believe himself to be her betrothed. Either way, it did not matter what Stephen believed, but

Gwen would not be harassed and threatened by the man. That he would swear to. He had, after all, sworn he would protect her. Ralph would think about the situation again later, now that his cousin had moved away from her.

First, the challenge of this mêlée. Ralph turned his head towards what he was about to face and took a deep breath under the metal helmet. Yes, he needed all his focus, strength and resolve if he wanted to succeed here. He rubbed the fabric of Gwen's token between his thumb and forefinger, hoping to extract some luck that she had imbued before tying the gloves to his wrist.

He stepped forward and sent a silent prayer to the heavens. He would give it everything that he had, this was his…his tourney to win. And the time was nigh.

The triumphant celebrations extended in the de Clancey tent later that evening. This time, however, his friends could honour his victory properly without the pretence of congratulating the acclaimed knight *Sir Thomas Lovent* in front of King Henry's court.

Soon, however, very soon Ralph would step out from behind the guise of his friend's armour…as himself. But for now, he would bide his time for just a little longer.

Ralph scanned the small space and smiled faintly to himself. It was a moment of shared merriment—eating, drinking with a gratifying sense of satisfaction, tinged with relief. He had won today and gained considerable loot in the takings, even after distributing some silver to Tom and their young stable lad. From ornate silver shields and expensive swords to a young foal and even ransom money. He took a sip from his mug and swiped his mouth with the back of his hand. But he could not have done any of it without the help of his friends and mentors whose belief in him exceeded his own and who went to exceptional lengths to support and aid him.

It humbled him to think that they did this for him, not that he understood why, nor that he really deserved their esteem, but even so… Words could never truly express the extent of Ralph's gratitude.

'You seem a little pensive, Ralph.' Isabel sat beside him on the small bench.

'Do I? I'm little taken aback by today's success, that is all.' He shook his head, sighing.

'Believe it, for you deserve this more than anyone I know.'

He covered her hand, giving it a squeeze in gratitude. 'My thanks, Isabel.'

Yet there must have been something in his manner as a furrow appeared in the middle of her forehead. Ralph knew too well that nothing much escaped Isabel de Clancey's perceptive eye.

'Come, this is an agreeable moment. A good moment. One you have worked hard for,' she said softly.

'It is,' he said absently, his voice sounding a little gruff.

'There is something else, is there not?'

An unfathomable feeling of desolation engulfed him, however hard he tried to shift it. It made him uneasy, detached even in such a congenial company of friends. He sighed and shook his head.

'No, all is well, I promise.' It was better to convince her that all his concerns centred around the reason for their celebrations, despite the win today. 'I cannot lose sight that this is just one mêlée, Isabel, even though it certainly helps towards covering some of my previous losses.'

'Yes, and from here on you can strengthen and build on your success.'

'I shall certainly try.' His smile became a little solemn. 'I want you to know that I couldn't have done any of this without any of you. You have stood by me when anyone else would have walked away. I'll always be indebted to you.'

'Please.' She waved her hand. 'I vowed from the moment I set eyes on you that I would do everything I could to help you after the way in which you were attacked and left to die. So, no, you owe neither me nor Will anything.'

But that was not true. He would always be honour-bound, his allegiances forged to Isabel, Will and every person here.

'Listen to me, Ralph…' she sighed '…you are close now. So close to getting everything you've set out to achieve. It is within your grasp, if you just reach out and grab it.'

Was it? He wasn't so sure. But there was also another who had always championed and believed in him.

Gwen…

He had not seen her properly today. Not since before the start of the mêlée. She had also been absent from the banquet, which had sent darts of concern through him. There had been something about her demeanour when she had spoken with his cousin that troubled him. Still troubled him.

Notwithstanding that, Ralph could not help but feel a little restless, a little hollow despite this achievement. It was always the same for him on occasions like this when he had a moment to reflect and ponder about his life, the past, present and also future itself. It left him morose, somehow bereft and unsettled, when he should be far more buoyed by the win. Damn, but he wasn't even certain what his future might hold. Not with any clarity. But it would be one without Gwenllian ferch Hywel. That much was certain.

She might not have married as he had expected her to, but had still chosen a different path for herself. One that she still intended to pursue and which did not include him. Ralph knew he should not care, not after all this time when so much had changed, and yet...

There had been a discernible closeness that seemed reassuringly familiar yet surprisingly different when Gwen had invited him to her chamber.

'Tell me your hopes and dreams...'

He had regretted asking her that nonsense. Yet, when Gwen had showed him her elaborate penwork on the parchment, she revealed much about herself in the process. The way she had held on to his hand, gently guiding him to align the marks he was making to her proficient ones. It was a glimpse through her eyes to the very heart of her enjoyment, the pleasure she gained. It had been fleeting, but it had been a window into Gwen's heart in some small way.

His eyes fell to his sword perched against the bench beside him and to the small length of woven green fabric—Gwen's token that she had made and embroidered. And that she admitted imparting a little of herself in her creations. And this...this small piece of her now belonged to him.

Ralph stood, with a sudden tangible desire to be alone, to ride somewhere away from here. Above all else, Ralph wanted...nay, needed to see her.

To see Gwen. To get the answers he so desperately sought.

'Yes. It is within my grasp, Isabel. And I hope I can take your advice and grab it.' He bowed with a real smile spreading on his lips. 'Now, if you'll excuse me, my lady.'

Chapter Twelve

Gwenllian expelled a big breath before she opened the wooden shutters to her window. She leant outside, drawing the cool night air into her lungs, and blinked. She had not expected this, not tonight after Ralph had performed spectacularly well in the mêlée. Yet the moment she heard a sound of something hitting her shutter, she knew that he was here, somewhere below. Her eyes adjusted to the darkness, trying to ascertain where Ralph was, but once again he was much closer that she had thought.

'Good evening, my lady.' His deep, low voice rumbled through her from somewhere beneath the canopied branches of the tree, close to the window.

'I did not think to see you, Ralph. Not tonight,' she hissed. 'I thought that you would be celebrating with the de Clancey retinue.'

'And so I was until I decided to take a diversionary tour of the castle.'

'Did you, indeed? And yet I believed you to be quite familiar with all it has to offer.'

'Alas, not familiar enough.'

She felt her skin prickle and flush. Lord, but her reactions to him were ridiculous.

'I had never realised you had such a penchant for hiding in the darkness.' Her lips twitched. 'Will you not step out from under it?'

'Very well.'

Gwen grinned as Ralph leant across and tilted his head, returning her smile. She marvelled how his handsomeness was not lessoned in any way by those scars zigzagging across the right side of his face.

'Good evening to you, too, Ralph. I am still trying to determine why you hide in shadows and under branches thick with leaves?' She had hoped her voice had been somewhat light and teasing, yet he replied earnestly.

'I know what I am, Gwen, what I was and what I still need to be,' he murmured softly. 'The scars that I carry may be grotesque, but they serve to bring back to mind everything that happened...lest I forget.' She watched as he rubbed his fingers over them roughly.

'I'm sorry, I did not mean to...'

'I know.' He smiled. 'And at least they don't scare every child I meet. William Tallany, for instance, admires them greatly.'

'I can imagine.'

It was remarkable that Ralph could dispense with any notion of regret despite the horrors that he must have experienced in Aquitaine when she could not move past the horrors that she had experienced at Kinnerton. That she still carried with her.

'So, tell me whether this diversionary tour of yours has been to your liking?'

'It has certainly been different.'

'Oh, how so?'

'Well, for one, being perched on a tree from this high vantage point does put a distinctive perspective on things.' He moved along the branch to get closer to her, balancing a little precariously. 'It makes a man realise how insignificant and fallible he is, especially if he were to fall.'

'Careful,' she said trying to keep the worry out of her voice. 'What was your other insightful understanding?'

'Ah, well, that would be for this. The opportunity to talk to you so freely.'

She bit her lip and dropped her head before turning her attention back to him. 'I must congratulate you, Ralph. You did splendidly well today, you know.'

'And yet I must come here directly for your congenial compliments as you were absent at the banquet or any-where else for that matter. I hope that you are well and that I am not intruding on your evening?'

'I am perfectly well, sir, and you are not intruding on anything.'

'I'm glad to hear that.' He dragged his long legs and dangled them over the thick branch of the tree that just about supported his large frame. 'In that case, could I tempt you to go for a ride on horseback…with me?'

'Now? At this time?' Her eyebrows shot up. She hadn't expected this. 'Do you not think it might be a little late for horseback riding?'

'Mayhap, but it seems also possible that this evening has not been diversionary enough.' He chuckled, look-ing so much younger and so much like the Ralph she re-membered.

'Sadly, I have no taste for such diversions.'

'Come now, it might be late and the time may not be conducive to riding, but where is your sense of adven-ture, Gwenllian ferch Hywel?'

'How well you say my name. Yet you must know that I left *that* on that cliff-edge near Kinnerton and the Welsh borders so long ago, when I almost toppled down the ridge.'

'Oh, Lord, I forgot about that!' He dragged his fingers through his hair. 'Do you remember how I caught you by the scruff of your cloak?'

'Yes, I do. It was both terrifying and so ridiculously funny. We collapsed into a peal of hopeless laughter, once you dragged me to safety.'

And into his arms… It had also been the first time that Ralph had kissed her—so sweet, so wondrous, filled with wistful promises of a future together. She heard him clear his throat, making her wonder whether he had been thinking about the same memory.

'I do remember that we got very lost on the way back to Kinnerton as the path we took had flooded.'

'And got back very late in the dead of night, much to your father's consternation. Had he not sent guards in search of us?'

'He had, if my memory serves, much to his chagrin.' He frowned but then lifted his head. 'Well?' 'Are you coming, my lady? Shall we get lost together?'

'I am not so sure it would be a good idea, Ralph.'

'Well, I must say, that is a shame.' He descended down the next branch below. 'Since there was a time when I recall that you'd welcome such an impulsive expedition, but no matter… I'm sure I'll enjoy my horseback ride just as much alone…with no other company but my horse.'

He let the moment stretch, emphasising his point further.

'Very well.' She chuckled. 'I'll come, but only so you do not have to suffer being alone and having no one but your horse for company.'

He smirked. 'I'm very much obliged to you, Gwen.'

'Wait while I dress as a squire, Ralph. I think it prudent to do so.'

'If you so wish, but hurry, my lady.'

'Only if you assist in helping me down. I have no head for heights, as you may also recall.'

'Don't worry, Gwen. I'll be here to catch you if you fall.'

They made their way carefully down the tree, around the castle wall and through the damp gatehouse shrouded under their dark cloaks, their heads bent low. Ralph fetched his huge black destrier and brought him around to where Gwen was standing, keeping watch.

'Here he is. Meet Fortis.'

'Oh, he's magnificent.'

Ralph grinned, dragging his hand up and down the animal's muzzle. 'That he is, are you not, my friend.'

Gwen tried to also pat the horse, but he jerked away. 'Temper? Or is he a little nervous?

'Probably a bit both.' Ralph chuckled. 'That could be why we get on so well. Isn't it, boy?'

'I see. And is he brave?' she asked, holding out her hand and allowing the horse to come to her, before she could smooth down its velvety flank.

'I believe so.' He nodded. 'I doubt I could have got through the many challenges I've faced without him.'

'How long has he been with you?'

'Since Poitiers.' He nuzzled the horse, scratching him along his neck. 'I reared him from when he was an anxious young foal, who no one seemed to care for.'

'Except you, Ralph. You always had a way with jittery animals.'

He shrugged. 'It was nothing that a bit of encouragement, patience and care couldn't solve. But don't be fooled by him. Beneath his gruff manner, he's a softy really.'

'Like his master?'

'I could not say, my lady.' He smiled wryly as he mounted the horse, holding out his hand. 'Shall we put him through his paces?'

'Yes. Let's.'

It was a wonderful feeling, galloping along the open fields, wrapped in Ralph's strong arms, as he gripped on to the reins tightly from behind her. She felt secure. She felt safe, here alone with Ralph, riding nowhere in particular in the dead of night. Gwen pulled the hood of her cloak down, and felt the cool night breeze against her skin.

The rush of riding at high speed across the hilly valley that gently rolled into the thicket under the full moon allowed her a sense of freedom that she rarely felt. This wonderful, exhilarating sensation that stirred her blood and put colour on her cheeks made her feel alive.

For the first time in a long time she was not weighed down by the burdens of her secrets.

'You're very quiet this evening.' She felt Ralph's breath brush against the side of her neck.

'I was just thinking the same about you.'

'Mayhap we are both consumed by our own reflections.'

'Or possibly that we are so enthralled by such vigorous exercise that it somehow removes the need for conversation.'

'Aye, just so.' He chuckled. 'That would be the reason.'

'In case that is a wrong assumption, what were these reflections of yours?' she said over her shoulder, without realising that he had leant so close his lips were a fraction away from the skin on her nape.

'My reflections are from the past, I suppose, merged with ones forged from being reacquainted with you again. Here at this tournament.'

'Then there is much to contemplate.'

'Either way, Gwen, I'm glad to be away from it all for just a moment, with you and Fortis as company.'

'Thank you. Yet I would have thought you'd have wanted to celebrate with your friends after your success earlier.'

'Trust me—' his deep low murmur rumbled through her '—there is no other place I would rather be than right here with you.'

As did she. God above, despite all her best intentions to stay away, Gwen was enjoying being here with Ralph far more than she should. It granted something precious to her, otherwise, bleak life. It must be the freedom of riding on horseback again, away from the stifling atmosphere of the tournament…as well other unpleasantness. But Gwen didn't want to be reminded of any of that. Not tonight.

They rode down the steep hill, still within the demesne of Castle Pulverbatch, and slowed to a canter as the path gradually led to a thick dense coppice.

'I wish I had thought to bring something to drink. I cannot think why I'm so parched.'

'Well, it's just as well that I brought some ale.'

'That is most thoughtful.'

Ralph dismounted and helped her down, his fingers flexed around her waist a moment longer than really necessary, the heat imparting from his hands spreading through her body. He caught her gaze and gave her a slow smile that made something inside her unfurl. This reaction to Ralph bewildered her and was something quite different, this breathlessness, to anything she had ever experienced when they had been younger. It befuddled her senses.

'Here.' He handed the flagon from his saddlebag. 'I think the exercise has brought on a glow to your face, Gwen.'

'And hence the necessity to cool down.'

'That is not what I meant, my lady.'

'No?' She raised the flagon before taking a sip. 'To your favourable victory today, Ralph. I'm very happy for you.'

She passed the flagon back to him, licking a drop of the drink from her lips, and watched as Ralph took a swig and swallowed as he moved to fetch something else from the saddlebag.

'I've also brought some provisions to sustain us.' His voice sounding strangely hoarse.

'It seems that you have thought of everything in advance of this diversionary endeavour to "get lost".'

'There's nothing like being prepared.'

'Yes.' She smiled. 'I'm embarrassed to say that I have come empty handed.'

'No need, I've brought everything we might want.'

Ralph passed a few parcels of food, wrapped in cloth and tied securely with string, his fingers grazing hers briefly, sending another wave of awareness through her. He cleared his throat, threw down a small blanket and allowed her to do the honours. She sat and unfolded the soft bundles. There was chicken, a small round of cheese, apples and rolls of bread.

A veritable feast under the moonlight.

They both tucked into the repast in silence. Gwen noticed his smouldering gaze on her as she nibbled a small portion of the cheese. She exhaled slowly, as her stomach flipped on itself. Oh, what foolishness. It was Ralph de Kinnerton who was sat across from her. Ralph, the boy she had known for most of her life.

Yet he was anything but a boy, he was a man in his prime. She gave her head a little shake and attempted to steer her thoughts back to a safer track.

'You certainly have come prepared.'

'I had to. In anticipation that anything and everything may occur.'

'Is that your usual strategy? This consideration to your life now or…' Gwen paused, unable to voice the other reason. That he anticipated how things might develop between them, even though they couldn't, she reminded herself.

'Or what, my lady?'

'Nothing, I just wanted to understand the extent of your preparations.'

He rubbed his jaw, his fingers lingering over his scars before answering. 'After surviving such a brutal attack, that frankly I should have foreseen, I now tread carefully in everything I do.'

'Even climbing up and down trees.'

'Especially that.' He winked. 'Everything is done with meticulous planning and gruelling practice, where once I would have relied far more on impulsiveness and trust.'

'Admirable.' She frowned. 'But surely your incredible advancement has not only built your resolve and tenacity, but the belief that you can also now rely on instinct as well.'

'You sound like Will.' He chuckled softly. 'Yes, instinct can come into play, but on its own can lead to impetuousness resulting in danger.'

'Ah, but not if you include the gruelling practice that

you mention. Along with intense discipline and the diligence needed to succeed.'

'Just so.'

'Yet this, tonight, seems far more impulsive than you give yourself credit for, Ralph.'

'I'm not a saint, Gwen, but a man…a warrior.' His words were low and husky. His smile, slow and sensual. It licked down the length of her body, making her shudder.

She flicked her eyes to his and caught the heat, that fervent desire that he seemed to find difficult to hide. It was unbidden, raw and unfettered, but it did not frighten her. And why would it? This was Ralph. A man who was so familiar and yet wildly different from the one she once knew. And one who made her long for things she should not long for. Good grief, he made her heart beat with such intensity she felt as though she might swoon.

'I hope you are not cold.'

'I am perfectly fine,' she mumbled, looking away.

Ralph appeared not to have heard her. He shot up and strode towards Fortis, retrieving a small woollen blanket from the saddlebag and draping it over her shoulders. His large hands skimmed her shoulders briefly.

'Just in case.'

'My thanks,' she said a little too breathlessly, trying to quell this growing tension between them. 'It is a little nippy, I suppose.'

Gwen took another bite of food, trying to compose herself and think of something…anything to say. She wondered whether he could sense these unwarranted feelings that she had. God, she hoped not. It would be unwise to draw attention to them, much less share them with him.

'I'm happy that this can now erase any doubts you may have had about your abilities, Ralph.'

'Ah, but has it?' He sighed deeply. 'The truth is closer

to this, Gwen, I harness any doubt that I have to what I hope can drive me forth.'

'I don't understand.'

'Living with the constancy of doubt, I can only do one thing other than throwing down my sword and shield in defeat—to use it to redress the balance in my favour.'

She raised her brow. 'That is an interesting way to view it.'

'Indeed. I realised that it was the only way for me. Either that or grow complacent, which would only lead to failure, something I can hardly afford.'

'Well, you are certainly succeeding, however you are doing it.'

'I do hope so,' he drawled.

Did the man even realise the effect he was having on her?

Gwen took a deep breath and stood. 'Show me.'

'I'm at a loss, my lady. What would you like me to show you?'

'Er…well…' Gwen grappled for something to say and went with the first thing that popped into her head. 'What about showing me a combative move?'

'I beg your pardon?' His lips seemed to twitch as though he was suppressing a smile.

She committed to her proposal, feeling none of it and knowing it to be the distraction it was. 'You are a valiant warrior knight. Show me anything you like that could be used in combat.'

'You would like me to show you, now? In the middle of the night?'

'I showed you how to make marks on a parchment, did I not?' She shrugged. 'I believe it is now your turn to return the favour, sir. Anyway, the full moonlight provides enough light out here in the open, does it not?'

'Indeed. How can I refuse?' He smiled, standing to face her. 'Very well. Let's see now, we need a couple of long sticks to act as swords.'

Gwen turned on her heel and scoured the ground in search of what they needed, using the brief lapse of time to temper her beating heart.

'Er... Gwen?'

She could hear him from behind, but waved her hand absently. 'Give me a moment, please, Ralph.'

'Gwen, if you'd care to...'

'I'm sure I can find a couple of sticks.' She moved further away.

'Gwenllian?'

She didn't reply, but continued to look, when a long stick perfect for what they needed landed at her feet, thrown from somewhere behind. She spun around, her forehead furrowed in the middle, and saw Ralph holding a similar stick to the one he'd thrown.

'Ah, well done,' she said, feeling a little foolish. 'You found them.'

He grinned. 'Shall we start?'

They went through a few basic rudimentary moves which were far more exacting than Gwen had considered. For some reason the words Ralph uttered did not seem to connect with the moves she was supposed to make. Or it could be more that her eyes were otherwise fixed to his lips, as if they were casting a spell on her, calling her to him. Enough! She frowned and tried to focus.

'Pardon me, but could you repeat that, please?' she said instead.

'Of course.'

'I never imagined it to be this difficult.'

'Ah, but I'm certain that a woman of your skill and ability can rise to the challenge.'

'I'm not so sure about that. I cannot remember everything you have said for me to do.'

'Try not to recall the actual words, only the feeling behind the sentiment. Allow yourself to be at one with your weapon.'

'I've always wanted to be at one with...*a stick.*'

'Come now, Gwen, focus,' he admonished. 'Stand with a little more space between your legs, so that you can move easily in any direction when need be. And try to be light on your feet.'

'Like this?' Gwen stood to attention, her legs apart.

'Very good.' He nodded. 'Now, lean forward, a little more, and hold your weapon out in front of you ready to strike, moving into it as you do. Either thrusting like this.' He motioned with his stick, moving it in the air. 'Cutting, like so. Or this—a slashing move.' He showed her each attacking stance.

'Then there's also the riposte.'

'Riposte?' She looked up. 'And what is that?'

'A counter-defensive move designed to befuddle your opponent.' He smiled at her knowingly. 'Here, try to use any of those three striking moves to attack me and I shall show you.'

She angled the stick to slash, cut and even thrust, but each of the newly acquired manoeuvres were countered and pushed away until Ralph swung around to a different position and lunged low on his knee and thrust his weapon forward with such force that it made her drop her stick.

'Like so.'

'A very effective move.'

'Precisely. Although this can be met with a counter-riposte after the parry is met head on, with another in response.'

'I see.' But not as much as she wanted to.

'The timing of each strike is also important, so that they are made with precision rather than being aimless, ineffective and redundant.'

They started to circle one another. 'Well, there is certainly a lot to remember.'

'Quite.'

For such a large man, it was quite disconcerting how easily Ralph prowled and moved lithely around her.

'There is also feinting, like so when I step back, lulling you into a false sense of feeling secure in your endeavour.'

'How provoking you are.'

'That is the whole point, Gwen.' He stepped back, his moves almost deceiving her. 'Good now, keep up the attack, changing and switching it up.'

'Like so?'

'Yes. Watch how I can turn your strike into a blunder, while switching the situation in my favour and overwhelming you.'

She tried to attack in the way he had shown her, but he was too quick for her.

'Very diverting, I must say.'

His lips twitched in an obvious attempt not to laugh. 'Shall we stop?'

He paused anyway, his grip loosening on the stick.

'No.' She lunged at him, hoping to catch him off guard, but Ralph was prepared for her clumsy attack. She saw mild surprise, but also a touch of approval as well.

'Very well, if you wish to continue.'

'I do.'

The slow, measured pace quickened, matching the vigour and this new rush of warmth flowing through her veins.

'That's good, my lady.' He stepped back, allowing her to push forward. 'However, you are lacking the necessary spark and spirit.'

She narrowed her eyes and attempted to replicate the fluid movements he had shown her moments ago.

'That's it, well done. Now, try letting go of all that tension that you have held on to, Gwen.'

Oh, Lord, did he know? Could he tell that she was carrying the weight of the past, being back here to the very place where it had all begun?

'Yes. All that unwanted aggravation that has been locked up inside you. Let it go, Gwen. Let it all slip away.'

His words pounded in her head and thrummed through her body with force. This unknown quality that was unleashed from within. Suddenly she was attacking with more ferocity and intensity.

And it felt surprisingly good. Surprisingly freeing.

They continued to step around each other in this fluid sparring dance.

'Is this enough spark and spirit?'

'Yes, very good.' He chuckled. 'However, I believe it is time we should stop.'

'I don't think so, not when I have just found my feet.' She hurled herself forward, knowing she was getting carried away, but what harm could it bring?

'Er... Gwen, you have certainly done well, but I think that is enough.'

'Not when I'm gaining an advantage.'

'Is that what you have?' He sighed, showing her clearly how deceptive her advantage really was. 'Let me tell you that there is a wild look in your eyes, my lady.'

'What of it? You inspired this display, did you not?'

'True.' He smiled. 'The fault lies with me, but we should now cease this display.'

'No, not yet.' Gwen was not done here. There was far more that she needed to let go of. Something inside had ripped opened and now there was no holding back.

'Come now, my lady, let us stop.'

Over and over she continued to thrash out, using the cutting and slashing moves to push him away.

'Enough, Gwen.' He shook his head. 'You cannot allow anger to govern you.'

'Is that what you had to do to master the anger you felt? The impulsiveness that you once had.'

He defended her attacks without much effort, making her push forward more.

'I had to learn to rein in and contain that anger so that I can use it to my own advantage.'

'And have you succeeded?'

'I am still diligently working on it.'

'Highly commendable.' She threw herself into attacking him with everything she had.

'Gwen, stop this,' he said softly.

But she didn't want to listen. All that anger, pain, grief and anguish that had been contained for so long needed release. That pent-up frustration needed to drain away from her. And it was actually working. Gwen continued to deliver more punishing thrusts, until the decision to stop was made for her.

Ralph moved so effortlessly and tripped her in an expedient, fluid way that one moment she was standing, the next she had fallen on top of him with a thud. How he had managed to turn so that he cushioned her fall, landing on the ground instead, she would never know.

'I'm sorry, my lady, but I fear that if I do not put a stop to this, I might end up getting clobbered.'

'Very unsporting. I cannot believe you just did that,'

she gasped, frowning at him. 'What new tricks you have learnt.'

And then quick as a flash he rolled them around so that now he was on top of her.

'True.' He smiled slowly. 'I sometimes surprise even myself.' And before she could grapple with his meaning, Ralph dipped his head and pressed his lips to hers, surprising Gwen as well.

Chapter Thirteen

This was not the first time that he had kissed her, but for all of Ralph's assured, assertive boldness it might as well have been. His lips were soft, sensual and warm as they learnt the shape of hers, far more than ever before. He began a slow seduction of her lips, showing her a different way than any before, as though his kiss could somehow erase the uncertainty that always dogged her. He was asking her to be bold and find her own courage. To forge a new beginning.

He stroked and caressed her lips, teasing her to kiss him back, willing her to take a chance. And then she did.

Gwen wanted to savour this, reacquainting herself with the pattern of his mouth and the languid impression it made on hers. A moan escaped her lips and he caught it in his mouth, smothering and growling in return. He cradled her head, tilting it up to gain better access as he coaxed her lips to open. Her eyes widened in shock as his tongue licked inside her mouth, tasting her. Hot, wet and incredibly delicious, tangling with hers.

This was unlike anything she had ever known, he was devouring her, consuming her. Everything altered and shifted with this kiss. It became carnal, wanton and heady. Her fingers dived into his hair, holding him close. He pulled away to nip her bottom lip, touching it with his tongue before sucking it into his mouth. He nipped, kissed and licked his way along her jaw, her neck, the slope of her breasts. His sinewy hard chest pressed against her, his hands grazing down her soft curves, around the small of her waist, flaring to her hips. Suddenly he stopped abruptly. His kisses, too, softened, becoming more probing, questioning. In answer she pushed gently against his chest and ended the kiss, trying desperately to steady herself and her tumultuous feelings.

Ralph moved away and sat beside her, expelling a long, slow breath. The silence stretched in the darkness as neither could voice what had caught alight so quickly and burned so vividly between them. It was bewildering and shocking to be so receptive to such earthly pleasures. Pleasures that she had forsaken and were not meant for her.

Heavens above, but Gwen was bound on another course and it would be well for her to remember that, rather than succumbing to these temptations of the flesh.

'Shall we return back, my lady?' His voice pierced through her conflicting thoughts.

Gwen turned her head and sank her teeth into her bottom lip, the lingering taste of Ralph still on her. She licked her lips and shook her head.

'Can we stay just a little longer?' She shrugged. 'It's a beautiful eventide and I'm reluctant to resume…well, everything I have to resume.'

'Very well.'

Gwen lay back on the blanket and stared up. The luminosity of the moon hung over the night sky, adding its own particular enchantment. Oh, yes, she wanted to soak up the magic of this evening just a little longer. It would be so easy to run back to her chamber and pretend that she hadn't enjoyed this interlude with Ralph. As though she could pretend to be unmoved by what had just happened, even it had been just a kiss.

In truth, it was far more than that.

Her body was still singing in the aftermath, yearning for more. But that would not do. Gwen should not have allowed it—not allowed a glimmer of something that could not be between them. It would be unfair to both of them. She might be intent on new beginnings, but it was not the one that Ralph had inadvertently alluded to tonight. Yet she was reluctant to move from this place and return to the path she had set out for herself.

Ralph sighed deeply and lay beside her, his head touching hers, wondering whether he should apologise. She had locked herself up again behind the wall she had built, so rigidly, that it was difficult to penetrate. Yet he had just moments ago.

Mayhap he should not have done it, but he couldn't resist her as she lay beneath him with that look of indignation on her face. He had to wipe it away and a kiss was as sure a way to do that as any other. He had not missed her reaction to him—that same desire and longing that coursed through his blood as well. And she had welcomed his kisses and returned them with so much ardour and passion that, in the end, he was forced to stop what he had started and allow her a moment to gather herself. Otherwise they would have both tumbled over a precipice, with no recourse. He did not want to take away that decision, especially after only recently reacquainting with one another again.

He opened his mouth to say words that needed to be

said when her hand found his, her fingers lacing through, giving them a gentle reassuring squeeze.

'Please do not say anything,' she murmured. 'Not about what just happened.'

'Very well.' But, no, he couldn't think of a way to dispel the awkwardness. His whole being, body and soul, was still throbbing with need. Ralph wanted her like no other time before. He wanted her at his side, in his bed, *together...*

Hell's teeth.

Instead, he would lie here beside her in the quietness of the night, with her hand in his, trying to push away these redundant thoughts.

'Do you know,' she whispered, breaking the silence, 'it has been a very long time since I stared at the night sky.'

'What do you see?' he whispered.

'A vast endless chasm.'

His lips tugged at the corners. 'Ah, I'm impressed at your observation.'

'I hope you're not mocking me, Ralph de Kinnerton?'

'Not in the least. I'm admiring such a lyrical ode to the moon, the stars and that endless night.'

'You ask to be privy to my thoughts and then deride them? For shame.'

'No, just a little teasing, I assure you.' He lifted her hand to his lips as she smiled, shaking her head.

'You know, Ralph, you were quite right earlier when you mentioned our insignificance compared to such incredible wonder.'

'Yet I was looking down from the tree, rather than up at the heavens. I was realising the enormity of what I still need to achieve.' He sighed. 'My observations were the magnitude of earthly, more temporal considerations rather than divine ones, Gwen.'

This was the moment that he could ask her to tell him everything. Disclose the very things that he still did not understand about Gwenllian ferch Hywel. He wanted so much to gain an insight, a possible reason why Gwen wanted to take the veil, and here was the chance. She could confide in him and explain her calling, using the same language, same passion that she had shown when she had described the processes needed to create the pages of her decorative parchment.

Yet, would she?

Ralph doubted it. For that same passion she showed in her intricate art where she evidently left pieces of herself, hell, even the way she kissed were from an earthlier proclivity.

Nothing, nothing in the way she behaved expressed a calling that he would assume that she would have. However hard he tried, Ralph could not see her take vows that would renounce worldly goods and devote herself solely to prayer.

Then again, it was possible that it had more to do with *him* and the difficulty he was having in accepting the idea of Gwen taking the veil. He found it hard to reconcile himself to that. The night's sky might be endless as Gwen described, but this, their time together, would soon be over.

Ralph allowed the silence to extend as he stared at those same damn stars, wondering on everything that had happened this night. He tried to settle into the tranquillity, this stillness that had descended after the gruelling difficulty of the mêlée, after sparring with Gwen… after kissing her senseless.

God, how he wanted to kiss her again, his whole body, tight with need.

Ralph should be at peace, lying on the ground beside

her with her hand in his, yet the questions were burning inside him. He felt anything but tranquil.

'Gwen?' He turned his head. 'Why didn't you come with me that night I left Kinnerton? Why did you stay behind?'

She swallowed uncomfortably.

'I... I believe I told you. Did I not?'

He could see it on her face. Her mounting anxiety flickered like a flame. Ralph felt like shaking her into talking to him, but tempered his voice instead.

'No, I'm afraid that I never did understand your reasoning. I still do not, my lady.'

She sat up and tried to untangle her hand from his, but he held on to it, refusing to let her withdraw. This was a way for Gwen to evade answering him again. But ever since they had found each other again, and become close, he had wanted to know.

Why had she not gone with him? It was a question that plagued him, even after all this time.

Ralph could still recall the heightened emotions of six years ago when he had been forced to hide in the woods outside Kinnerton Castle. His cousin had taken control of the whole area after Ralph and a few of his men had gone to bring back his father's body, after the old lord had died in vain trying to plead his innocence from the charges of treason. And by the time Ralph had returned, his ancestral castle and lands had been lost. Ralph remembered getting a message through to Gwen, with great difficulty, to meet him in the woods and the relief he'd felt at seeing her well and unharmed. But then it had all gone disastrously wrong when she had refused to run away with him.

Ralph had been raw with grief and so enraged by his cousin's betrayal that he'd believed everything Gwen had said that night when she told him to leave without her. And eventually he had, taking with him all the bitterness, anger and resentment, which also extended to the woman who was sat beside him now, for six long years.

However, everything had changed once Ralph met Gwen again, here at this tournament. His understanding of that night had somehow shifted. He had a certain knowledge now that he did not back then. For one thing, Gwen had not, under the guise of duty, harboured a cold ambition to be the Lady of Kinnerton, without caring who its lord would be, as he was led to believe. That had been the reason given back then.

Now he knew better. Gwen's refusal to leave with him and escape the imminent peril at that time had been for different reasons entirely. Circumstances that she was now reluctant to discuss. Again, he could not understand why. It had been just as dangerous for her as it had been for him, yet when Tom had asked her on his behalf, at that encounter in the hall, Gwen had dismissed the notion, simply stating that her reasons were to *protect Ralph*.

He had been so shocked to see her again here at the tournament and wanted nothing to do with her initially, but he hadn't really acknowledged what she had said that night at the banquet.

Ralph had been so adamant about maintaining his indifference that he had not allowed himself to question what she had said more deeply. It had been since their friendship began to thaw and become more companionable that these uneasy questions about Gwen and that time had come to the fore once again.

'Tell me, Gwen. What did I need protection from?'

He watched as the colour from her face drained and she slowly turned her head to meet his. 'I… I am not sure what you mean.'

'You told Tom that you stayed behind to protect me. Remember?'

Of course she did.

'What does it matter now?'

'To understand more. That is all.' Ralph cupped her cheek with his hand, his fingers grazing her cheek. 'As I said, I never comprehended the reason why you had not run away with me back then. And when you explained it had been to shield me...well, you can imagine how it shamed and humbled me to know that. The question is what or whom you believed you were protecting me from? And why you didn't confide in me at the time?'

'How has this conversation come about?'

'My intention is not to make you uneasy.' He shook his head. 'But know that this has not been discussed. I am as much in the dark now as I was back then.'

'Then pray, let's leave it. Let us not spoil this evening by talking of such darkness.'

He could not do that, not after finally broaching this conversation. 'Was it my cousin? Did you believe that you were somehow protecting me from Stephen le Gros?'

Ralph watched as her jaw clenched and a slight gasp escaped her lips at the mention of the bastard's name.

She snatched her free hand from his grasp and stood, walking back towards Fortis. 'I cannot believe that you would foul the night air by uttering his name.'

He followed her and stilled her elbow. 'How, Gwen? How could you have ever protected me from him?'

Somehow he knew that her reluctance to explain what had happened had something to do with Stephen le Gros. And his heart sank at the thought.

She turned slowly around to face him and eventually spoke. 'He made a promise that if I stayed and I did not leave with you, that he would let you leave Kinnerton peaceably.'

He looked at her through a narrow gaze, trying to add meaning to her words. Understand the events from six years ago.

'How did you make him keep his bargain?' She remained silent. 'Gwen?'

She lifted her head. 'I... I promised to marry him.'

He raised his eyebrows. 'But you did not.'

'No, I did not.' She hissed through her teeth. 'I managed to run away before he could force me to, gaining the protection of the Crown, who were keen to profit from my lands.'

'I see.' Yet there was something niggling at him. Something that was still missing from what she had just disclosed.

Gwen stepped away, taking a deep shaky breath. 'Can we please go back? I find that I'm a little fatigued now from this diversionary outing. Sadly, my sense of adventure has long deserted me as I feared it would.'

Chapter Fourteen

Ralph swirled the wine in his mug, fascinated by the rich colour of ripened berries, before swigging it back. Rather than the sweet tart taste he expected, it tasted foul.

'Do you not think you have had enough for one night, my friend?' Tom yawned, sitting upright, dragging his hands through his hair. Ralph felt a niggle of guilt, knowing he had probably woken him up.

'Go back to sleep, Tom.'

'What is the matter? You have been dour and irritable all day.'

'Nothing,' he muttered, pouring more wine into his mug. 'Is this a new batch?' he said, trying to change the subject.

'I would not know.'

'Here, try some.'

'My thanks but, no. I drank enough at the banquet, earlier.' Tom rubbed his forehead. 'And you should mayhap think about getting some sleep before the *mêlée à cheval* on the morrow.'

'How right you are.' Ralph sighed before knocking back the wine and wiping his mouth with his hand. 'You are a good friend to me, Tom, do you know that? Not that I deserve it.'

Tom shook his head. 'Whether you deserve it or not, Ralph, you'll always have my fealty. You know that, after…well, after what you did for me in Poitiers.'

'That was nothing and the debt you believe you owed me was paid a long, long time ago.'

'Hell's teeth, Ralph, are you worried about the practice today because, cometh the hour tomorrow, I know that you'll be there with your sword in hand, blustering your way though.'

'Bluster, eh?' He smiled faintly at that.

'You know what I mean.' Tom frowned. 'Tell me, does your current mood have anything to do with Lady Gwenllian? I noticed that she was absent from the banquet earlier.'

Ralph had not seen her since their interlude the night before, when it had all begun so promisingly after she had agreed to their midnight outing. They had ridden out in the moonlight, sparred with sticks, kissed breathlessly, talked and stared at the night sky. It all, however, ended in discomfort, with a chasm between them as they rode back to the castle in silence.

Since last night, Gwen had avoided him, making it clear that although she might care for him, there could be nothing more. That all there was between them was his promise to escort her on her journey to taking the veil. Nor had he gone in search of her or sought her outside her arched window. It seemed that Ralph's attentions disconcerted her. Yet there was something more, something more disturbing about her reluctance to talk about the past and in particular their last night at Kinnerton that bothered him.

'I feel like a blind man wandering around in the dark,

when it comes to Gwen.' He lifted his head. 'All I know is that it all goes back to my cousin.'

'It would. You saw the way he behaved that first night when she came to talk with me.'

'Yes, but there's more to it than that, but I just cannot see what it is.'

'Whatever it may be, it can surely wait until after the *mêlée à cheval*, do you not think?'

'Yes. It can wait.' Ralph swallowed the remainder of his wine and grimaced. Lord, but it tasted bitter. But then everything did.

The extreme conditions on the day of the *mêlée à cheval* were absolutely horrendous. The rain had been thrashing the open fields so hard that visibility was becoming impossible for every knight on the field the following morn. And it was not letting up. The shallow fog added its own opaque film of obscurity.

God, but how different this place was from the last time Ralph had ventured out in the demesne with Gwen a few nights ago, underneath that clear moonlit sky—not that he had seen her since then, or this morning. Then again, who would venture out in this dire weather?

Ralph felt the annoyance thrum in his veins. He must turn all his attentions to the reason he had come back—to win silver from this damn tournament in an attempt to claim back Kinnerton—and stop incessantly thinking about Gwen and his last encounter with her. Yet it was easier said than done in this deluge that was threatening to bury them in heavy mud.

Hell's teeth, what a nightmare.

Ralph blew a frustrated breath from beneath his helmet, barely able to see anything from this vantage point. The splattering thick mud was so thick and dense that

Fortis had difficulty getting through it, yet the animal was equable and more reliable than Ralph was currently feeling. It was astonishing, but the terrible weather was the least of his troubles.

Ralph blinked several times and widened his eyes in an attempt to survey the area around him, but his field of vision was progressively getting blurred, not that it was easy to see in any case. As well as his blurred vision, his insides churned around, coiling and twisting in agony. He leant forward, hoping to gain more support from the saddle seat and Fortis's neck, but he felt progressively unsteady.

He did not feel well. It had started last night when he had writhed around in his pallet, unable to sleep. He hadn't disclosed his symptoms to anyone, believing that it was a bout of apprehension after being so distracted at practice. He hoped that the malady would pass, if he ignored it. But it had not. The longer the day wore on the worse he felt.

He swayed slightly just before he saw a knight in his periphery charging at him with his sword. Ralph's heart palpitated as he drew his sword up in a line of defence. Even his trusty sword, however, felt as though it was carrying the weight of the world. What was happening to him? He felt like a sot, inebriated to the point that he couldn't control his faculties. But Ralph had not drunk that much, had he? The other man was suddenly there, attacking him with his blunt sword which Ralph somehow defended. God, but now he saw double, nay, triple the knight. The man tried to force Ralph back in an attempt to unhorse him, but he just held firm. For now.

Christ above, he could not hang on for much longer. He countered another strike of the knight's sword as it clashed against his in the rain. Again and again the bastard came at him, but Ralph defended himself against each blow, before drawing his horse close enough so that he could strike him when he least expected it.

Fortis managed to jump through the squelch of mud that had rendered his movement to a halt momentarily so that they could get away before another counter-attack. But the respite had been far too brief.

Ralph was not sure how he managed to remain mounted on his horse as he swayed violently, moving back and forth, unsteady and unsettled. From somewhere to his right, he felt a blow and he was jolted so hard, he fell from his horse, the soft muddy ground cushioning his fall. He managed to get to his feet, staggering forward in search of his horse in the mayhem, but he could not see him.

Oh, God...oh, God... Where was Fortis?

Ralph could not afford to lose his horse. Fortis? Where was he?

He might have been taken or, worse, injured. He looked in every direction desperately.

'Fortis?' Ralph muttered. His name stuck in his throat. 'Where the hell are you, boy?' But he was nowhere to be found.

His boots were stuck in the mud, making progress impossible. He started panting and shaking uncontrollably, knowing he could not move anyway. God above, but he was gripped by something intense, dark and deadly.

Ralph sensed someone approach and spun around to the left, only to feel someone punch him hard on his back and again in his stomach, the fine chain hauberk absorbing some of the shock, but not enough. Not nearly enough.

Ralph was pushed to the ground and repeatedly jabbed with something solid and hard. He swung his sword and got to his knees, managing to get to his feet, only for something to come at him in full force, knocking him down again. This time he could not get up. His chest rose and fell rapidly. He could just make out that the green fabric Gwen had gifted him dancing in the breeze. He reached out, grappling in the air, trying to catch it, but it was out of reach. Always out of reach. A heavy-booted foot trampled on it, pushing it into the mud and dirt as it drew closer.

'That is a warning for now.' Ralph heard a voice hiss from somewhere close by. His vision was now hazy and faint. 'Stay away from Lady Gwenllian ferch Hywel, do you hear, Lovent. Next time you go anywhere near my betrothed, I'll kill you myself.'

Ralph received another round of kicks and jabs on his head and stomach just for good measure. He tried to lift himself up, but something suddenly struck his head, snapping it back. God, but he felt as though he was dying.

His breathing became more and more laboured and his mouth tasted something acrid and foul. He tried to get up, but it was impossible to even move. He could hear the muffled voices from somewhere far away in the distance before everything descended into darkness.

His delirium brought hot and cold sweats. His skin felt prickly, as though something sharp jabbed at him repeatedly. As though he were blighted by pestilence. He felt itchy. He could not rest. If only he could sleep. That he would for eternity, but there was still something that he had to do, wasn't there?

God, but his mouth was dry, like the rough side of a tree bark. His head felt as if it might split in two, the pain unlike anything he had ever known.

Ralph's eyes opened wide at a sudden screech of pain

that he heard from somewhere close by—or had it come from his own lips?

Gwen? Was she here with him in this dreadfully dark place?

'I had to protect you, Ralph.'

It was her voice.

'No... I don't want you to. Come with me. You'll be safe with me. I would look after you.'

'I had to do it...'

'What did you have to do?'

'I had to protect you... It was the only way.'

The words spun around in his head, making him retch. It was like a punch in the gut.

'No!'

'I had to.'

'Please, stop. Please...'

Again and again he heard the voice in his head.

'I had to do it.'

'At what cost?'

'I had to protect you.'

Ralph's head felt as though an anvil had been struck against his skull repeatedly. The sharp persistent pain was only made a little more bearable when something cold, wet and soothing was delicately placed over his forehead, eyes and the top of his head. A hand—a woman's, he sensed—was stroking his hair back reassuringly. The wet material had now shifted to his chest, rubbing down his aching battered body.

'Gorffwys dy ben blinedig, o farchog dewr...'

She sang in a soft melodic voice. He felt far from being a brave knight, but weary—yes, he felt that in his bones.

'Cysgu fy nghariad...'

Sleep, my love? Was he dreaming of a love lost in faraway places filled with fables, mist and dragons? Could he be the one to slay them? He rather doubted that.

Where was he? He could recall a glimmer of being pulled from that torrent of violence in the middle of the mêlée after being savagely struck and beaten. He had been made to purge his body from some vile, putrid humour—that he could also just about remember. The memory of being in agony, his stomach twisting and knotting in turmoil as he retched. It felt as though he had been gutted from the inside.

Ralph's eyes flickered as he turned his head a little, but it felt too heavy to move. He tried opening them, a moan escaping his lips.

'Rest easy, Ralph.' It was a calming, comforting voice. And it belonged to a woman he was surprised to see at his side after the way in which they had last seen each other.

'Gwen? Where… Where am I?' His mouth was so dry.

'The tent that you share with Sir Thomas.'

'The mêlée. I… I was ambushed and then I…' he muttered.

'Hush, you're safe now. Lords Tallany and de Clancey rode out and dragged you out of that muddy field. Sir Thomas had to be stopped from coming after you as well.'

'Tom?' He tried opening his eyes again. 'Is he here?'

'No, but he will return shortly.' She placed the wet sponge back on his head.

'Rest for now, Ralph.'

He exhaled and closed his eyes, finally falling into a deep slumber.

Gwen had taken a vigil beside Ralph's side from the moment he had been brought back from that awful, bloodied field. It was inconceivable that Ralph had nearly perished out there at the hands of thugs who brought their standing as knights to shame. It had only been by chance that William Geraint had somehow been alerted to what had happened and acted swiftly, otherwise things might have ended very differently.

As well as being ambushed, Ralph had also consumed something noxious that threatened and weakened his body: he had been poisoned. The aftermath had been mayhem as the de Clanceys and Lord and Lady Tallany had brought a complaint forward, denouncing what had happened in the mêlée and seeking a judiciary counsel. Yet with the severity of the grim weather during the mêlée, it was impossible to ascertain what had happened without actual proof of foul play.

But Gwen knew the one man who would happily break the sacred code of knights and would do so again and again without any hesitation—Stephen le Gros. She could not prove it, but knew he was the one man who would resort to foul play for his own gain. Had he not warned her? Had he not shown his jealous streak?

God only knew what the man was capable of if he discovered that during the mêlée, Thomas Lovent was in fact Ralph. Unless, of course, he had already found out that his cousin was alive. Gwen dismissed that, knowing that to be impossible, as she would otherwise have heard about it by now.

Her gaze flicked to the man sleeping on the pallet. She watched as his chest rose and fell breathing deeply. He had come in and out of consciousness these past two nights, oblivious to Lords Hugh and William's privy meetings with the Earls of Chester and Hereford and the young King Henry, without much success. They had wanted the mêlée to be declared invalid on the grounds that tournament codes had been broken, but this had been met with objections.

The interim had at least allowed Ralph to get well and regain his strength, now that Lady Isabel had given him a tincture that had expelled everything from his body. He would be weak, but he was alive, thank God.

'Gwen?' he mumbled, stirring. 'Are you still here?'

'Yes, Ralph.' She watched him, relieved to see he was finally awake. 'Where else am I going to be?'

'Where is Tom?' His voice was barely a whisper.

'He is being inconspicuous in another de Clancey tent, since the general belief is that *he* is the one in this condition and not you. Do not worry, he will sneak back later.'

'I see. How long have I been like this? And where's my horse? What happened to Fortis?'

'Easy, Ralph. You have been like this for the past three days and two nights. And Fortis… I'm afraid he has been kept in lieu of payment for the loss at the mêlée.'

'By whom?' He pushed himself to sit up. 'Oh, God, not Fortis. It's all over then.'

'No, Ralph.' She laid her hand on his arm. 'Even now, as we speak, Lords de Clancey and Tallany are speaking with the privy council on your behalf.'

'I need to get up.' He tried getting out of bed, but Gwen placed her hand on his arm. 'I need to…'

'You do not need to do anything other than get well and back to your old self.'

He gently removed her hand. 'I'm much better as can you see, my lady.'

'I am sure you are, but you still need your rest, Ralph. Everything can wait until later.'

She caressed his forehead and smoothed back his dark hair. Her fingers grazed the deep, distorted, gnarled skin on one side of his face. It was astonishing what this man had gone through these past few days and also in the past at the hands of men intent on bringing him down. Ralph's courage and tenacity never failed to amaze her even though she was once again struck by the fragility of life. She had almost lost him again, so soon after finding him alive. It didn't bear thinking about.

She sighed deeply. 'May I get you anything?'

'Water, please,' he muttered and sank back into the pallet.

Chapter Fifteen

Gwen returned to Ralph's tent in the de Clancey area the following morning after matins, with her prayers solely for Ralph's speedy recovery. To her surprise, however, he was no longer in his tent. Instead she encountered Thomas Lovent who informed her that Ralph had felt much better and had gone to the stream for a wash.

She had not accepted the offer of waiting for Ralph under the amused gaze of his friend so had decided to return to the castle. But somehow her feet seemed to take her on a somewhat different path than on the periphery of Pulverbatch Castle.

Gwen found herself walking into the dense woodland on the edge of the demesne lands. She glanced around to make sure she was unobserved before stepping on to the wooded path—a path she had last ventured upon when she had met Ralph again for the first time and discovered that he lived and had survived his ordeal in Poitiers. It made her uneasy to know that again his life had been under threat, albeit inadvertently as he dissembled as another man. Yet, once it came out in the open that Ralph was alive, Stephen le Gros would double his effort to bring about his cousin's demise.

She smiled faintly to herself as she passed the great big oak tree, her fingers grazing the trunk, and moved to follow a narrower path taking her deeper into the woods, the dense thickets and overgrown brambles on either side before it opened out to the gently sloping grassy bank beside the stream. Tall branches provided shelter all around the enclosed clear water that pooled and rippled to a narrow gurgling stream that gradually meandered its way between two large trees and somewhere beyond her periphery. It was as though time had stood still, preserving this little secret haven from all who were unaware of its untouched beauty or even its existence.

Gwen pulled down a branch and looked out, her eyes resting on the man whom she had sat beside, holding his hand and mopping his brow as he lay in a state of delirium on his pallet.

Standing with his back to her and submerged in waist-high water, Ralph de Kinnerton looked like the epitome of health and virile masculinity now. No one would have believed that only a few days ago he had been so unwell. Ralph looked revived and remarkably well, diving under the water before re-emerging and flicking his wet dark hair to the side.

He must have heard her footfall as he turned around quickly, a dark, instinctively predacious look crossing his eyes before his features softened as he realised it was a friend and not a foe who was disturbing his peace.

Her breath hitched in the back of her throat, as he gave her a small smile and moved towards her, dragging his wet hair back with his hands. Water droplets ran like rivulets down his jaw, his chest and his huge arms. He kicked the water up as he emerged from the water, his hose sticking to his thighs.

What was wrong with her? The poor man had just

gone through a terrible ordeal and all she could do was become hot and a trifle bothered about the way the hard ridges of his body glistened as he came out of the water.

And it was not as though she hadn't seen his naked chest before either. Only a day ago he had lain incapacitated on his pallet under a thin blanket. But, of course, she had been far more preoccupied with worry about his recovery to fully appreciate the state he was lying in.

But now…well, it was quite different.

She returned his smile, chastising herself with these inappropriate musings, especially at such a difficult time. Oh, for goodness sake, she had declared that she would soon take the veil and here she was ogling at the sight of Ralph's sculpted bare chest and wide shoulders.

Yet it was impossible to ignore his magnificent state of undress, so she averted her gaze instead.

'Good morrow, my lady.'

Gwen dragged her eyes back, ensuring that they remained fixed on his face and nowhere else. 'Good morrow to you, Ralph. I can see that you are much better than when I last saw you?'

'Indeed.' His voice seemed suddenly distant and flat.

Her eyes darted around before settling back on him. 'It has been a very long time since I ventured this far into these woods and to this idyll.'

'For me, too.' He nodded toward the deeper waters of the stream. 'And if my memory serves, it was here that I taught you how to swim, Gwen. Or was it waters closer to Kinnerton?'

'It was here.' Gwen flushed, pushing the memory out of her head. She did not want to be reminded of those happy recollections.

'Ah, I thought so.'

'Even with its familiarity, should you be alone here,

after what happened?' She didn't want to remind him, but after the attack at the mêlée it might have been prudent not to come here alone.

'Stephen and his men believed that they attacked Thomas Lovent, who is probably gambling with a few of the de Clancey knights as we speak. And as my friend informed me himself, he is damn well able to look after himself.'

'What about you, Ralph?' She moved a little closer to the edge of the stream, the clear water lapping gently at her booted feet.

'I thank you, but I'm perfectly fine.'

Gwen blinked, looking around the beautiful yet peaceful area secluded from the outside world. It was still as confined and hidden as it had been in the past. But the fact that it still offered a sense of privacy and shelter from anyone intent on disrupting and ruining the peace did not mean it could not happen. Anyone could find this haven if they looked hard enough.

'Even so, after what happened, do you not think there is a need for caution?'

'I believe we have now passed that stage.'

'What do you mean?' She frowned. 'What do you intend to do?'

He shook his head as he picked up his tunic from the ground and put this on. 'Nothing that you need to worry about, Gwen.'

'That is something I cannot do.'

'I thank you for your care and concern, but I'm fit and hale in body and dispirited in everything else.' He grimaced.

'Surely you cannot blame yourself for what happened.'

'Can I not?'

'The fault, I believe, lies with your cousin and not you, Ralph.'

'I know, but I should have foreseen that he would attempt something like this, but I became too complacent.'

'I'm sure your powers of foretelling the future are admirable, but you could not have known that this would happen.'

'But I should have, since it is Stephen we speak of. I know that he somehow tampered with the wine that had been left in the tent or gave an order to do so and I know that he was responsible for what later happened in the mêlée, when every damn knightly code was broken.' He exhaled through his teeth. 'But neither I, nor anyone else, can prove that he was responsible.'

'What will you do?'

'There's little I can do except to, somehow, attempt to remedy the situation.'

'I know everything may seem lost, but I'm sure that you'll find a way through.'

'I have lost everything…including…' he swallowed '…including Fortis, whom I reared since he was a foal. God, but I don't know how I'm going to replace him.'

'I am so sorry.'

He shrugged, looking away. Gwen could only imagine how difficult it must be for Ralph, knowing that he had lost something as precious as his dependable horse. If only there was something she could do to help.

She lifted her head. 'You must believe that all is not lost, Ralph.'

He reached up and brushed his fingers against her cheek and down the column of her neck, sending a shiver down her spine. 'Your faith in me means more then you'll ever know. And right now, that is all I have. Your faith and my blind hope.'

'Don't say that. You have much more than that,' she whispered.

He dropped his hand to his side. 'Do I? I do not know any more. My endeavours here were always going to be difficult and hard. An arduous challenge with no certainty of success.' He sighed.

'But not impossible.'

He shrugged. 'I suppose nothing is beyond the bounds of possibility. Although, as I said, my blind hope seems to rise every time I face adversity.' His laugh seemed hollow, bitter even.

Yet there was more to it than Ralph gave himself credit for. He was now a powerful warrior who could match any other in skill, resolve and fortitude. Every time he had been knocked down in life, he just got back up, refusing to give up.

She reached out and touched his arm. 'I would call it courage, Ralph.'

'Would you?' His eyes fell to her hand, reminding her of the need to remove it. 'I'm a fool to believe in the conviction that if I train harder, focus better, be more persistent and assiduous, then somehow everything will fall into place. But the truth is somewhat different. Far more onerous.'

'You are not, nor have you ever been a fool, Ralph de Kinnerton.'

'Oh, I beg to differ,' he said, shaking his head. 'You asked me what I would do now. Well, let me tell you, Gwen—the time has finally come for me to face Stephen.'

'Oh, Lord,' she said, unable to hide her concern. 'Would that be a wise course of action now? Just after being attacked in the underhand way you were?'

'Absolutely. What could be better than inflicting the element of surprise when Stephen least expects it. When he is so confident of his claim on Kinnerton and on you, may I add, with impunity. Especially since he has the ear of the Earl of Hereford. Indeed, my cousin believes that no one would now stand in his way. But he is wrong.'

'You will be careful?' She tilted her head up at him and took in his handsome face, marred by his gnarly scars, and his dark brown eyes, intense and impassioned.

'I'm no longer that petulant, impulsive and, yes, foolish boy. That boy has gone and gone for good.'

'I rather liked him, Ralph. He was also kind, considerate and he cared about so many things that most men, frankly most lords, seldom do.'

His eyes locked on to hers, a curious sort of look in them. 'Is that so?'

'Yes,' she murmured. 'Tell me, Ralph. What happened to him?'

'I'm afraid to say that he had to grow up.'

'Well, that is a shame, since he did not need to alter as much as you might believe.'

She watched as the strain in his eyes eased. 'For all that I have lost, at least I have found you again, Gwenllian ferch Hywel. Mayhap you are right. His hands wrapped around her waist, pulling her close, his damp tunic against her. 'Mayhap all I need is right here, after all.'

His left hand, callused and rough, cradled her cheek, his thumb brushing against her lower lip, dragging back and forth. She heard him gasp softly as the tip of her tongue licked her lip. Just as he bent his head, tilting his head close to hers, a sudden splashing noise in the stream jolted her, making her take a step back.

She spun her head around to find young William Tallany splashing towards them in the shallow water of the stream, with Lady Isabel's dog, Perdu, yapping as he followed him.

'I was not actually alone here. There, you see…' Ralph smirked as he waved his hand in their direction '…my protectors.'

'Good day to you, William Tallany,' she said, bending to pat Perdu.

'Gwen! Good day to you.' He beamed at her. 'Were you about to kiss Ralph?'

'Ah…well… I…' Her gaze flicked to Ralph, who was covering his amusement behind his hand, then back to William who was staring up at her, waiting for her to respond. 'No, I was not.'

'Well it looked as though you were.' William shrugged his little shoulders before picking up a stick for Perdu. 'If you are going to kiss, I shall have to look away.'

Ralph shook his head. 'Sharp as a lance is our William Tallany. Never misses a thing.'

She flushed and elbowed Ralph gently in the chest as he began to chuckle. 'You're not exactly helping,' she muttered from the side of her mouth.

'Allow me a moment with my young protector.' He grinned before bending down to address William. 'Now, young sir, I believe you should cease your impertinence in the presence of a lady.' Ralph smiled, mussing up William's hair.

'What is "pertinence"?'

'Being rude.' Ralph nodded blandly. 'You cannot gallivant about the woods, asking fair ladies impolite questions about kissing.'

'I need to know, Ralph, in case I have to avert Perdu's eyes.' He scowled, covering his eyes with his hands. 'Mama and Papa are always doing the kissing thing and it's 'gusting!'

'One day, you will think quite differently about that, my little friend. I assure you.'

Ralph brought himself to William's level. 'Besides, I cannot be kissing a lady who is soon to be entering a convent to take the veil.'

'But Gwen's too pretty to be a nun.' William scratched his head. '*And* she did like to dress as a squire, although I suppose she has a dress on now.'

The young boy pointed at her attire.

'Now, what did I say about being impertinent to a lady?' Ralph admonished.

'And it is true, William, I shall soon leave here and enter a convent. You won't tell anyone, will you?'

'Oh, no. Not more secrets. I cannot remember all of these secrets.'

'I'm sure you can manage one more, my young sir.'

'Maybe if you kiss her, she'll change her mind,' William whispered to Ralph.

Ralph stood back up, and pinned Gwen with his heated gaze. 'Mayhap it might.'

Gwen flushed as she looked away, trying hard not to laugh. Oh, Lord, it was a mistake to come back to this peaceful spot. With all these confusing new feelings for Ralph, she felt anything but at peace.

'Are you sure this is the course you wish to take?'

Ralph looked around the tent at each of the men who had stood shoulder to shoulder beside him. From Hugh de Villiers, William Geraint to his friend Thomas Lovent.

'Yes.' He nodded at each of them. 'It's time that I made an appearance as myself. Especially at this time when the Earls of Hereford and Chester are still in counsel with King Henry about the legitimacy of the *mêlée à cheval* and its aftermath.'

'It is likely that the outcome of the mêlée would still

stand, Ralph, despite everything Will and I have tried to put forth.'

'And I thank you for it. All of you for everything you have done for me.' He tried to swallow a knot that had formed in his throat. 'I do not know how I can ever repay any of you, but know that you shall always have my fealty, until I draw my last breath.'

'Well, let us hope that it shall not be too soon.' Tom smirked, shaking his head. The solemnity in the tent suddenly lifted and became lighter.

'Indeed.'

'At least not until after this tournament officially ends.'

'Of course.'

'And I for one am happy to finally take my place as myself, the real Thomas Lovent.'

'Not that you couldn't at those hugely difficult moments such as attending the evening banquets.' Will smirked.

'Or basking in all that glory when *Sir Thomas* did exceedingly well.' Hugh slapped Tom on the back.

'Well, apart from those times and you are right, my lord. It has been exceedingly trying.'

The four men laughed before Will moved forward and clasped Ralph's arm.

'I hope you know that the reasons that I, for one, have given you my assistance have been more than gaining your fealty, my friend, although I would gladly have it. For one thing, my lady wife would have had my head if I refused to help you.' He smirked. 'But, no, in truth, the sense of injustice that you faced never sat well with me. Not after everything that happened to you, Ralph.'

'Thank you, my lord. I don't know what to say.'

'There's nothing to say.' Hugh stepped forward. 'Except that I feel the same as Will. This kingdom would do better with honourable, valiant men like you, Ralph. To that end, I would stand with you whatever happens.'

God, but Ralph felt the sudden rush of emotion. He was indeed a fortunate man to count these men as friends and allies.

'Well, not for me,' Tom drawled, folding his arms across his chest. 'I am only in this for the coin.'

They all laughed again, the moment's sincerity all but broken.

'Naturally. What more is there in life other than coin?' Will winked.

'Apart from the love of a good woman.' Hugh grinned.

'I can drink to that.'

The two lords filled their mugs with more ale as Tom pulled Ralph to the side for a seemingly private discourse.

'There is a surprise for you, my friend, but do not look so concerned. This is a good one. Very good.' He flicked his head to the entrance of the tent. 'Come.'

They took their leave, pulled their hoods over their heads and walked around to the winding path that led to the area where the de Clancey cattle were stabled. It dawned on Ralph that this would be one of the last times that there would be the need for their subterfuge when venturing out. That was if, God willing, everything went to plan. Soon he would be standing beside his friend as *himself*—as Ralph de Kinnerton, the man he was destined to be, worthy to stand against anyone. And he could not have done it without his friends and, in particular, Gwen. Their belief in him and his strength of character determined the man he had now become.

'What is this, Tom?'

'Why don't you go inside and find out?'

Ralph rushed forward, his heart pounding. 'Is he here?' Ralph turned, his face filled with relief. 'Fortis?'

Tom leant against the wooden frame housing the horses. 'Indeed.'

'How?' Ralph leant in, placing his head against the muzzle of his horse. 'How in God's name did you manage to get him back?'

'It is somewhat of a mystery.' He heard his friend's laughter.

'How in heaven can I ever repay you, Tom?'

'But it's not I that you owe anything to, Ralph, but another.'

'Will?'

'No, not him either.'

'Hugh, then.' He sighed deeply.

Either way it would take much coin to repay him. And yet for all the coin in the land, Ralph had thankfully got his faithful horse back. That counted more than Ralph could say, after the disastrous last few days where he had almost perished. And losing Fortis had been the most arduous thing about the mêlée—the most difficult to accept. They had been through quite a lot together and now, just like that, as if by magic his horse had returned back to him. It was nothing short of being unexpected and so very welcome indeed.

'No, Ralph. Wrong again. I would guess someone fair and not a man, if I were you.' Tom smirked.

'Gwenllian?' Ralph's eyes widened in surprise as Tom nodded. It could not be. 'Hell's teeth—Gwen? But how?'

Ralph looked at his friend with a look of bewilderment on his face. How on earth did she do it and without mentioning it to him earlier when he had seen her by the stream in the woods? It was unbelievable that she was able to do something as expensive as this. More and more questions tumbled in his head.

'I have no idea, my friend, but mayhap the lady could enlighten you herself.'

'I do not know what to say. I'm truly speechless!'

'I believe the usual thanks should suffice, my friend.' Tom chuckled.

'Oh, I intend to.' Ralph shook his head, as he ran his hand up and down Fortis's muzzle one last time before heading out towards the castle.

Chapter Sixteen

Gwen walked down the narrow hall that led to the ante-chamber. She opened the wooden door and let herself into the empty chamber, placing the lit torch into the metal sconce. Before she had the opportunity to turn, someone had grabbed her from behind, covering her mouth with their hand, and pulled her across behind a wooden beam in the dark corner. Her heart began to pound in her chest as she tried to remain calm.

Oh, God, please let it not be him! Not Stephen.

'I cannot believe that you would still choose to go anywhere alone, my lady.'

Ralph!

'I am going to remove my hand very, very slowly, but I would appreciate it if you would not scream, Gwen.' His low voice rumbled somewhere close behind her, tickling her neck.

His hand slowly left her mouth, leaving her inhaling deeply. 'What do you think you're doing, Ralph de Kinnerton?' she hissed. 'You scared me half to death!'

Gwen spun around and found herself looking at him with his finger to his lips, imploring her to talk quietly. She looked around in every direction before pulling the sleeve of his tunic and motioning for him to follow her to the chamber she shared with Brida in the furthest corner.

They scrambled inside, closing the wooden door hastily behind them.

'Why are you wandering around the castle alone?'

She raised her eyebrows, slightly confused by his presence at this time of night. 'May I remind you that this part of the castle keep has a guard and is not supposed to allow men anywhere near it. Especially ones who skulk around in dark corners, ready to pounce on young maids.'

'You wound me!' He gave her a look of mocked outrage. 'I do not skulk, Lady Gwenllian. I was being careful not to alert anyone to my presence here. And it was just as well now that I have tested the security here, because I have to say that it is most inadequate.'

She stepped closer to him closing the space between them. 'Is that so?'

'Yes,' Ralph whispered, his hands circling around her waist, pulling her closer. He dipped his head and breathed in her hair. 'It should have been much, much harder for me to breach the keep, but I found it surprisingly easy to gain access.'

'And now you are here and have managed to sneak into my chamber of all places at this ungodly hour.' She looked up as she placed her hands on his chest. 'I would like to enquire why?'

'You really do ask too many questions, my lady.' His lips quirked up as he pulled her closer to him.

'I believe that this was the only question I have asked you. Why are you here, Ralph?'

'To see you, of course.' Even in the relative darkness of the chamber she could see the curl of his smile rise even higher. 'Should I go? Am I intruding on your solitude?'

'Nothing like that. I just wanted to understand the

urgency in seeing me now. Could it not wait until the morrow, sir?'

His hand moved up and down her spine, leaving in its wake a shudder that she had difficulty suppressing. Ralph dipped his head, his warm breath merging with hers. All she had to do was tilt her head a little and their lips would touch. She licked them instead.

'No, I fear I could not wait to see you.' His left hand had now made its way around to her face, stroking and caressing her skin. 'Do you know that you must have the softest skin, Gwen?' He ran his fingers through her hair, wrapping a flaxen tendril around his fingers.

'I am not sure I can understand the haste in breaching this area of the keep with such urgency, just to pontificate on the softness of my skin.'

He lifted her head a fraction higher, his fingers beneath her chin. 'A man likes to revere such things.'

Gwen smiled despite herself. 'Really, Sir Ralph, you make little sense. What would you do, I wonder, if Brida were to walk in right now and find you here?'

His unwavering gaze awakened a sensation that unfurled itself in the pit of her stomach, making her far more aware of every tingling sensation.

'I would bid her a good evening,' he smiled. 'Where is the ever-faithful Brida, anyway?'

'She offered to stay and assist with one of the ladies here, Lady Matilde, all night. In fact, I am just returning from attending to her as well.'

Ralph pulled away, the mirth in his eyes replaced with a look of concern 'I hope all is well with the lady?'

She nodded pulling away. 'Nothing but a malady of the heart, I believe.'

'I see.' He sighed. 'Well, the lady is fortunate to have friends who comfort her in her, ah, difficult moment.'

'While there is sadly no cure for her misery, she is young and would eventually overcome her affliction.'

It took a moment for Gwen to realise what she had just said. Ralph released her and he frowned.

'Is that…is that what happened to you?'

'I…well.' Gwen looked up to find Ralph studying her intently. She dropped her gaze back to her hands.

She had tried so hard to overcome her own heartache over the man standing opposite her and yet the truth was that she had never quite managed to do it. Her feelings for Ralph, even after everything that had happened between them, had never really changed, no matter how hard she tried. He still made her heart soar, even though she had tried to forget about him and everything they had once shared.

Gwen cleared her throat and swallowed uncomfortably. 'We were not talking about me.'

Ralph dragged his fingers through his hair and gave her an eloquent look.

'No.' He flashed her a quick smile. 'Although it is because of you and what you have done that I came here to see you tonight.'

'So not for the softness of my skin?'

He smirked. 'Lovely and fair as your skin may be, I had to come tonight to express my eternal gratitude for returning Fortis to me.'

'Ah.' She raised her eyebrows. 'So, you have found out about that already.'

'I'm speechless, Gwen. I cannot believe that you did this for me.'

'Could you not?' She reached up and caressed his face, just as he had done moments ago. 'What are friends for, after all?'

His hand covered hers, turning it over, and he planted

a kiss on her palm, without taking his eyes off her. 'Mayhap a little more than what friends usually do, my lady.'

She shrugged. 'Yes, but mayhap I am just more of a generous friend than I realised.'

Would it ever be possible to be just friends with Ralph? There could be no future between them and yet she could not stop thinking about the man. She could not stop caring and, God help her, longing for him. Even though it was hopeless for her to allow anything more to develop between them.

'Your generosity is not in question here.' His arms came around her waist again, anchoring her to him. 'What I need to know is why you did it.'

'Quite simply, you needed him back and I managed to facilitate that.'

'As easy as that?' He shook his head. 'Horses are expensive, Gwen.'

'I am aware of that. But I wanted to get him back, knowing how valuable and important he is to you.'

She had to stop herself from adding that there was very little she would not do for him.

He kissed the tender skin of her wrist. 'I am in your debt, my lady.'

'You think too much about it, Ralph. My benevolence stems from the necessity of a horse for our journey later to the convent.' Even to her own ears her voice sounded breathless.

'Naturally.' He nipped her delicate skin. 'And with what, may I ask, did you manage to acquire my necessary horse?'

Ralph ran his fingers through her hair, twisting a tendril around his fingers before letting it fall away.

'I exchanged my parchment scrolls.'

He snapped his head up. 'You did *what*?' The shock in Ralph's face was palpable, his hand flexing around hers.

'The knight in question, Sir Geoffrey de Clun, admired them greatly and agreed to the transaction.'

'Oh, my God, Gwen.' He searched her face for answers. 'Tell me you did not resort to *that*?'

Gwen's brows pinched in the middle. 'I do not understand your reaction, Ralph. I thought you would be pleased to have your horse back.'

'Oh, I am.' He nodded. 'Believe me, I am. This is an incredibly considerate thing that you have done. I am indeed a lucky man to have such a benefactor, but at what cost, Gwen?' He raised her hand and pressed his lips to each finger. 'Your painstakingly beautiful work on the parchment. You gave them up like that?' He clicked his fingers.

'You make too much of this. Really, it was nothing.' Her voice sounded husky even to her own ears.

'I beg to differ, my lady.' One of his hands moved around to cradle her head, while the other stroked her cheekbones and her neck before moving to brush her bottom lip. 'It is everything.'

Gwen's lips parted as her tongue tentatively touched the back of his thumb. She heard him draw a hissed breath in through his teeth before swiftly bending his head and covering her mouth with his. This kiss started in the same way as the slow, languorous one they shared that night in the moonlight, but swiftly changed and became more probing, seeking and demanding. It questioned her about things she would rather forget even for a short time.

It was all at once heated, wet and breathless. All at once ravenous and consuming. Oh, but it wasn't nearly enough, not nearly close enough. Gwen wanted so much more of him. She was shocked at the expedient way things had suddenly shifted between them.

But it had been this way between them from the first moment Gwen had glimpsed his dark, shadowy silhouette in the woods. The moment when she had been made aware that he had lived. That he had survived.

At the time the physical changes to Ralph had not only stunned her, but scared her a little. Her own visceral reaction to this altered version of Ralph, who was taller, larger, leaner and stronger than ever before, frightened and confused her. All his sinewy hardness left no room for any soft edges and he was very much a man. A man in his prime.

Gwen had initially believed that the reasons to being afraid were these raw masculine changes in Ralph but, no…that was a lie she had told herself. She knew that now. It was her own reaction to him that she had been afraid of from that very first night when she had seen him again. This frisson that swept through both of them, pushing them together, even if it was for just one night.

This night.

Because that was all it could ever be.

God, but she had almost lost him again. It had been far too close.

She clung to him and kissed him back, with such a need to taste him. To slide and tangle her tongue with his.

'Easy, sweetheart.' He smiled against her lips.

But Gwen took no heed, her urgency for him grew and soared. Her hands visibly shook as she slipped them under Ralph's tunic, yearning to touch the smoothness of his skin. The hard, rippling contours and planes of his chest and stomach muscles. Her fingers grazed the light dusting of hair on his chest that ran down in a line below his hose. A nervous laugh tore from her lips as she helped him tug the tunic up and over his head. A lock of his dark hair fell over Ralph's forehead as they both stood staring at one another. The tension dragged for a long, quiet moment. Her breathing was ragged, had quickened, punctuated by the thrum of her own heartbeat. She watched in fascination as the wide expanse of his bare chest rose and fell rapidly.

Yet it was when Gwen lifted her head that she almost swooned. His eyes held an unfettered desire that glittered in their very depths, a surge of emotion smouldering with so much longing and need. She reached out and slid her hands up his chest and around his shoulders. And then it happened. She was pulled into his arms, her breasts flattened against his rock-hard chest, his mouth crashing on to hers. His hands dug through her hair, gripping her on either side of her head as he deepened his assault on her mouth. She met him with every measure, following his every move.

Lord above, what on earth was happening to her? She was pinned to the spot, a small flame igniting from deep within and spreading throughout her whole body. Her legs were unsteady, wobbly, incapable of supporting her. Everything seemed to turn and shift, making Gwen feel as though she were about to stumble and fall.

Ralph's hands dropped to her waist, his fingers circling around, giving her a slight squeeze. She gasped into the heat of his mouth as he lifted her off her feet and carried her to the bed, without breaking the kiss. He lay down beside her before his hands, lips, teeth and tongue explored her mouth, her jaw, down the slope of her neck and along the swoop of her collarbone. He ran a finger down the throbbing vein and sucked her quivering pulse, his other hand gliding down her body, exploring her every curve. Gwen's whole body was now alight with wonderment and need. Ralph tugged her bottom lip with his teeth, sucking it before his kisses softened. He pulled away on a shudder.

'Tell me to stop, Gwen, and I will.'

'I cannot seem to,' she panted.

'We must, otherwise it shall become too late.'

She turned her head and nipped the taut skin along his neck. 'What if we don't want to stop?' she murmured.

'Do you know even what you're saying, sweetheart?'

'Yes.' She frowned, opening her eyes. 'Of course I do.'

'So, you know what this would mean?'

She reached out and touched his jaw, feeling the hard muscle under the stubble and skin. 'Must I derive meaning from what we are doing?'

'Yes,' he hissed, turning his head to kiss her palm. 'We would be bound together otherwise. Would you have me take that choice away from you?'

'No, Ralph.' She drew his hair back with her fingers. 'You would not be taking that from me.'

'Think what you are saying, Gwenllian.'

'Yes,' she whispered. 'I am asking you to stay with me here tonight.'

It was neither by design nor by fault that they had ended at this precipice, when she had acquired Fortis for Ralph. They had always been hurtling towards this bittersweet moment from that first moment.

'Is this truly what you want?'

Gwen lifted her head and pulled his lips gently between her teeth. 'Yes…oh, yes.'

She loved him, that was the truth. Gwen loved him with every part of her being, but she would not share her life with Ralph de Kinnerton. This she knew with clarity. Yet she would have this moment with him. Yes, *this* she could take.

Then she would let him go. And keep the night close to her heart.

'Kiss me, Ralph.'

And he did more ardently, with more intensity than she could ever have imagined. God, but he made her feel boneless. She lay beside him with her hands on his shoulders, sliding them around his neck, pulling him close. They continued to stroke and touch him all around his back, before dipping around the curve of his back and on to his firm round buttocks, still covered by his hose.

Oh, yes, she wanted him even though Ralph would never truly be hers. Gwen was resigned to that. But mayhap she could show him the constancy of her love, since she could not put these feelings to words. How thoughtless would that be to both of them, otherwise. No, she would let only this night guide her emotions, however sinful it might seem.

Soon this part of her life would be all but over and she would have nothing left other than the empty shell of her heart. But what happened between them, she would remember for the rest of her days.

Oh, yes, she could show him on this night what she truly felt about him. She would bare her soul to him. Only for tonight.

Somehow, as they tumbled and touched, learning the secrets of one another, they had managed to divest every layer of clothing. They lay in each other's arms with the novelty of having skin to skin, flesh to flesh. Was it her heart pounding against her ribs or his?

Ralph shifted his body on top of her, nudging her legs apart and settling within. He lifted one leg and lightly kissed his way up, using his lips, the slide of his tongue and lightly nipping her with his teeth. He wrapped one leg around his body before touching and kissing her other leg, his fingers trailing over her sensitive skin. His large hands moved to her neck, grazing across her chest and along the slope of her breasts, moving lower and lower, circling over her stomach. Heavens above, Gwen didn't know whether she could take much more as he flicked his tongue over her nipple, drawing one into his mouth and sucking lightly, before turning his attention on her other breast, his heavy hooded eyes fixed on to hers. His scent—a mix of soap, herbs and musk—was intoxicating.

Something was unfolding and pooling within her core.

'This may hurt a little,' Ralph whispered, his lips against her skin.

'Don't stop.' Gwen's eyes flew open. 'Please do not stop.'

The light in the sconce and from the fire in the hearth flickered over their entwined bodies, adding its own luminous glow. She arched her back as he entered her body, stretching and filling her. Gwen felt a tug and pull and sharp burst of pain before it was replaced by another, altogether different sensation.

'Gwen?' Ralph stilled as he lifted himself up and watched her for a moment. 'Are you...is everything well?'

She opened her mouth, but the words dried on her lips. Instead, she smiled and nodded her head, her eyes filling with tears. They were joined as one, how could she not be? Yes, she was very well indeed.

'Look at me.' She felt Ralph's hand caress her cheek. 'I want to see you.' Her eyes fluttered open to find that he was smiling at her with so much tenderness that it made her heart squeeze. 'I love you, Gwenllian ferch Hywel.'

'And I you.'

'Yet there are tears?'

She nodded. 'Of joy.'

'I feel the same.' He leant forward and kissed her softly on her lips. 'Are you in pain?'

'No...no, I promise you I am well.' Any lingering discomfort was slowly subsiding as she became more used to the feel of him.

'I am glad to hear that.' He kissed her neck, sliding his tongue along the length and nipping her earlobe. 'Shall we resume?'

'There's more?'

'Oh, yes, sweetheart.' He lifted his head and grinned at her. 'A lot more.'

Chapter Seventeen

Ralph started to move inside her, covering her lips with his in a long sensual kiss. Her legs wrapped around him as he increased the pace. Soon they were finding their own way through the ebb and flow of the hazy, lush wonderment of their heightened passion. This giving and receiving of pleasure. They laced their fingers together, clinging on to one another. The fervour of their rapturous elation reached an unexpected height, a single, pure moment of ecstasy.

Gwen had believed that tiny pieces of her soul were left in the decorative parchments and woven fabrics she created, but they were nothing quite like this—for she had exchanged a much larger part of herself tonight.

Could Gwen ever have imagined that this—what she had just experienced on this bed—would turn out this way? No, how could she know? It was something that she only ever believed could be used to manipulate and control. To hurt and dominate.

But not this. Never with Ralph. Not after what has passed between them, these feelings that centred around something so strong and so potent it blew everything else away, leaving only the most powerful and perfect canon of emotion. Love… And God above knew how much she loved the man who was holding her now so gently, kissing her damp forehead.

'Saints above, but I have no words to describe what just happened.'

'Nor I.' She could feel him smile against her skin. He rolled over, twisting his head around to look at her, his fingers threading through her hair.

'You are a beautiful woman, Gwen.' He gathered her in his arms. 'And I hope you appreciate how much this unexpected night together means to me.'

'For me, too, Ralph.' She flushed, leaning on her elbow as she touched and traced the fullness of his lips. 'Our time together… I shall never forget it.'

'I am glad to hear it, my lady.' He caught her finger lightly between his teeth and winked, before swinging his long limbs around the bed. 'Stay abed while I attend you, Gwen. You must be sore after what just happened.'

He flashed her a quick, sheepish smile and walked towards the tall wooden coffer. He rung out a cloth from the large washing bowl filled with water and brought it back to her.

'My thanks, Ralph. I shall take that.' Gwen bit her lip as she sat up, her long hair tumbling around her. She pulled the coverlet higher to cover her nakedness and pressed the damp cloth along her thighs and between her legs where she did indeed ache.

'This interlude this eventide has, I hope you appreciate, changed everything.'

'I think not. I love you, Ralph, with every breath I have in my body. I want you to know that,' she murmured as she reached out and cupped the scarred skin of his jaw, feeling the uneven, rough surface of his skin. 'But my plans for the future remain unaltered.'

He sat on the bed beside her, seemingly bewildered. 'Even after what has just passed between us?'

'Yes,' she whispered. 'Even after that.'

And just like that the harsh realities of finally succumbing to her desires for Ralph came to the fore. Even before the residual warmth from her body was only just receding. Too soon. It was far too soon for her to confront and face the decisions she had made.

She looked up and caught him staring at her for a moment. A muscle twitched in his jaw.

'I see.' He sighed, raking his fingers through his hair. 'You are determined on your course then. To be alone?'

'There is nothing else for it. Nothing that I can do.'

'You can marry me as we both once wanted. We can bind our lives together as your father and mine had always planned. Hell's teeth, Gwen, it's what I had hoped you still wanted now that we have been reunited. And what I want more than anything in return.'

There might have been a time when she had wanted the same, but not any longer. It could not be. She had reconciled herself to the fact it was impossible for them to be together. Their show of love tonight was something she would never forget, but it was not enough to erase the shame that she had felt for allowing Stephen le Gros the liberties that he had taken with her. What that man stole from her from that bleak time could never be replaced or recovered. It would crawl and spread inside her like a dark humour, eating away at her. And it would eventually emerge, seeping out in all its contorted ugliness, and come between her and Ralph. And Gwen would not do that to him. She could not tie herself to Ralph, just to trap both of them in a marriage that would inevitably become a dreadful nightmare.

'No, I… I no longer want that with you, or anyone else for that matter.'

His eyebrows furrowed in the middle before he gave his head a shake. He stood up and began to dress. 'You sat beside me, mopping my brow after what happened at the mêlée, you bought my horse back, you take me to your bed and you say you love me, Gwen. Yet you claim that you cannot marry me.'

'No, that I cannot do,' she whispered as she exhaled a shaky breath. 'Let me say that I would do all of that again if I had to. And, yes, I do love you and always will, Ralph de Kinnerton.'

'Forgive me then, my lady, for I do not understand you.' He dragged his tunic over his head and picked up his sword belt, tying it around his waist. 'I do not comprehend what this night was about.'

'It was about giving in to our carnal desires, our wants and needs.'

'And nothing more than that?' He crossed his arms across his chest. His eyes fixed on to hers. 'Remember it is me you are talking to, Gwenllian ferch Hywel.'

'I do not know what you want me to tell you.'

He spoke after a long moment of silence. 'The truth, Gwen. Surely you owe me that.'

She lifted her head. 'I have been nothing but honest with you.'

'Are you certain about that, my lady?'

'Yes.' How in heavens had this evening descended to this quarrel? 'I really do not comprehend what you mean.'

'Do you not? God's breath, Gwen, look at you.' He stepped forward, standing in front of her. 'You are the most beautiful, generous, intelligent, loyal woman I know. Your goodness knows no bounds, my lady, but let me speak freely here and say that you are not, nor have you ever been, meant for a life behind the walls of a convent.'

'You do not know that, Ralph.' Her head dropped low as a single tear fell to her cheek. She quickly brushed it away, annoyed with herself. 'You know nothing of my life these past six years.'

He got on his knees on the floor in front of her, lacing his fingers through hers, the pad of his thumb gently grazing her knuckles.

'I do realise that, and I wish to learn more about you and the time we were parted, Gwen, in the hope that I can understand what made you change the direction of your life so drastically,' he whispered softly. 'It is this that I cannot understand. And now after what has unfolded between us tonight, I am even more convinced that you have not been forthright with me. For some reason you are convinced that you have no other option available to you then to take the veil and I am asking you to tell me why that is.'

'I… I…' She blinked, unable to answer him momentarily. 'It is my calling, Ralph.'

'I do not believe you.' He grazed her cheek with his finger.

'Then I am sorry that I cannot convince you. But it is, nevertheless, the truth.'

He shook his head, frowning. 'Will you not talk to me, Gwen and tell me the real reason behind all of this? Tell me what it is that you are afraid of.'

She wanted to tell Ralph. She wanted to explain everything that happened and why she had not run away with him all those years ago, but somehow the words were stuck in her throat. She did not know how to voice them.

'How did you protect me, Gwen?' She looked up and found him watching her intently. 'How did you protect me from Stephen le Gros, all those years ago? Besides the promise that you would marry him, which I wish you had never made, by the way. Indeed, I wish you had had more faith in me to protect you and had run away with me, instead.'

If only it had been that simple. She screwed her eyes shut before opening them and shaking her head. 'Oh, Ralph, do you not see it was impossible for me to do that? I could not take the risk of anything happening to you.'

'I know, sweetheart, but at what cost?' He rubbed his fingers on his forehead. 'Forgive me for saying this, but I sense that there's more in the way you protected me, and allowed my safe passage, than the promise of marriage to Stephen, which never came to pass, anyway.'

Her stomach twisted and knotted in apprehension. This was a question he had asked before, on the night they had ridden in the moonlight. The night he had kissed her again. And just as then, Gwen could not answer him for the shame and guilt she still felt in her bones. But she knew now that Ralph's suspicions regarding his cousin and her reluctance to answer him meant that she had little choice other to explain everything to him now.

God, but how she hated having to revisit that awful moment in her life when fate had intervened adversely. But now after finding Ralph again here at this tournament, it almost seemed as though they had returned back to the beginning of that tumultuous time when both their lives changed indefinitely.

'I did everything I could to protect you back then, Ralph,' she muttered, not quite knowing where to begin. 'In the aftermath of your father's death, Stephen had secured the whole of the Kinnerton garrison and he would have made good his promise and killed you and the few men loyal to you. I could not allow that to happen.'

'And you have my thanks, now and back then. But there's something missing here.' He exhaled through his teeth. 'Something that might explain your reticence to a future you once wanted.'

'Life and circumstance ultimately change our perspectives and the very things we once wanted.'

'And what were the circumstances that changed everything for you, Gwen? He brushed his fingers over her hand. 'Can you not tell me whether you were obliged to promise more to ensure my safety back then? More than marriage.'

She looked into his eyes which seemed far more cautious and pensive, but also hopeful and trusting.

Oh, God...

How would they change once she told him the truth? Would he look on her with contempt and half-veiled disgust after what she would tell him? Mayhap this was also a reason why she had given herself to him. Why she had wanted this one precious unsullied night with Ralph before the reality of their situation tumbled around them. Before the truth served to pull them apart as it surely would, with nothing but derision and scorn left between them.

'Gwen?' He lifted her chin with his fingers as he whispered softly, 'What are you hiding?'

They both jumped when a quick knock was followed by Brida opening the wooden door of their chamber and striding in. 'Ah, poor Matilde has finally settled to sleep and I...' Her friend suddenly realised that she was not alone as her eyes flicked from her to Ralph. 'Oh, I apologise sincerely. I did not mean to intrude on your...well, allow me to remedy the situation. I'll leave and return later.'

'No need for that, Mistress Brida. Please come.' Ralph

sighed. 'I was just leaving, myself.' He leant forward so that only Gwen would hear. 'I hope to continue this discourse later, my lady?'

'Of course,' she lied.

'Until later, my lady. Mistress Brida.' He sketched a deep bow. 'I bid you both a pleasant night.'

'Yes, goodnight, sir.'

Gwen slumped back in the bed, unable to look at her friend and hoping the coverlet would swallow her whole from the embarrassment she felt with Brida catching her in such an exposed manner. She might be discreet, but how mortifying to be found in such a state of dishabille. What must Brida think of her? Yet none of it was as dreadful as having to continue the uncomfortable conversation with Ralph de Kinnerton. She groaned inwardly. How had this night come to pass in the way it had?

Chapter Eighteen

How had Ralph managed to handle the previous evening with Gwen as badly as he had? He felt like a dolt in the way in which he had behaved in the warm aftermath of their lovemaking. The whole evening had been a surprising pleasure-bound journey of discovery where they had explored one another in the most intimate manner. Yet, somehow, it had ended with Ralph enquiring as to the real reasons why Gwen would not be true to her heart and marry him just as she had always intended. He had beseeched her for the truth about how she had protected him from his cousin six long years ago, instead of running away with him, because he knew it had to be more than her promise to marry Stephen.

He had made perfectly valid points, with perfectly legitimate questions. But immediately following their intimate relations?

No. That had not been well done of him.

Ralph could kick himself for being an inconsiderate fool. As well as being insensitive to her needs afterwards. Like a simpleton he had blundered his way into getting Gwen to explain her aversion to marriage to him or anyone else. Instead, he should have coaxed her to speak to him about it all at a later time—not that they had much time left at this tournament. Even so, after everything that had happened, Ralph should have behaved with far more decorum.

God above, he would never forget how she had looked in the height of their passion or how she had given herself so completely. Whatever happened between them last night would be etched on his mind in perpetuity. The way her beautiful fair hair tumbled around her, the sweet scent of her soft skin that reminded him of a dewy summer night. The way she kissed him, explored his body and had responded to him, matching him in every way.

Oh, yes, he would treasure last night for the rest of his days.

'You are very quiet this morn, my friend.' Tom tilted his head and gave him an impassive look.

'Apologies, but there is much on my mind.'

'I can well imagine.'

They were striding through the gatehouse of the castle, for a meeting with King Henry, the Marcher Earls, knights and nobles. The time had come to explain the reasons for their contrivance.

'Are you nervous, because I confess that I am?'

Ralph nodded. 'Yes, but I am glad that this is all finally coming out in the open. I have hidden behind your good name for far too long.'

'You have, but let me just say that you have certainly elevated my name much further than I during this tournament.'

'I doubt that.' Ralph chuckled as he pulled his hood over his head. 'Although it is true that when I dissembled as *Sir Thomas*, I made quite a good left-handed sweeping strike across the body.'

'Ah, but then that was something that I instilled in

you.' They climbed the stone stairs and made their way up the great hall.

'Is that so?' He stopped outside the huge wooden door, manned by two guards.

'Absolutely.'

Ralph snorted as he turned and clasped Tom's arm. 'Either way, I would like to convey my heartfelt gratitude for everything you have done for me.'

'Will you stop? You shall put me to blush.' Tom extended his arm and clasped Ralph's arm as well. 'Besides, you know that I only helped you for the silver.'

'Of course you did.'

'Naturally.'

'It's been a privilege, my friend.' Tom motioned towards the door. 'Well, are you ready to step inside and face the inevitable indignation?'

'I believe so.' Ralph nodded. 'Yes, let's do it.'

Ralph knelt beside his good friend on the cold stone floor strewn with rushes in front of the assembled group of men in the great hall. His sword lay in front of him, his head bent reverently low in front of the young King Henry and the most powerful men in the kingdom who loomed above as they sat on the dais. He felt beads of sweat on his forehead as he stared at the floor. The palms of his hands were clammy, but he resisted rubbing them together while he felt the deafening beat of his heart pierce through the eerie silence of the room. The only light was from the torches flickering on the wall sconces dotted around the large chamber.

'You did what!' the Earl of Hereford bellowed. 'And you, de Clancey and Tallany allowed this...knew about this duplicity? This mockery?'

Ralph felt Will and Hugh walk and stand either side of them.

'We supported this man in his bid to claim his birthright, but it was never an attempt to dishonour anyone at this tournament,' Will said.

'What else could we possibly derive from such actions?'

Ralph lifted his head and addressed the Earl of Hereford, who sat on one side of the King and the Earl of Chester on the other.

'I wanted the privilege to be able to pay the heavy scutage settled on my castle and its lands many years ago with anonymity and in the guise of a knight. As my friend here, Sir Thomas Lovent.'

'What we fail to understand is why you would feel the need to behave in such an underhand manner. To conduct your affairs and enter this ennobled tournament that exemplifies our chivalry and honour in such secrecy. This has been badly done of you all!'

'I implore you to listen to my reasonings, my Lord Hereford.'

'Why should we do that? You have made fools of everyone here.'

'I beg pardon, Sire…my lords…but that was never the intention. Our conduct was never nefarious.' Ralph looked from the King to the other more seasoned men sitting beside him, making sure he looked each of them in the eye. 'Otherwise, why would we have come on our own behest to inform the Crown of our conduct?'

'Why indeed?' the Earl of Hereford snorted.

King Henry stamped his foot. 'I wish to hear this man. Stand and make us privy to your reasonings, sir.'

The two knights stood up and bowed before Ralph spoke. 'There is a very good reason as to why Sir Thomas and I switched our identities, Sire. I did not want my existence, the fact that I'm alive and escaped death, to be known until a time that was more prudent. As it is now.'

'This is preposterous,' the Earl of Hereford snapped, getting out of his seat.

'Let the man speak, for God's sake, Hereford,' the Earl of Chester, Ranulph de Blondville, said in irritation before addressing Ralph. 'Why would that be, sir? Did you believe your life to be in some sort of danger?'

'Yes, it already had been. But once I joined the retinue of my Lord de Clancey, it was also the opportunity to gain advantage. One that would escape the notice of my enemies.'

'As you said, with the guise of anonymity?'

'Just so, my lord.'

'I see.' The Earl of Chester narrowed his eyes. 'Who are you, sir?'

Ralph took a deep breath before speaking. 'I am Ralph de Kinnerton, the rightful lord of Kinnerton Castle.'

There was an audible gasp as Ralph had predicted there would be with such a proclamation. His eyes darted around the chamber and settled briefly on Stephen le Gros, who had drained of colour, spots of greyish puce appearing on his face. The corners of Ralph's lips lifted faintly as he saw the shock etched on his cousin's face. The man, however, quickly recovered himself.

'That is a lie!' Stephen cried. 'My cousin, Ralph de Kinnerton, whom I would like to remind the court was one time accused of being a traitor, is dead.'

'Silence!' the Earl retorted. 'We are not in session at the King's Court for you to vociferate your protestations, sir, and, as I may recall, it was *you*, Stephen le Gros, who accused your young cousin of being a traitor!'

That should have silenced the man, but Stephen had always had the knack to deflect an awkward situation.

'And you think this is him, my lord?' Stephen pointed at him, barely hiding his contempt. 'Do you think this man even looks or behaves like my cousin, Ralph de Kinnerton? He is so disfigured that he must be an imposter!'

With that the hall was suddenly filled with a huge commotion and uproar as many voices clamoured to be heard. Ralph turned, looking in every direction as many of the men who stood around the periphery were openly either disputing or agreeing with Stephen's allegation.

But against this he stood tall, resolute, facing forward, with his stance never wavering. Ralph could not show any of these men that inside he felt as though he were faltering under the pressure.

'Silence!' The Earl of Chester stood, casting his gaze around the hall. 'What is this rabble we have here?'

The din eventually quietened until there was only a lingering hum of uncertainty hanging in the air.

'You were saying that you are Ralph de Kinnerton, the only son of Walter and Maud de Kinnerton.'

'I do, my lord.'

'And is there any way you can prove your claim, sir?' The Earl of Chester gave him a short nod of encouragement.

'Yes, do enlighten us, as I must confess that you do look nothing like the boy I once saw beside Lord Walter de Kinnerton,' Hereford sneered. 'He was vastly unremarkable, as his own father privately mentioned to me. You see, we were acquainted.'

Some of the men including his cousin sniggered, evidently amused at the Earl's base comments, but Ralph had to hold his nerve and not cower. With a muscle ticking in his jaw, his fists clenched at his sides at being reminded of his own father's perception of him, Ralph tried to retain his composure.

Damn, must he continually be reminded of how lacking he once had been?

He caught Tom's eye, and saw a barely visible nod of his endorsement. Ralph sensed that the same would be true of the other two men who stood shoulder to shoulder with him—Will and Hugh.

God, but he was a lucky man to have friends and allies like these men. Ralph squared his shoulders and exhaled deeply before responding.

'You are quite right, my lord, when you describe the boy I once was, but that was over six years ago when my whole life was turned upside down and I was forced to flee my home in peril.' Ralph pinned his gaze on to the Earl of Hereford who had always endorsed Stephen le Gros. 'And I may have left as a boy, but I have returned a man—I hope a worthy man as the Lord of Kinnerton.'

'And yet you have hardly proved anything regarding your claim?'

'That is because the scoundrel is an imposter!' his cousin bawled, chiming in.

'Sir Stephen, you will have your chance to refute any claims this man may have regarding his kinship with you, but if you blurt out once more, then I shall have to ask you to remove yourself from the hall. Do you understand, sir?'

'I do, my lord, but you can appreciate my indignation at having this man claim to be my dead cousin, Ralph de Kinnerton.'

'Oh, believe me, I am very much alive,' Ralph retorted.

'Ah, but that is just the point, as it will take far more than just sheer faith and belief to confirm your true identity to us, sir, especially as your cousin here repudiates your very claim.'

Hell's teeth, but this was ridiculous. How was he supposed to validate his claim?

'What would you have me say, my Lord Hereford?' He made a pointed look at the Earl. 'That I carry my father's seal, his signet ring of the Lords of Kinnerton? Or should I divulge details about Kinnerton, castle and all its surrounding areas or my knowledge about its security arrangements that only the constable would be privy to? Or should I regale you with stories of my childhood, talk about my mother, my betrothal? Mayhap you prefer I present the court with my personal belongings, which I still have in my possession? Would any of these convince you that I am who I say I am? Or do you intend to take the word of a man who, after all, had much to gain from my downfall as well as my father's?'

'That is an outrage!' Stephen's snarl echoed through the hall. 'I have been acting sergeant of Kinnerton, with my Lord Hereford as its Sheriff for over six years, collecting the burden of heavy tax from peasants so that I can somehow pay the Crown its due and finally become its Lord, as my uncle always desired me to be. His heir apparent.'

There was a stunned silence at this disclosure. On the one hand it exposed Stephen le Gros's ambitions to enhance his own position at the expense of hardworking men and women who toiled the land, but also the backing of Hereford who stood as Kinnerton's Sheriff.

Ralph's shoulders tensed at the mention of his father's favouring his cousin over him. But then he realised something that he had always overlooked before. If what his cousin disclosed had been the case, then why had the man been so eager to lend his support to usurp the man who claimed him as his heir apparent? It did not make sense.

'And yet you, along with many others, later accused my father of conspiring against the Crown. An accusation that was never actually upheld even after my father's untimely demise,' Ralph declared, flicking his gaze to his cousin.

'My Lords, you cannot allow this upstart, this imposter who has brought this great tournament to disrepute to throw these vile accusations.'

'Indeed.' The Earl of Hereford turned to the young King, who had been listening to the proceedings. 'How can we believe the words of this charlatan, Sire?'

'This man can certainly prove that he is, in fact, Ralph de Kinnerton, Sire,' Hugh said, lending his support.

'Indeed, I can also affirm the truth of that statement for all the reasons given.' Will nodded. 'My wife, Lady Isabel de Clancey, can also attest to helping Sir Ralph after he was ambushed and brutally attacked in Aquitaine, leaving him with the scars you are now witness to.'

'All very interesting, yet this does not prove that you knew Ralph de Kinnerton before, when he lived in his ancestral home, to affirm that the man we now see before us and *that boy* are one and the same.'

Ralph exhaled through his teeth, realising the truth of Hereford's observation. After all, it was his word against his cousin's.

'But mayhap I can, my lord.' Gwen's soft yet determined voice suddenly burst through from the back of the hall.

Ralph turned, his jaw dropping as he watched in awe as she strode gracefully but with purpose, her head held high, with her maid following behind her.

His heart soared as he pondered the marvel that was *Gwenllian ferch Hywel.*

God, could this woman be any more magnificent as she was here in the hall. Once again acting on his behalf.

The Earl of Hereford stood and stepped down the dais. 'Lady Gwenllian, how fortuitous for your arrival in the hall at this very moment, but this is a privy council, which prohibits women from attending, as you well know.'

Gwen made a deep curtsy as she addressed the men who sat on the dais.

'I do know, my lord, and I apologise profusely for disturbing the proceedings here, but believed that since I am someone who knew Sir Ralph de Kinnerton for over ten years, my evidence might be welcomed, under the circumstances. That is, if you would grant me the opportunity to speak at this council?' she said.

'I am afraid not, my lady. We would not be in need of your testimony here.'

'No, my lord, wait.' The young King Henry stood and walked down the dais to approach Gwen, who swept into a low, graceful curtsy as the young monarch made a bow in return. He extended his arm and ushered her further into the hall, by the foot of the dais. 'I would like to hear this evidence. Please continue, Lady Gwenllian.'

'My eternal thanks, Sire, my lords.' She dipped her head deferentially. 'As you may know, I was the ward of Lord Walter de Kinnerton and went to live in Kinnerton Castle after the death of my beloved father, Hywel ap Rhys of Clwyd, as a young girl. Here I came to know my betrothed, Ralph de Kinnerton. We grew up together and would have married had the disastrous circumstances of six years ago not intervened.' She paused and straightened her back. 'But I can tell you, as God is my witness, that this man before you and the boy I knew are one and the same. He is, indeed, Ralph de Kinnerton.'

'So the man before you had revealed his true identity before doing so to us?'

'Yes, Sire, he did, but only because I became suspicious of who he was. I will say that although he has altered physically, this man is nevertheless who he claims to be.'

Ralph caught Gwen's eye briefly and smiled faintly.

'Thank you, Lady Gwenllian, for your affirmation in support of this young man, who does indeed look like his father the more I look upon him,' the Earl of Chester agreed, lending his support. 'Subject to confirming the evidence that this man, or should I say Sir Ralph, has stated, I think we can all stand in agreement, can we not, Sire?'

Ralph found that he was holding his breath, waiting for what seemed like an age before King Henry finally nodded. 'Yes. We believe that you are indeed Sir Ralph de Kinnerton, but you will need to vouchsafe your claim.'

'I would happily do that, Sire.'

'Good. Very well, I think we can surmise everything by what you have declared and upon presenting your father's ring and personal belongings and recounting tales of Kinnerton to the scribe.'

'But, Sire…my liege! This is most irregular. You cannot accept the testimony of…a woman,' Stephen ground out, but was silenced by the young King holding his hand out.

'And yet we have, Sir Stephen. Your objection has been duly noted, but know this…' The Earl of Chester pushed forward, addressing his cousin. 'If we find out that your grievance stems from a stance to discredit Sir

Ralph for pernicious and dishonourable reasons, then charges shall be brought against *you*.'

'Sir Stephen le Gros understands that, do you not?' the Earl of Hereford said between clenched teeth. 'However, Sire, there still remains the unresolved issue of the way in which Sir Ralph brought this tournament into disrepute.'

'Hardly that,' Chester countered. 'And he explained the reasons for that, did he not?'

'Yes, I believe he did.' King Henry nodded.

'I thank you, Sire.' Ralph stepped forward and knelt before the young King and bent his head. 'If I may also ask about settling the matter of Kinnerton Castle and its environs as well.'

'You have some nerve, young man,' Hereford blustered.

'I hope you can appreciate, my lord, that Kinnerton is my ancestral home and I have finally raised the silver scutage hanging over it. I can now, with your approval, reclaim it.'

This was not quite true as Ralph still had much of the difference to make up, but he would raise the feudal relief somehow. Having the attention of King Henry and the most powerful Marcher Lords in England was far too good an opportunity to pass by.

'Must it be settled? Surely the castle can stay part of the Crown's estates.'

'Sire, that would not do.' The Earl of Chester turned to the King. 'Llewelyn of Wales grows stronger by the day. We need stability and security in the marcher borders, held together by powerful lords who can lead cohesively in this province.'

'Which is why the right candidate is Sir Stephen le Gros, who also has the support of his men and the Kinnerton guards,' Hereford argued.

'Even with so many voices of dissent about the hardships at Kinnerton, eh?' the Earl of Chester asked of Hereford, who looked away. 'Oh, yes, I have heard much about it.'

'Besides, would that not be unlawful, Sire?' Ralph made sure that this question was addressed directly to King Henry. 'Since I am the rightful heir of Kinnerton.'

'As his father before him had always wanted?' Gwen added.

It seemed that Gwen was of the same mind as him, appealing to King Henry. This was, after all, something the young monarch might share in common with Ralph, coming into his reign at such a young age with so many still doubting his ability.

They waited a while as King Henry rubbed his chin, his mood pensive before he got up and walked down the dais to stand in front of Gwen, who curtsied once more.

'You are quite right, my Lady Gwenllian, my father King John did everything he could to secure the smooth succession of the throne.' King Henry raised her back to her feet and dipped his head over her hand. 'That is despite all the problems of the Barons' conflict in his own reign, so I do understand.'

He then ambled back on the dais and stood directly in front of Ralph. 'The only way to settle this, Sir Ralph, so that it can be resolved once and for all, pending the return of the silver owed to Crown is...' he took a deep breath '...for you and your cousin to engage in one-to-one hand combat and bring about an end to this tournament.'

There was an audible gasp.

'That is an inspired idea, my liege,' said Chester, nodding at the King.

Hell's teeth! Was this some kind of game to King Henry, who was, after all, many years younger than himself and who still probably craved the spectacle of the tournament? Yet the idea did have merit. Combat with Stephen would give Ralph an opportunity to show his prowess and give anyone who still doubted him a chance to prove himself.

'I accept the challenge, Sire, my lords.'

'As do I.' Stephen stepped forward, but making sure he was as far away as possible from Ralph.

'Very good. Then it is settled for tomorrow noon,' the King declared as the hall began to cheer.

'If I may, Sire?' the Earl of Hereford interjected. 'Surely we cannot allow Sir Ralph to leave this hall without a penalty for abusing the terms of this tournament, otherwise we would be inviting nothing but shame and ridicule?'

God, but the man was an obsequious ass.

'Ten silver marks should surely cover that, Hereford.' Chester frowned.

'He already owes silver to the Crown. No, what would suffice would need to be something far more appropriate.'

Ralph stepped forward. 'Then I would suggest that I provide alms for the monastery of your choosing, Sire, and spend a night in the dungeons here. Would *that* suffice, my Lord Hereford?'

'Yes,' the Earl sneered. 'I suppose that would.'

Chapter Nineteen

Ralph exhaled as he looked around the small, dark, dank, foul-smelling dungeon in the underbelly of Pulverbatch Castle. He kicked up the dirty rushes on the ground as he heard the rattling of chains, turning to find a guard coming through the narrow passage beyond the arched doorway inserted with thick metal bars, carrying a lit torch. Then Ralph saw her behind the man... *Gwen*.

She was here in this awful place to see him. His chest tightened just as she finally came into view, on the other side of the metal bars.

'Gwen? What are you doing here, my lady? This is no place for you.'

She stepped forward and nodded at the guard who passed her the torch. 'You can have only a moment, Lady Gwenllian,' the guard said, before moving to walk outside the narrow hallway.

Gwen turned back to face Ralph on the other side of the metal bars. 'I had to see you, Ralph. To make sure that you were well.'

'I am better for seeing you.' Ralph slipped his fingers through the gap and smiled. 'Thank you for coming to the hall earlier today. Without your testimony, I very much doubt that I would have convinced those men of my true identity.'

'It was the least I could do to lend my support in my own small way.' She reached out and laced her fingers with his.

He shook his head. 'You must know that it was far, far more than that, Gwen. I am once again indebted to you.'

'No, you are not.' Her lips curled upwards faintly. 'But I did come here to say that I am so proud of you, Ralph de Kinnerton. You handled the situation with a lot of courage in front of King Henry and the Marcher Earls.'

'I am not so sure about that.' He shrugged. 'But I shall need all the courage I can muster tomorrow with Stephen.'

Her brows furrowed in the middle. 'And must you fight him?'

'I'm afraid there is no other way to prove my worth to those men.'

'But this is Stephen le Gros we are discussing,' she hissed. 'The man has no honour and would stoop to any lengths to gain advantage.'

'Trust me, I shall be ready for him.' He smiled briefly, touched at her concern. 'There is really no need to worry, Gwen.'

'That is going to be difficult to do under the circumstances.' She sank her teeth into her lower lip. 'I have something for you—a token that I hope will bring you luck tomorrow.'

Gwen pulled out the length of material from her drawstring pouch, which she draped over her arm, the richness in the embroidery gleaming in the dappled light from the torch. Ralph could see that it was the token Gwen had given him before the *mêlée à pied*.

'Where did you find it?' he said in surprise, gliding

his fingers across the length that she held out. 'I believed that I had lost it after the disastrous *mêlée à cheval*.'

'I confess that it had not been easy to find as it had been embedded into the mud after the mêlée. But Brida and I found it after a thorough search of the area.'

'And then laundered and brought it back to its former beautiful state, from what I can see.'

'With an extra addition down the centre, if you take a closer look.'

Ralph blinked, running a finger down the centre, and realised there had been an additional piece of fabric that had been carefully stitched on. He knew instantly where the material had come from.

It was the first token Ralph had ever received from Gwen. It was the only item in his possession that he knew held some significance when he woke after being ambushed in St Jean de Cole. So much so that he wore it constantly around his wrist until it had become worn and weatherbeaten. It was the blue and purple strip of material he had churlishly returned back to her that first time he had spotted her, after years apart, on the eve of the tournament sitting in the royal spectator area.

'I cannot believe you kept it.'

His fingers grazed over the softly textured material. 'It's strange, but those first few days after I woke from the ambush in St Jean de Cole, it was this piece of fabric that kept me going, in the midst of my confused mind. I somehow knew it was a link to the past. To *you*.'

She swallowed as she nodded. 'Well, I hope now that the new and old pieces have come together, it would also serve as a token for tomorrow. And also the future. Your future.'

'It shall.' He squeezed her fingers gently, taking her

beautiful token. 'I thank you for your kindness, my lady. It means a great deal.'

'It is nothing, I assure you.'

'Yet, for me, I am assured that it's everything and more.' He smiled softly, looking over the token. 'I'm glad that you did not throw away the original token you gifted me.'

'I very nearly did, when I believed you to be dead and with your friend Sir Thomas seemingly presenting it back to me. But then I realised that I could not do that, Ralph.'

'After the way in which it was returned, I would not have blamed you if you had.'

'How could I?' She sighed. 'For me, it was also a link back to you.'

He lifted her hand through the bars and pressed a kiss to the back of her hand. 'Forgive my initial reaction, Gwen. I was frustrated, angry and carried a lot of hurt from that time.'

'Due to my decision not to run away with you six years ago?'

He nodded. 'Indeed. You deliberately wanted me to think the worst of you.'

She swallowed uncomfortably. 'I suppose I'm quite persuasive, when I have to be.'

'True, and it certainly worked—I believed that about you, all those intervening years. Yet in reality you did what you did to help me get away.'

'Yes.'

'To protect me by giving me more time to do so?'

'Indeed.' Gwen untangled her hand from his and took a step back. 'It's getting late. I must be going.'

'Wait, a moment longer, Gwen.' Ralph ran his fingers through his hair. 'Please do not go yet. However painful it is, I hope you know that you can tell me anything.

Let us not have what happened six years ago still stand between us.'

'This is hardly the time.' She turned her back on him. 'Can we not discuss this after your combat with Stephen tomorrow?'

'I may not have another chance. Besides, do you not believe that I have waited long enough to know what happened between you and Stephen? Ever since I've been reunited with you, this has gone round and round in my head, as I pondered on the nature of the promises you were forced to make to him back then.'

'This is not what I wish to discuss, rather something I prefer to forget, Ralph.'

'I can imagine, sweetheart.' He walked to the bars, studying her and noting the stiffness to her body. 'I realise that your decisions back then were not only difficult, but what you believed to be right.'

'Yes,' she whispered. 'It was the only way I could assure your safety, otherwise, he would have hunted you down, as I explained before.'

He realised then the stark reality of what Gwen had believed to be true and his heart twisted in anguish for the decisions she had had to make.

'And as I said, I am grateful for what you did, Gwen. You are truly a remarkable woman.' Ralph exhaled. 'However, there is one thing I would like to know. I need to know what you had to do for that assurance.'

Ralph wondered whether she would actually tell him and, just when he believed that her silence would not break, she finally spoke.

'The first thing I did was to convince you, Ralph, of my indifference to you, which was actually much harder than I initially believed. However, the expediency for you to get away played its part and eventually you were forced to leave Kinnerton without me.' She took in a deep, shaky breath before continuing. 'In truth, I was relieved that you left, otherwise Stephen claimed that he would have killed you in front of me which I believed he would have. However, as always with Stephen there was so much more that he sought.'

'Go on.'

'Must I, Ralph?'

'I would like to know what happened so that I can understand the past better. So that I can understand you.' And the hard choices Gwen had made.

Ralph hated having to ask her of this, knowing how difficult Gwen found talking about that awful time in their shared past, but he had to know exactly what happened. Only then could he be of any help to her.

'He…he brought shame on me, Ralph, insisting that I would soon have to marry him, anyway, so he…oh, Lord, this is so difficult to say. He touched me. He despoiled me and he would have done more had we not been interrupted. Had he not been called away with the need to quash certain factions of Kinnerton men who still supported your father…or rather you.'

He drew breath slowly through his teeth as he grappled with what she was finally telling him, but there was more as she continued.

'Then he marked me, here at the base of my neck.' Her voice was filled with a slight tremor, as she turned her head and swept her veil and the hair beneath on to one shoulder, exposing the back of her neck. She rubbed her fingers down from her hairline. 'It's quite faint now, but he…he used a dagger to mark his initial into my skin, in the hope that I would never forget to whom I belonged— as he reminded me,' she said sadly.

There was a dull ringing in Ralph's head and his stomach twisted in a knotted coil of cold fury and a certain feeling of helplessness for all that Gwen had gone through. God, but had he not expected something like this? He had predicted that there was something missing from what she had said, yet this was far more and far more depraved than he had ever imagined.

Now for it to be finally voiced made Ralph's blood roar with rage to think that Stephen le Gros had touched Gwenllian, the loveliest, kindest and most caring woman he knew and against her wishes, with sullied hands that could only belong to someone as foul as his cousin.

And what made this all so much worse for Ralph was that it had all happened while he had thought the worst of Gwen and her reasons for not running away with him. For six long years, he had believed that she had somehow put her ambitions for wanting to become the next Lady de Kinnerton above anything else. And while she had been put through that dreadful ordeal, at the hands of his cousin, Ralph had run away like a worthless coward.

God's breath!

The shame he felt for not protecting Gwen when she had needed him threatened to consume him. Lord only knew how much when he had failed her so utterly and completely.

'Ralph?' Her soft voice pierced through his morose musings. 'Won't you say something?'

'Yes.' His voice sounded shaky even to his own ears. 'But let me say that no words can truly convey the regret and outrage I feel for what happened to you, Gwen.'

'It was not your fault, Ralph.'

'Was it not?'

'No.' She shook her head. 'But I hope that what I have recounted here explains the difficult choices I was forced to make. And ones I must continue to make after this tournament draws to a close.'

Yes, he did. He had foreseen that there was a lot more to the path that Gwen had chosen and his assumptions were sadly correct. Her desire to take the veil now took on a huge significance that made him want to weep at her feet for all that she had endured. And in truth, if he had been listening closely, mayhap he would have understood her difficulties better, despite the fact that he had pushed Gwen to relive that painful moment from the past again. Yet there was more from the manner in which she had spoken. Gwen had not just disclosed this to explain the shame, guilt and pain she felt about what had happened resulting in her decision to enter a holy order. But because she was also telling him that there could never be anything between them. Had she not been saying this all along? That their love was not enough to overcome the past.

Damn Stephen le Gros to hell.

All of it had begun and ended with the bastard.

The guard emerged again from the narrow passage outside to take her away from this gloomy, damp place. Just as well, since Ralph could not presently look at her knowing how much he had let her down. How much he felt the blame of what had happened.

He heard Gwen step away to leave when he turned to her once again.

'I must go now. Until tomorrow, Ralph, try to manage to gain some rest.' Her voice was now dull, void of any emotion. So much so, that he wanted to reach out to her.

'I am sorry, Gwen. I should have protected you better against a man like Stephen.'

'As I said, it was not your fault.' She shook her head, giving him a sad smile. 'How could it be?'

Very easily.

Ralph waited until she had gone before he pounded his fist against the stone wall again and again, welcoming the sharp pain as the cold jagged edges of the wall grazed and cut his hand. He sank on to the floor and covered his head with his hands, feeling the enormity of what Gwen had just divulged. She might not believe that he was to blame, but he felt the responsibility for what had happened to her all the more. He felt it keenly, knowing that she had done it…yes, to protect him.

Hell's teeth, that took on a very new and dark meaning now.

And yet Ralph knew whose fault it actually was. Who was to blame for all their misfortune. His cousin—Stephen le Gros.

As Ralph sat there on that filthy floor, he made a vow to himself that he would never allow anything like this to happen again. As God was his witness, he would rather die, than allow anyone to harm even a hair on Gwenllian ferch Hywel. The impending one-to-one combat with Stephen on the morrow suddenly took on a far more ominous stance, but it could not come soon enough.

Yes, everything had begun and ended with his cousin and tomorrow Ralph had a moment with destiny, to end it once and for all.

Gwen left the horrible cavernous dungeons close to tears, but she would not allow them to fall. No, she would hold her head high, meet with Brida outside the dungeons and make their way back to the keep. Only once she was back in the privacy of her chamber would she then give in to those tears.

She had always known deep in her heart what Ralph's reaction would be, once he was made aware of the truth about that terrible time, all those years ago. And she had not been wrong since he could hardly hide his bitterness, anger and even disappointment. Ralph could barely look at her once she had informed him, the sudden difference in him so very tangible.

Mayhap in time it would even alter the way in which he viewed her and Gwen would not be able to live with that. No, she did not want to see resentment and eventually disgust masked on Ralph's face. His vile cousin would constantly be between them. It would never do. A future between them would always be doomed.

She stepped out into the night and took a deep breath, allowing the clean, crisp air to replace the putrid smell from the dungeons.

'Is everything well, Lady Gwenllian?' Brida stood outside the underground opening, waiting for her.

No, nothing would ever be well again. 'Yes, I suppose, all things considering.'

'Sir Thomas is here to provide escort.' Her companion flushed a little as she nodded in the direction of Ralph's handsome friend.

'Indeed, my lady.' Sir Thomas Lovent bowed before walking to her side. 'Ralph ensured that while he might be ensconced inside a cell, you would still need protection from his cousin, should the man want to seek retribution for your part in the hall earlier.'

'Yes, you were very brave, Gwen.'

It would be her one last act in helping Ralph before she set off on her journey to the convent. A journey that Gwen realised she would now have to make without Ralph's escort. Mayhap she had always known deep down that it would be too much of a struggle for them both to travel together. That their intense attraction would always be an impediment to what needed to be done. To go their separate ways. Well, there was nothing for it. She would inform Brida of the changes to their plans. They would now get away after Ralph's one-to-one combat with his cousin on the morrow, whatever happened.

'I do not know about that, but I'll be glad of the protection you provide for us, sir.'

'It shall be my pleasure, my lady.' He nodded. 'And just to give you further peace of mind, there'll be de Clancey guards dotted around the keep and outside your chamber, courtesy of Lady Isabel de Clancey.'

'Then please pass on my thanks to the lady, until I am able to convey them in person.'

'I'll be happy to.' He strolled beside her. 'And how is our mutual friend?'

She sighed. 'As well as can be expected, when you consider that he's spending the eve of the most important combat against Stephen le Gros in a dungeon.' She frowned. 'Was there nothing that could have been done about it?'

'I'm afraid not. I tried to share the burden with him, but Ralph would not have it. He insisted that it was his penance and only he would spend the night in that hovel.'

'But it is hardly fair.'

'I agree, yet it was the only way to appease a man as powerful as the Earl of Hereford.'

'So, while Ralph has to sleep in that rat-infested hovel, as you put it, his cousin can spend the night on a warm comfortable pallet.'

'Let it not trouble you, Lady Gwenllian. Ralph has slept in worse places without it impacting his performance. You forget he is a seasoned warrior.'

'I shall try not to, sir, but it still worries me greatly.'

'I understand.' He gave her a reassuring smile as they approached the entrance to the keep. 'I shall leave you here and bid you goodnight, my lady, Mistress Brida. Until tomorrow.'

Yes, it all rested on what would happen on the morrow.

One thing was certain; she was not going to get much sleep this evening either.

Chapter Twenty

Gwen sat in the canopied spectators' area with the royal party, twisting her hands in her lap nervously. As predicted, she had a very difficult night, tossing and turning, anxious about the event about to commence and unfold. It was not a cold day, yet she could not stop shivering and breathing unevenly.

She scanned the area and caught Lady Isabel de Clancey's eyes further along the way, sitting with Lady Eleanor Tallany and her young son. It seemed that they were just as nervous as she, which for a strange reason was quite comforting, knowing that she was not the only who cared for Ralph and the outcome today.

Gwen smiled and inclined her head when she realised that she was being beckoned over to sit with them. 'Gwen, Brida, come and sit with me!' William Tallany said loudly.

The two young women shuffled along to sit with their small group and greeted one another before sitting down beside them.

'I wanted to thank you, Isabel, for providing the guards around the keep yesterday. It meant that I could go to my bed feeling far more secure than I otherwise would have.'

'Oh, it really was nothing.' Isabel shrugged. 'And it was the least I could do after what you did. I am told that without your statement of support for Ralph, he would have not been successful in convincing the Crown of his true identity.'

'I could hardly sit by and allow that to happen.'

'No.' Isabel smiled knowingly at her. 'I suppose you could not.'

Gwen sobered. 'Lady Isabel, I believe that you are under a misapprehension regarding Ralph and myself.'

'Do not distress yourself about such trifles and I am sure that you are right.' Her smile deepened briefly before it slipped away. 'Look, they are about to commence.'

Gwen snapped her head around to watch Ralph stride towards the royal stands, his hauberk mail armour worn over a gambeson, carrying his shield and helmet in one hand and his gleaming metal sword in the other. He seemed every part the raw, menacing, powerful warrior exuding strength and confidence. And he had never looked more wonderful. He walked with purpose, his cousin on one side as he reached the dais in front of where King Henry sat in his royal regalia, flanked either side by the two Marcher Earls of Chester and Hereford who maintained their roles as hosts of the tournament.

The men knelt with their swords in front of them, solemnly making an oath to God, to the King and to the rules of the combat they would soon engage in.

Gwen kept her eyes on Ralph de Kinnerton, the man she loved deeply, but had to forsake. She noted that he had wrapped her token around his wrist and hoped that it would bring him the fortuity that he deserved. He got to his feet and met her eyes briefly before turning his attention to his weaponry. It amazed her that this man, who seemed so assured and confident, could be the same as the one who had spent the night in that stinking dungeon.

Either way it mattered not, when her heart clenched tightly at the sheer sight of him. When tiny wisps unfurled in her stomach, just by being near to him.

She reproached herself, knowing it was futile to continually acknowledge these feelings. If last night proved one thing, it was that they were not destined to be with one another, however much they both might desire it. The life-changing events from the past made a future together a sad impossibility.

'Do not worry about him, Gwen,' Isabel muttered in her ear. 'I'm sure he shall prevail.'

'I hope so. His cousin is also skilled and would not think it beneath him to use underhand tactics.'

'That may well be true, but Ralph will see through anything. I am certain.'

She nodded. 'I'm sure your estimation is right and I'm glad that his night in the dungeon does not seem to have had a detrimental effect.'

William Tallany turned to her and responded earnestly. 'That is 'cos I made sure Ralph had lots of honey cake when he came out of that *hellhole*.'

'William! Where did you hear such coarse language?' his mother reprimanded.

'Papa said it.'

'And yet it's not the proper thing in front of ladies,' Eleanor said as William shrugged an apology, making them all smile, breaking the tension briefly.

'Well, in any case, we shall soon find out, but do not forget that today Ralph fights for honour and the chance to have Kinnerton restored to him in front of the most important men in the land. And as himself, without another's mask.' Isabel squeezed Gwen's hand.

'Yes, very true.'

It also meant that, above all, she hoped Ralph would be victorious after overcoming adversity with everything that he had endured. He deserved nothing less.

Ralph felt darts of apprehension and tension flicker down his spine. This momentous occasion that he had, in some way, been waiting six long years for had finally arrived. His day of reckoning with Stephen le Gros.

God, but the man was vile and reprehensible. He had betrayed his father and been instrumental in his downfall, taken Kinnerton, betrayed Ralph and tried to bring about his demise, time and again. But above all, he was the man who had hurt Gwenllian ferch Hywel in the most abhorrent, unspeakable manner. All because of his insatiable greed and lust for power. But Ralph must not think about her now, could not be distracted by his thoughts of her. He must channel his own anger.

Ralph allowed this to penetrate his mind again and again, reminding himself of everything that Stephen had done. All the futile pain and destruction the man had caused.

They stood adjacent to one another, kneeling in front of King Henry and the Marcher Earls, making an oath of peace to King Henry. They then turned to face each other with a perfunctory bow as customary under the chivalric knightly code. And then it begun…immediately with their clashing swords.

Stephen came at him with a succession of attacking strikes, sweeping his sword across his body, pushing Ralph back into defending himself. Neither man spoke as they were both wrapped in these initial encounters, trying to gain the measure of one another.

Over and over Ralph turned and tilted his sword to

defend the onslaught of Stephen driving and pushing his attacks forward, ruthlessly. It mattered not, as Ralph was ready for the relentless wave of strikes, noting with satisfaction that not only did he match his cousin's strength with ease, but he held him back with such force and determination that it was making Stephen become increasingly subdued, his movements slightly laboured.

Still, he would not underestimate the man who was known for his cunning. The clash of the metal blades continued as his cousin lunged forward, swiping and slashing his sword across, making Ralph spin around to his side to engage in the riposte and counter-attack. Oh, yes, he also had a few tricks under his gambeson.

'Not bad, my young cousin. Not bad for someone like *you*,' Stephen muttered from under his helmet.

'Someone like me? And pray what is that, Stephen?'

'Now, I would not want you to run off crying, Ralph. Not in front of all these people, including the gullible young King, come to witness this little family squabble. But come now, Ralph you know exactly what I mean. It seems you have been busy these past few years. Why, you could barely hold a sword before, let alone yield it.'

'I have certainly lived through the most arduous of years,' Ralph said, swinging his sword around his body effortlessly.

'I suppose you must have,' his cousin said uninterestedly. 'And yet I cannot help being a little disappointed.'

'I am sure you must be, since all your attempts to stifle me have only ended in failure.'

'Have they?' He chuckled. 'We shall see. To think that after all this time and effort, you're still going to lose, Ralph. Oh, yes, how very disappointing and predictable you are.'

'I do not think so.' Ralph would not allow this man

to crawl under his skin like he used to and spread his venom. 'I am no longer the boy you used to know and manipulate for your own gain.'

And to prove his point Ralph stepped back and removed his helmet. The hum of the crowd's gasps and murmurs enveloped them. Stephen had no choice but to follow suit and take off his helmet, throwing it at Ralph's feet.

'Yes, this is better. At least I can now see the pathetic look on your face when I bring you down.' He thrust forward suddenly, taking Ralph by surprise. 'Boy or man, it makes no difference to me.'

'True, why hide beneath the veneer of respectability or even chivalry? You have never possessed either.'

'God's breath, Ralph, you are a bore. You were back then as well, if memory serves, an insufferable dolt.'

Ralph countered another attack with one of his own, regaining the upper hand as he pushed the other man off his course. 'You know, this was always something I never understood about you—your hatred for me. The fact that you bullied and intimidated and then set out to spread lies about me to anyone you could. Why? What did I ever do to you?'

'You surely cannot expect me to answer such trite nonsense.'

'But then you would say that, since you always took pleasure from another's misery, misfortune and hardship, borne out of this strange need to subjugate others.'

'It is called being a strong, ruthless leader, Ralph— something you have never understood. Nor could ever be.'

'I suppose, by crushing your opponents by any means?'

'Exactly, my young cousin. It is the way of the world.'

'You are right, that is something I can never understand. And as the head of our family—with our motto of

Honore et Fide Imus—you have brought nothing but dishonour and disgrace. Look what you have reduced us to.'

'What *I* have reduced us to?' His cousin's eyes widened. 'If you were not such a simpering weakling, Ralph, I would never have had to do any of it.'

'What a convenient excuse.' Ralph laughed without any humour. 'God, to think that I did nothing other than admire you, revere you when I was young. Damn it, I looked up to you as though you were my older brother.'

'Yet that was precisely the point,' Stephen sneered as he brought his sword forward, striking out. 'I was not your brother, Ralph, but a lowly cousin. One who was given all of the advantages with none of the rewards.'

Ralph defended himself aggressively. 'Is that what all of this has always been about—the rewards you felt were your due?'

'What else?' the man spat. 'Your fool of a father made me believe as though I would be his heir, the way he always he showed his partiality and preference. Constantly parading me in front of his sergeants, sheriffs, even lords and earls. Soon I came to believe it.'

'Then that was your own foolish mistake, as it was never true.'

They continued to dance around one another, the tension stretching and building between them. Stephen attempted to push him back and subdue him, but his efforts were repulsed as Ralph countered every blow with far more aggressive parrying ones of his own.

'It was your father's fault for making me believe that. The man had always sought my advice and never yours, Ralph. And as he had constantly berated your shortcomings and defects, I only mimicked *his* continual disappointment in *you*.'

Ralph ground his teeth, knowing that there was some

truth in that. Everything he had done was always seen as some sort of failure and flaw in his sire's eyes. He had never been good enough for the man.

'That may be so, but it changed nothing, Stephen.'

'That is where you are wrong because it changed everything. How was I to know when your father made me think the opposite? Eventually I asked him to legitimately declare me as his heir, but do you know what my uncle said? That he already had an heir. Can you believe it, after everything he had said and done to the contrary?'

Ralph turned swiftly to deflect another strike. 'So, you decided to become turncoat and denounce him as a traitor.'

'He had enemies enough who wanted to join with me, so it was hardly difficult to convince anyone of my uncle's deficiencies or, come to mention it, *yours* as heir apparent.'

'God, but you are an arrogant, presumptuous ass, Stephen.'

'Am I? How droll,' he said on a chuckle. 'And yet I still maintain the necessity of what I did.'

'Is that so? Did you somehow command Kinnerton well in the past six years?' Ralph bent his knees and lunged forward on the attack. 'Because from what I understand you have done nothing other than line your own purse while mismanaging the castle and demesne lands.'

He did not miss the flicker of anger in his cousin's eyes. 'That is nothing other than idle talk. Besides, I do not answer to you, my young cousin.'

'We'll see.'

'We shall.' The man turned on his heel and swung his sword up from a downward motion so quickly that the blade nipped Ralph's scarred cheek.

Hell's teeth but Stephen was using a sharp sword instead of a blunt blade as proscribed for tournaments such as this.

'How very predictable that you have resorted to cheating, Stephen.'

'When there is so much at stake, I cannot afford to take any chances.' He shrugged. 'I suppose you shall now want to halt this and whine and whinge about it all. Either way I shall still triumph over you.'

Ralph knew that he should alert the Crown of his cousin's flagrant rule breaking, since a man as erratic and unreliable as Stephen le Gros in a volatile situation like this could cause any manner of disturbance. Especially, as he'd said himself, when he had so much at stake.

But Ralph could not do it. He had endured so much at the hands of his cousin, so much that he had had to overcome and survive. The very real danger of sharpened swords did not alter anything now. Ralph felt numb to it. After all, he had suffered the man's verbal and physical intimidations when he was young. He had survived the assault and ambush in Aquitaine and, more recently, at this very tournament, he had survived being poisoned while taking a beating by Stephen and a few of his cronies.

'You keep your weaponry, if it gives you comfort, but it makes no difference to me.'

'I see that you are still as naive as ever,' Stephen scoffed.

'Better that then to use trickery to get ahead.'

'Whatever you say, cousin. But tell me, out of curiosity, did it hurt? In Aquitaine?' The man jabbed forward as Ralph felt a small trail of blood trickle down his face. 'I can assume it must have, just as I'm convinced of the hideous consequences that I can see before me.'

'You should know all about that, Stephen—after all, you caused it.'

'How remiss of me, as I had hoped to cause more,' he jeered. 'It looks so sore in its disfigured ugliness that I wonder how the lovely Gwenllian even looks on you.'

The very mention of Gwen's name on Stephen's lips made Ralph stiffen immediately. How dare the man even attempt to use her good name after everything he had done. Gwen was Ralph's weakness, but he could not allow himself to fall for his cousin's trap, however difficult it might be. He understood that it would be best to ignore Stephen's mocking. But, of course, the man was not finished yet.

'Although it was vexing that the lady came so readily to your rescue, but then she did always leap forth to save lost puppies like you, Ralph.' He struck out, turning to shield from Ralph's attack, a slow smile curling on his lips. 'Oh, do I sense a little anger here? Could it be possible that you know how unworthy you are of Kinnerton, but more importantly that you're undeserving of her—of Gwen?'

The men continued to circle around one another before engaging again with a quick succession, clashing swords.

'Suddenly so quiet, Ralph. What has happened? Have you lost your tongue?' Stephen's voice seemed to drip with scorn. 'I do hope it is not something I said about Gwen that has made you as tense as you are.'

Ralph continued to keep his silence, knowing that he did not want to discuss anything regarding Gwen. Not with a man like Stephen. It would be disastrous to allow his cousin to draw him in, flaming his anger and fury to such a magnitude that it could threaten to consume him. That would not serve him well in the middle of a combat when Ralph needed his wits about him. Unfettered anger that could spill out of control would never do in this situation.

'I would wonder what a woman like Gwen would truly think about that scarred ugly skin of yours, when one considers the glorious smoothness of her own,' Stephen sneered. 'And lord knows how I explored that creamy soft suppleness myself.' He chuckled. 'Did she ever tell you about that, Ralph? Did she tell you about how I gave her the most inexplicable carnal pleasures—as she also gave to me? Oh, I can still recall her little sighs and moans of delight as we explored one another. That and the way she looked in our moment of intimacy.'

The sudden ringing in Ralph's head became more and more constant and relentless. He knew he should not rise to the man's taunts, they were just untruths, but it was increasingly difficult to do. He did not want to imagine his cousin's filthy hands anywhere near Gwen, but the fact remained that the man had touched her. He had defiled her.

Stephen le Gros had broken an oath that should have been sacrosanct as a knight, when he preyed on someone who was not in the position to fight back and had not sought his attentions. His cousin had behaved with depravity when he had frightened Gwen into doing things against her will.

God's blood, but he had to be punished.

Ralph felt the anger quickly flare and disperse through his veins, hot, blazing and fierce, pumping through his blood. He wanted to roar and rage at Stephen, but he knew he had to temper his anger in the way that would be conducive in this combat. In the very manner that William Geraint and Hugh de Villers had ground into him.

Ralph took a deep breath as he took a step back and squared his shoulders. His eyes narrowed on his opponent, knowing that Stephen was about to come at him with another set of attacking thrusts and strikes. But his cousin was a little slower than he had been at the beginning. Ralph's plan to allow Stephen to go on the continual attack was beginning to yield, since he could feel the tiredness emerge in the man's strokes.

It was his moment to take Stephen on swiftly. Ralph led his cousin into a false sense of believing that he now had the better of him. But it was time to show him otherwise.

He thrust forward on the attack, but was blocked by Stephen.

'Come on, my young cousin, is this all that you possess?' he barked. 'Is this all you can do?'

Ralph took a few steps back as his opponent lunged forward and, just as he did so, Ralph swung around to the side and completed the feint by using a fluid parrying strike that took Stephen totally by surprise. The man stumbled and fell back on to the grassy plain, his jaw widening at the expediency of his defeat as he looked up to see the tip of Ralph's sword pointing at him.

'No, I believe this is!' Ralph retorted on a deep breath, with a faint smile on his lips. 'I believe you have lost, Stephen.' He kicked his sword away from him and picked it up.

Ralph breathed a huge sigh of relief as his cousin was for once speechless, confounded and seemingly unable to comprehend what had just transpired.

It was over, thank God. Ralph was victorious. He had triumphed over his terrible adversary in a resounding manner. The dull noise of cheering enveloped him as he gave the defeated man one last glance before striding back towards the royal spectator stands, with many now on their feet.

Yet it seemed there was to be one last stand. Ralph's innate instinct kept peril at bay as he sensed a sudden footfall behind him. He quickly swung around to find Stephen running at him with a dagger, his face contorted into savage viciousness. Ralph stood with his legs apart and waited until the man was close before he bent his knee and swung his feet around, taking Stephen's legs from under him and tripping him up. Once again, the man was thrown to the ground.

'You have lost, Stephen.' Ralph looked down at his cousin as he removed his dagger from his hands. 'And you are beginning to look very foolish in front of King Henry and the Marcher Earls.'

'I cannot let this happen,' the man said through gritted teeth.

'But you have little choice.' He gave him an implacable smile. 'Concede, Stephen, concede with some semblance of graciousness and dignity.'

'That would be convenient after everything that has happened,' he spat. 'You have taken everything from me—Kinnerton, even Gwenllian!'

'You never understood, did you?' He shook his head in disgust as he leant forward. 'They were never yours to begin with, Stephen.'

With that Ralph marched off, unable to spare another moment with the man who had caused him so much grief and misfortune.

Yes, it was finally over.

Chapter Twenty-One

Gwen stood up clapping, tears streaming down her face, as she watched Ralph stride with purpose back towards the royal party. After many, many long years and after so much pain and hardship, Ralph de Kinnerton was finally vindicated. He had triumphed over his deplorable cousin and in front of the King and the Marcher Earls and Lords, casting any last shred of doubt about his abilities as a warrior lord away.

She felt her heart might burst from her chest as she dwelled on Ralph's decisive, emphatic win. She was so proud of him. Isabel turned to her and gave her a huge hug as William Tallany jumped up and down beside her.

Gwen watched as Ralph knelt in front of King Henry, who stepped down from the dais followed by the Earls of Chester and Hereford. He declared Ralph champion and, as the new Lord of Kinnerton, handed him a scroll with the royal stamp and then placed the ring of the Lords of Kinnerton back on Ralph's finger. A befitting ceremony would later be sanctified and legitimised in church, but this felt somehow more symbolic.

Before long they were once again cheering Ralph as Lords de Clancey and Tallany, as well as Sir Thomas, greeted and congratulated Ralph personally. Gwen followed the women down from the dais to extend her congratulations. She watched in amusement as Ralph threw a delighted William Tallany in the air before sitting him on his shoulders, the little boy's legs dangling either side of his neck. She took a tentative step forward, suddenly feeling a little shy and self-conscious in front of so many people.

Ralph caught her gaze and grinned, the warmth of his smile extending to his eyes, making her stomach flip over itself. Nothing, not even his visible scars, could ever diminish his vitality and spirit. Ralph de Kinnerton was an extraordinary man to come through the enormous trials that he had. She returned his smile, giving him a quick hug and muttering words of congratulations. He gave her another penetrating look and opened his mouth, about to say something, before some other person vied for his attention. Yes, there would be many who would seek his attention now that he had taken his rightful place as the Lord of Kinnerton.

Her heart swelled with love for him. But it was precisely the very fact that she loved Ralph de Kinnerton that prevented Gwen from taking any step to be by his side. Stephen le Gros might have been defeated, his threat finally quashed, but he would always somehow come between them. She was pragmatic and realistic enough to know that. She sighed as she quietly slipped away from the area, allowing room for others wanting to pay homage to Ralph. She would be in the way as many people clamoured to see him.

Lost in her own musings, Gwen found herself in a quiet area between the castle and the open fields of the tournament as she meandered back. She picked up her pace, sensing that she was being followed. Yet every time she turned around and darted her gaze in every direction, there was no one anywhere near her. It was likely to be her imaginings, though she now wished she had been a little more prudent and not so hasty to get back to her chamber on her own. She should have at least said something to Brida or Lady Isabel, but the need for quiet reflection had suddenly overwhelmed her.

The leaves on trees that lined the path to the castle whistled in the breeze as Gwen reached the castle gatehouse. She exhaled slowly through her teeth. Her head dropped as she rubbed her forehead, relief flooding her veins. It was quite a ridiculous reaction when she considered how wonderful this day had turned out to be. But she was too premature as she was yanked violently by the arm as she stepped outside the stone gatehouse. She was pulled down a narrow, deserted pathway with a hand harshly covering her mouth.

'I want you to be very, very quiet, my dear.' It was Stephen le Gros's voice from somewhere close behind her. He was clasping her arm with such ferocity she could feel his fingernails digging into her flesh.

'I want you to listen very carefully to me, do you hear?' His face loomed from behind and was too close for comfort. 'I shall let go of my hand, but only if you agree to my conditions. We shall walk together, quietly but very efficiently, and leave this damn castle. We shall then mount my horse and get away from this infernal place. Otherwise, I am afraid I shall have no choice other than to use this.' She could feel the tip of some sharp weaponry against her back.

Stephen's own unique scent enveloped her senses, making Gwen want to retch. Her stomach recoiled from his very touch. But she had to think quickly. She acquiesced to his demands by nodding her head, as he pushed her back in the direction of the gatehouse.

She made a muffled noise from beneath his sweaty palm grasping her tightly.

'Oh, no, my sweet, not yet.' He trailed his lips along the side of her face, making her want to pull away. 'You see, I could not allow *him* to take you from me. You belong to me, Gwenllian. Never forget that.'

They rounded the corner and, before she knew what had happened, a strong, tightly coiled arm swung out and smashed his elbow in Stephen's face with astonishing accuracy. She was pulled and lifted away from the man and deposited behind another, by Ralph, who was now standing and pointing Stephen le Gros's own dagger at him, having retrieved it from the ground.

'You broke my nose! You broke my nose,' Stephen whimpered.

'You are lucky that I did not break more than your damn nose!' Ralph thundered.

Gwen blinked, wondering whether she had ever seen Ralph de Kinnerton in such a blaze of fury. He looked as though he was just about hanging on to his temper by a thread.

'Are you all right, Gwen?' he asked slowly, his eyes still fixed on his cousin who had fallen to the ground, clutching his bleeding nose.

'Yes, I am well. Thank you.'

'Good.' Ralph bent down and grabbed Stephen by the scruff of his tunic and pulled him to his feet, the sharp tip of his dagger against his neck as the other man visibly sagged and squirmed. 'Now what should I do about you, Stephen? Tell me whether anyone would truly mind if you wound up dead in some ditch nearby?'

Gwen gasped from behind, detecting the palpable

anger that Ralph was finding difficult to restrain. Slowly but surely the rage from within him seemed to be unravelling.

'No,' she said softly, placing her hand on Ralph's sleeve. 'Stephen is not worth your troubles.'

'You know as well as I what this bastard has done in the past and what he was about to do again.'

'Yes, but it is over, thank God,' she muttered. 'Do not allow Stephen to get locked inside your head. If you end his life, now, in this way, then it will become a stain on your conscience. You do not need to do that, Ralph.'

'But he tried to hurt and take advantage of you again.'

'And because of you he did not succeed.'

Indeed, she finally felt free of the wretched man—of his threats, manipulations and intimidations, which in truth exposed him to be weak and deficient. Gwen realised then that she need never be fearful of Stephen le Gros again.

Ralph dragged his cousin along the pathway and dumped him on the ground.

'Listen to me, you vile, pathetic bully.' He scowled. 'I shall escort you to the gatehouse and out of this castle where you will leave for good and never return. I never want to set eyes on you again. If you come anywhere near here, Kinnerton or especially Gwen ever again, I shall kill you. It is that simple. Do we understand each other?'

Stephen gave a single nod as Ralph continued to drag him back to the entrance of the castle. He pushed him through the gatehouse and ensured that the man mounted his horse and left with just his accompanying squire who had been waiting patiently for him.

Incredibly they both stood side by side as they saw the last of Stephen le Gros, without his usual loyal supporters propping him up. One by one they had swiftly turned their backs on him, after Ralph's decisive win. The man was now alone and dejected in the world, as he deserved to be.

Gwen's forehead furrowed in the middle. 'Do you believe that Stephen will keep to his promise?'

'That is not easy to predict when one considers who we are discussing.' Ralph turned around to face her. 'But I hope so.' He studied her for a moment before continuing. 'What I would like to know is why you ventured back to the castle alone? Surely you knew the dangers that you might possibly face.'

'Yes, of course, but in that moment of euphoria after your triumph, I overlooked that possibility. I thank you, by the way, for coming to my aid.'

'Always, Gwen. Never doubt it.' He fixed his gaze on to hers, making her flush. 'But you still haven't answered why you left so suddenly.'

Gwen did not quite know how to respond. All she knew was that in that moment she had needed time to be alone and reflect on her future, now that Ralph's seemed, finally, to be resolved. And to make her last final arrangements before her impending journey to the convent. In any case, Gwen never dreamed that she would be missed for such a short time.

She shrugged. 'It was nothing of import and I hardly know now.'

'I see.' He sighed. 'And you are sure that you are well? Stephen did not hurt you?'

'No, I am perfectly well, I thank you.'

'Good,' he muttered, as they descended into an awkward silence.

'I had better go,' she said finally. 'I am sure Brida would be wondering where I have got to.'

'I hope to see you this evening, my lady, at the banquet to celebrate today's success.' He bowed over her hand.

Gwen knew that she should not stay. It would be best to prepare for their journey on the morrow, but that look in Ralph's eye made it impossible for her to refuse.

'Of course, I would not miss it for the world. Until later.' She inclined her head and made her way back inside the castle.

The evening banquet that served as a celebration of Ralph's victory and his restored castle and lands was the most spectacular that had been staged during the tournament. Torches had been lit, with garlands of seasonal greenery and flowers decorating the trellis tables that were covered in linen cloths. Trenchers of mutton, beef and pork with delicate spiced sauces to accompany the meat had been laid out on the tables. Warm rolls of bread, rounds of cheese and small savoury pastries were stacked on to platters, along with dried and fresh fruits. And, of course, the tables groaned with plenty of ale and silver goblets of red wine.

'Are you unwell, my lady, only you have hardly touched your meal?' Brida hissed from beside her.

'I just am not particularly hungry, that is all.' Gwen sighed, placing her meat knife down. Indeed, for some strange reason, her stomach seemed to be knotted in a perpetual state of nervous apprehension.

Brida lowered her head close to hers, so her voice would not carry beyond Gwen's ears. 'Try for something. After all, the choicest cuts have been selected for our trencher.'

Gwen forced herself to take small bites of food, knowing her friend was right, but everything tasted dry in her mouth, despite the obvious care and attention that the meal had been prepared with. What was wrong with her? It was as though she anticipated something this eventide, although she had no possible notion of that. She surreptitiously glanced in the direction of Ralph, who was sat with King Henry, the Marcher Earls, and William de Clancey and Hugh de Villers. Thomas Lovent also sat with the noble men, laughing and talking boisterously. It seemed everyone present on this eve was vying for Ralph's attention.

Gwen could not be happier for him, he deserved nothing less. Yet she could not help but feel a little empty inside, knowing that soon their lives would pull away from one another, once they went their separate ways.

She sipped her spiced wine and returned her attention to her meal, just as musicians assembled at the end of the hall and began to strum their instruments before beginning to play. Their first few ditties were famous melodies from Poitiers. Gwen attempted to join in with the merriment and clapping. The next, however, was something so unexpected that she snapped her head up, blinking in a daze. It was a beautiful Welsh ballad sung to the most beautiful melody. And Gwen remembered it instantly from the far reaches of her mind.

She began to hum the tune as she tried to remember the beautiful words sung about a warrior returning to his love and waiting on the hillside to be reunited with her after many long years apart.

Ar y llechwedd hwnnw y byddwn yn cwrdd â fy nghariad eto.
Sut y byddai'r tymhorau'n mynd heibio cyn y gallem fod gyda'n gilydd eto.

Gwen could recall how her mother would smooth back her hair and sing it to her as she tried to coax her to sleep, when she was a child. The memory was so potent and immediate that it brought a lump to her throat.

There was only person present in the hall who would know of this faded memory which was so utterly precious to her. One of the very few she had left of her mother. Gwen lifted her head and caught Ralph's eyes watching her with such ardour that she felt her cheeks heat.

She felt so touched that he had remembered this that her eyes unexpectedly filled with tears. Feeling annoyed with herself, she quickly turned her head and wiped them away with the back of her hand before anyone could bear witness to anything so mortifying. And in the middle of a celebratory banquet as well. Really, it was all too embarrassing.

Gwen turned back around to find Ralph standing in front of their table, looking down on her, his dark eyes glittering. Oh, but how handsome he looked, standing there with a ready smile and his dark hair combed and swept back. His long, muscled legs were encased in dark hose and braies, and with it he wore a matching linen tunic with a blue quilted gambeson, belted at the waist, that moulded to the contours of his broad shoulders and hard chest.

'My lady,' he said softly, holding out his hand to her. 'Would you care to dance?'

Gwen exhaled slowly and nodded, not quite trusting herself to speak. She rose to her feet and took Ralph's outstretched hand. They moved to the centre of the hall as others also gathered there. Hugh and Eleanor joined them, as did William and Isabel. Gwen even spotted Thomas approach Brida, whom she noticed refused the poor man with a vigorous shake of the head.

Yet none of that seemed to signify. The way Ralph was looking at her was as though no one else existed but them. It made her feel as though she would swoon with this strange hopeless longing she knew she could not give in to. She must stand strong and think of the sadness that would eventually come if she gave into her desires now. It was best to keep this contained as though they were mere friends and nothing more.

The melodic music enveloped them as they circled around one another in graceful, fluid moves.

'You seem quiet this evening, Ralph.'

'Am I?' he muttered from behind her as he flexed his fingers around her waist and lifted her up before lowering her back down. 'I had not noticed.'

'I am not surprised. This has been an incredible day.'

'Indeed.'

'Tell me, how do you fare?' she said as she moved around him and another couple before coming back around and resting the tips of her fingers on his.

'Very well, now that I am finally able to have a moment with you.' He winked at her, giving her a wicked smile before his mirth faded to be replaced with a look of contemplation. 'And what of you, Gwen? I hope that you are now able to put Stephen and his subsequent demise behind you?'

She considered this question before eventually answering. 'It's strange but now that the nightmare of constantly watching and worrying about him seems to be at an end, I feel...you'll laugh when I say this, but I feel a little numb from it all.'

'That is not something that would provoke my levity.' Ralph frowned. 'Not after everything that he put you through.'

'That he put *us* through,' she corrected.

'Yes.' He moved away from her in the dance sequence before turning back. 'And the feelings you describe are understandable. However, I'm hopeful that it soon will pass.'

'Yes, I am sure it shall.' She smiled. 'I would not want to be continually bound to him in such a meaningless way.'

'That would not serve you well.' He slid his hand over her fingers and slowly pulled her towards him. 'In time Stephen le Gros would all be forgotten.'

'And we should start tonight by never mentioning his name. For too long he has dominated our shared past.'

'I can accede to that.' He laced his fingers with hers and gave them a gentle tug. 'Come, let's get away from here for a moment.'

'What? We cannot do that,' she hissed. 'This banquet has been given in your honour, with King Henry, the Marcher Earls and other dignitaries present.'

'No one shall notice.' He grinned sheepishly. 'Besides, I have been in discussions with them all day. I believe I can surely now have a moment alone with you, if you would honour me with your company.'

Gwen blinked, wondering whether it would be wise to be alone with him. But knowing that this could be the last time she conceded. 'It would be my pleasure.'

They continued the group dance, but gradually pulled away a little at a time until they found themselves at the side of the hall.

'Come along.' He chuckled as they stepped outside the hall.

No, it would not be wise at all.

Chapter Twenty-Two

It was a cool, quiet evening with a clear night sky festooned with stars. Ralph seemed to be in a hurry as he tugged Gwen's hand through to the outer bailey.

'Where are we going in such haste?'

'You'll see. Come.'

They continued along the path that brought them to a stone gatehouse.

'We're leaving the castle? At a time like this?'

'No better time than here and now, Gwen.' Ralph's lips twitched in the corners. 'Besides, we shan't be going far.'

They made their way out of the castle and around the castle curtain where she was surprised to find Ralph's squire holding his horse's reins.

'Not going far, did you say?' She crossed her arms as she shook her head. 'And this excursion does not seem as spontaneous as I believed it to be.'

He ran his hands down Fortis's smooth flank. 'I admit it has been done quite by design.'

'So it would seem.' She chuckled softly as she stroked the animal's muzzle.

'However, we shall not be venturing far. Just far enough.' He held out his hand to her. 'Shall we?'

'Yes.' She nodded. 'Let's.'

They mounted Fortis and turned the horse around before galloping away from Pulverbatch Castle. Gwen sat side-saddle in front with Ralph's protective arms wrapped around her.

'By the by, I wanted to ask whether you had anything to do with selecting the beautiful Welsh ballad earlier?'

'I may have.'

'Thank you, it was one my mother used to sing to me.'

'I recall you telling me.'

'I am surprised you remember something as insignificant as that, after all this time?'

He pulled the reins, making the horse come to a halt and leant over her shoulder, his breath close to the side of her neck.

'Not so insignificant, Gwenllian. And I hope this night is filled with yet more surprises.'

The low timbre of his voice sent a frisson of excitement through her as well as a touch of confusion. What surprises?

'Then, my lord, allow me to say that I am touched by your courtesy and thoughtfulness.'

'It was my pleasure.'

They continued to gallop through familiar woods and even a low-level stream, riding further west, with the moon and the stars as the only guiding beacon of light.

Finally, Fortis climbed a hilly mound that brought them somewhere Gwen had not believed she would ever see again—Kinnerton Castle, far across the valley yonder and perched on a low hill, but still visible.

It was standing in magnificent splendour, with a motte surrounding the high curtain walls and five stone towers including the keep linked together in fortification. It looked peaceful now, this place that had been the cause of so much turmoil and upheaval.

They both stared out into the night, lost in their own private contemplation of old memories now faded in dreams.

'I cannot believe that this is the same place I have been dreaming of, for so long. It seems so much smaller than I remember and only but yesterday when we were last here,' Ralph muttered softly. 'And yet also a lifetime ago, as well.'

She nodded. 'So much has happened since then. So many changes, both good and bad.'

'And here we are…back again.'

She wrapped her arms around herself as the breeze whipped around her. 'Why are we here, Ralph?' She frowned. 'Why have you brought me here?'

'Because this is the place where it all began and where everything must now surely be settled.'

Ralph jumped down and helped her dismount.

'Yes, for you this is a proud moment to savour. To know that all your endeavours, all those hopes and dreams you spoke of have finally become a reality.'

'But not for you, Gwen?' He caught a stray tendril from beneath her sheer veil and tucked it behind her ear.

'No.' She sighed. 'My path, as you know, will take me on a different route. Far from here.'

'And you would be happy then, once you reach that journey's end?'

'Must our lives be measured by the extent of our happiness?'

He stared at her for a long moment before answering, 'I do not see why they can't. But mayhap the pertinent question is whether you believe you have the right to be happy?'

No. She did not. Happiness was not something that she considered to be of any importance in her life. 'All I seek is a little comfort. That would suffice.'

'I'm afraid I do not agree.' He turned her around slowly to face him. 'I believe that you are worthy of more than that.'

'Stop this, Ralph.' She screwed her eyes shut. 'Do not make me want things that I cannot have.'

'Why?' he murmured. 'Why can you not have what your heart desires?'

This was something she did not want to contemplate. It would open a chasm of want and need that she had shut out and contained for so long, it might otherwise threaten to burst open.

'Gwen?' he said softly. 'Sweetheart, look at me.'

Her eyes fluttered open to find Ralph looking at her with such intensity that it made her pulse trip over itself. The truth was that what he offered tempted her so much that she wanted to reach out and take it, but she could not do it. It would end up hurting them both in the end and she could not bear to gain his eventual disgust.

'I love you Ralph de Kinnerton.' She swallowed. 'But you and I cannot have the ending we once hoped to have.'

He raked his fingers through his hair irritably. 'Just say the word, Gwen, and I shall escort you to whichever convent you wish to go, if it would be the means to your happiness.'

'Why would that be of any consequence?'

'Because it matters to me. *You* matter to me, for the love of saints.' His eyes held a storm of emotions still warring with the injustices of the world. But just as quickly it faded. 'You say you love me, yet you are prepared to relinquish that love.'

'Only because I have no other choice.'

'Oh, I think you do, but you stubbornly refuse to see it.'

'That is neither fair nor true.' She moved away, looking over the valley beyond. 'Don't you see that this is for the best? I am convinced that, one day, you shall come to realise that.'

'Will I indeed? I very much doubt it.' His lips twisted in annoyance. 'What is it that you think you are doing, Gwen? Protecting me, again?'

'Not just you, but both of us, I imagine.'

'Oh, sweetheart.' He reached out for her and she went to him. 'Whatever you may believe, I want you to know that you deserve happiness and more than that you should be cherished and loved.'

Her heart thumped rapidly against her chest as she shook her head sadly. 'I thank you, Ralph, but it is not a question of that.'

'Yet it could be,' he said softly as he rested his chin on her head.

'Love will not be enough.' She pulled away a little and sighed. 'We may wish to banish Stephen le Gros and never speak of him again, but he will always, always be there between us.'

'Only if we allow it.'

'Mayhap not now, but some day it will. What he did to us—to me—shall snake its way between us and spread all that spleen and venom. And I cannot bear for you to come to despise my shame, which you eventually shall.'

'You paint a less than flattering picture, Gwen, but you should try for a little more faith in me.'

How was she to explain that it had nothing to do with

that, but more an understanding about how these powerful emotions would inevitably develop?

'I never took you for lacking in courage,' he murmured, tilting his head up.

'On the contrary, Ralph, leaving you will take all the
courage I have left.'

He shook his head before releasing her. 'Then I fought
him for nothing. Then ultimately Stephen has won, regardless of it all.'

'You must not say that. You have achieved so much
since your return. You have restored your family honour and you're now the legitimate Lord of Kinnerton. It
is a great cause of celebration, Ralph, and I am so very
proud of you.'

He moved to stroke his horse, patting him before lifting his head to the heavens.

'And yet I did not fight him just for my family honour
or even to regain Kinnerton.' Ralph turned to look at her
with such intensity, his eyes glittered in the evening light.
'I fought for every indecent look, every unwanted touch,
every intimidation and every injustice my cousin perpetrated. Above all, I did it all for *you*. Only you, Gwen.'

Her lips trembled as she tried to say something, the
words stuck in her throat. He stepped forward and took
her hand in his, brushing his callused fingers over her
knuckles.

'God, but it pains me more than you can ever know
that I was not able to protect you against Stephen as I
should have back then, especially after what it cost you,'
he said hoarsely, his head bent low. 'But allow me to say
that you are a remarkable woman. What you did, what
you call *your shame* was the most selfless, brave and yes
courageous thing that anyone has ever done for me. You
saved my life, Gwen. Time and time again. And yet, how

do you suppose I can ever reconcile and repair the damage that my cousin has done?' He lifted his head. 'By either letting you go or eventually despising you, apparently. Neither of which I can readily do, incidentally.'

'Oh, Ralph.' Her eyes swam with tears. 'I do not know what to say.'

'You can say that you trust in my words and believe me when I say that none of this—Kinnerton or being its lord—means anything without you. That the notion of being without you rips at my soul. That I would do anything to convince you that I am in earnest.' He turned her hand around and placed his larger palm over hers, their fingers entwined. 'Tell me, when are you going to let me in because I love you, Gwenllian ferch Hywel? You are the very beat of my heart.'

She stared at their fingers laced together. 'As you are mine, Ralph de Kinnerton.'

'Then marry me, Gwen. Consent to be my wife.' He cupped her cheek and tilted her face up. 'Have faith in a future of our making and take a chance on happiness that could be ours. I would do everything in my power to give you that. In fact, I would give you those stars that you're so enchanted by and throw in the moon as well. But know this—my love for you is more like the vast sky that holds them together, it is enduring and never ending.'

She was stunned into silence. For as long as Gwen could remember, a dark cloud of uncertainty and bitterness had hung over, resulting with the inevitable separation that pulled them apart for six long years. Was it now really possible to breach that, if only she would reach out and grasp it? Could the strength of their true and binding love for one another be enough to forge a new future, as Ralph said, of their own making?

There was only one way to find out. Besides, Gwen

was tired of fighting her feelings and her deep longing to be with Ralph, which she had been doing from the first moment she saw him again by their tree in the woods near Pulverbatch Castle. She had tried to convince herself that theirs could only be a friendship, that anything else was an impossibility.

But then she had not known how Ralph would truly view what she had endured for him. Incredibly, he had thought her brave and courageous, a remarkable woman.

Mayhap she needed to be brave one more time and trust in him and his love.

'Yes.' She lifted her head and gazed into his eyes. A slow smile spread on her lips. 'I'll marry you, Ralph de Kinnerton. And I do not need the stars or the moon—just you.'

Before she knew what had happened Gwen was pulled into a warm embrace, as Ralph bent his head and covered her lips with his in the most tender kiss that almost made her knees buckle.

'I suppose I can now seek those hopes and dreams you once asked me about,' she teased.

'Yes, sweetheart, and far more besides.'

Chapter Twenty-Three

The day that Ralph de Kinnerton married Gwenllian ferch Hywel of Clwyd in the small chapel at his birthplace of Kinnerton Castle was a wonderfully bright and sunny day. The short journey from Pulverbatch Castle to Kinnerton was made in a cavalcade by the young King Henry himself, as well as the Earls of Chester and Hereford. Their friends, William and Isabel de Clancey, Hugh and Eleanor Tallany as well Sir Thomas Lovent and Gwen's companion Brida O'Conaill also attended the ceremony, solemnised by Hugh Foliot, the Bishop of Hereford.

The moment the music soared to herald the arrival of the procession outside the chapel would be etched in his mind for ever. Ralph stood waiting on the steps outside the chapel, with a small posy of wildflowers bound with a ribbon made by Gwen's fair hands as he first glimpsed his bride walking to meet him.

Her flaxen hair was tightly bound under a delicate silky veil topped with a simple gold circlet. She wore a vivid blue woollen kirtle dress with long fitted sleeves, the same shade as her eyes, edged in intricate gold embroidery and worn over a cream tunic. He stood mesmerised as he watched Gwen, who had never looked lovelier than on this morn. And on a day when she would utter vows that would bind them in union for ever. Except perhaps when she looked up at him and smiled. His breath hitched in his throat as he felt that smile through every vein of his body. God, but he loved her.

The moment was naturally broken when the short cape he wore, with the crest of Kinnerton over a dark blue padded gambeson, was tugged at the edges.

'Psst, Ralph? Ralph?' William Tallany whispered, looking a little flustered. 'Do I give Gwen the ring now when she gets here or later on?'

'I thought your lady mother told you.'

'She did, but I have since forgotten,' he hissed loudly.

Ralph rubbed his forehead and sighed. 'Later, when we have both said our sacred vows.'

He returned his gaze to Gwen as she continued to make her way towards them, only to notice William shuffling nervously by his feet.

'What is it now?' Ralph asked from the side of his mouth.

'I need to go. Now.' William stepped from one foot to the other.

Ralph shook his head in disbelief. He knew it had been a bad idea to allow the boy to be involved in the wedding procession, but he did not have the heart to say no, once William asked with such joyous excitement.

'Did you not use the piss-pot beforehand?'

'I did, but I have to go again.'

He met Tom's bemused gaze as he tried not to laugh out loud himself. 'I'll take him, while you wait for your bride.'

'Do not let him lose that ring, Tom. I need it!'

'Naturally.' His friend winked. 'And do not worry, we shall get back before anyone notices our absence.'

'See that you do and before he causes any mischief.'

'I would never do that,' William said, outraged.

'Of course not.'

And, thank God, he kept his word, as the marriage ceremony proceeded without any further interruptions. Well, except when Isabel de Clancey's dog somehow managed to get in the chapel, making William Tallany giggle uncontrollably despite his mother's chagrin and embarrassment.

None of it mattered in the end and it certainly made this splendid day far more memorable—charming, even. And to top it all, Ralph had finally married the woman who held his heart and completed him.

Later, when they both sat on the dais watching the fool flanked by their many guests, he leant over to Gwen and whispered into her ear, 'Happy, my love?'

'Yes, more than I could ever imagine.' She beamed at him. 'And it is all because of you.'

He lifted her hand to his lips and shook his head. 'It is finally because we are where we should always have been—here in Kinnerton,' he muttered, his eyes scanning the huge hall before returning to hers. 'Together.'

'I never thought it could be possible.'

'Ah, but life can be full of possibilities if you happen to look for them.' He winked. 'Which reminds me. Here, I have something for you.'

He passed her rolls of vellum tied with a ribbon that he beckoned a maid to bring.

'What is it?' Her forehead creased in bewilderment as she looked at the rolls and then at him.

'Best to open them and see.'

Ralph smiled as he watched Gwen's stunned reaction. She opened the scrolled rolls to find that they were her beautifully crafted parchments of pen and the artwork that she had used to pay for Fortis.

'I never thought to see these again, Ralph. How in heaven's name did you manage it?'

'Have I not told you that I'm pretty good at making conciliatory bargains? Besides, I made Geoffrey de Clun an offer he could not refuse.'

'I dare not think what that means, but thank you.' She kissed his cheek. 'This means more than you can ever know.'

'Well, I could hardly let those little pieces of yourself that you imbued on these scrolls to be misplaced.' He shrugged. 'They belong with the rest of you.'

'As I belong to you. And you to me?'

'Always.' He grinned before he returned her kisses. 'And for ever, Gwen.'

* * * * *

*If you enjoyed this story, be sure to read
the first two books in Melissa Oliver's
Notorious Knights miniseries*

The Rebel Heiress and the Knight
Her Banished Knight's Redemption